Praise for

MEDICINE WALK

"An essential read. . . . Superbly written."
— *NOW* magazine (NNNN)

"Richard Wagamese has become a master. This brilliant novel is his heart song, his crowning achievement thus far."
— Joseph Boyden

"Richard Wagamese's novel renders the Canadian wilderness with staggering insight and beauty. The same can be said for his understanding of the fragility, wildness and resilience of the human heart. Magnificent."
— Lisa Moore

"A deeply felt and profoundly moving novel, written in the kind of sure, clear prose that brings to mind the work of the great North American masters, Steinbeck included. . . ."
— Jane Urquhart

"[A] touching story about relationships, reconciliation, hope and heartbreak."
— CBC.ca

"Wagamese is one of Canada's best writers. . . . [He] exhibits profound sympathy for the human condition and deep faith in the redemptive thrust of the story. . . . *Medicine Walk* is a spiritual biography that transcends time and place, history and heritage to speak to all with hearts to hear."
— *Guelph Mercury*

MEDICINE WALK

RICHARD WAGAMESE

EMBLEM

McCLELLAND & STEWART

Cloth edition published in 2014
Emblem edition published in 2015

Emblem is an imprint of McClelland & Stewart, a division of
Random House of Canada Limited, a Penguin Random House Company

Emblem and colophon are registered trademarks of McClelland & Stewart, a
division of Random House of Canada Limited, a Penguin Random House Company

Library and Archives Canada Cataloguing in Publication is available upon request

ISBN: 978-0-7710-8921-3
ebook ISBN: 978-0-7710-8920-6

This is a work of fiction. Any similarity between the characters in this book and
persons living or dead is purely coincidental.

Typeset in Sabon by M&S, Toronto
Printed and bound in the United States of America

McClelland & Stewart,
a division of Random House of Canada Limited,
a Penguin Random House Company
www.penguinrandomhouse.ca

7 8 9 10   19 18 17

 Penguin
Random
House

For my sons,
Joshua Richard Wagamese
and Jason Schaffer.

Let the snake wait under
his weed
and the writing
be of words, slow and quick, sharp
to strike, quiet to wait,
sleepless.
– through metaphor to reconcile
the people and the stones.

—William Carlos Williams, "A Sort of a Song"

HE WALKED THE OLD MARE OUT OF THE PEN and led her to the gate that opened out into the field. There was a frost from the night before, and they left tracks behind them. He looped the rope around the middle rail of the fence and turned to walk back to the barn for the blanket and saddle. The tracks looked like inkblots in the seeping melt, and he stood for a moment and tried to imagine the scenes they held. He wasn't much of a dreamer though he liked to play at it now and then. But he could only see the limp grass and mud of the field and he shook his head at the folly and crossed the pen and strode through the open black maw of the barn door.

The old man was there milking the cow and he turned his head when he heard him and squirted a stream of milk from the teat.

"Get ya some breakfast," he said.

"Ate already," the kid said.

"Better straight from the tit."

"There's better tits."

The old man cackled and went back to the milking. The kid stood a while and watched and when the old man started to whistle he knew there'd be no more talk so he walked to the tack room. There was the smell of leather, liniment, the dry dust air of feed, and the low stink of mould and manure.

He heaved a deep breath of it into him then yanked the saddle off the rack and threw it up on his shoulder and grabbed the blanket from the hook by the door. He turned into the corridor and the old man was there with the milk bucket in his hand.

"Got any loot?"

"Some," the kid said. "Enough."

"Ain't never enough," the old man said and set the bucket down in the straw.

The kid stood there looking over the old man's shoulder at the mare picking about through the frost at the grass near the fence post. The old man fumbled out his billfold and squinted to see in the semi-dark. He rustled loose a sheaf of bills and held them out to the kid, who shuffled his feet in the straw. The old man shook the paper and eventually the kid reached out and took the money.

"Thanks," he said.

"Get you some of that diner food when you hit town. Better'n the slop I deal up."

"She's some good slop though," the kid said.

"It's fair. Me, I was raised on oatmeal and lard sandwiches. Least we got bacon and I still do a good enough bannock."

"That rabbit was some good last night," the kid said and tucked the bills in the chest pocket of his mackinaw.

"It'll keep ya on the trail a while. He's gonna be sick. You know that, don'tcha?" The old man fixed him with a stern look and pressed the billfold back into the bib of his overalls.

"I seen him sick before."

"Not like this."

"I can deal with it."

"Gonna have to. Don't expect it to be pretty."

"Never is. Still, he's my dad."

The old man shook his head and bent to retrieve the bucket and when he stood again he looked the kid square. "Call him what you like. Just be careful. He lies when he's sick."

"Lies when he ain't."

The old man nodded. "Me, I wouldn't go. I'd stick with what I got whether he called for me or not."

"What I got ain't no hell."

The old man looked around at the fusty barn and pursed his lips and squinted. "She's ripe, she's ramshackle, but she's ours. She's yours when I'm done. That's more'n he ever give."

"He's my father."

The old man nodded and turned and began to stump away up the corridor. He had to switch hands on the pail every few steps, and when he got to the sliding door at the other end he set it down and hauled on the timbers with both hands. The light slapped the kid hard and he raised a hand to shade his eyes. The old man stood framed in the blaze of morning. "That mare ain't much for cold. You gotta ride her light a while. Then kick her up. She'll go," he said.

"Is he dying?"

"Can't know," the old man said. "Didn't sound good but then, me, I figure he's been busy dying a long time now."

He turned in the hard yellow light and was gone. The kid stood there a moment, watching, and then he turned and walked back through to the pen and nickered at the horse. It raised its head and shivered, and the kid saddled her quickly and mounted and they walked off slowly across the field.

———

The bush started thin where the grass surrendered at the edge of the field. There were lodgepole pines and firs where the land was flatter, but when it arched up in a swell that grew to mountain there were ponderosa pines, birch, aspen, and larch. The kid rode easily, smoking and guiding the horse with his knees. They edged around blackberry thickets and stepped gingerly over stumps and stones and the sore-looking red of fallen pines. It was late fall. The dark green of fir leaned to a sullen greyness, and the sudden bursts of colour from the last clinging leaves struck him like the flare of lightning bugs in a darkened field. The horse nickered, enjoying the walk, and for a while the kid rode with his eyes closed trying to hear creature movement farther back in the tangle of bush.

He was big for his age, raw-boned and angular, and he had a serious look that seemed culled from sullenness, and he was quiet, so that some called him moody, pensive, and deep. He was none of those. Instead, he'd grown comfortable with aloneness and he bore an economy with words that was blunt, direct, more a man's talk than a kid's. So that people found his silence odd and they avoided him, the obdurate Indian look of him unnerving even for a sixteen-year-old. The old man had taught him the value of work early and he was content to labour, finding his satisfaction in farm work and his joy in horses and the untrammelled open of the high country. He'd left school as soon as he was legal. He had no mind for books and out here where he spent the bulk of his free time there was no need for elevated ideas or theories or talk and if he was taciturn he was content in it, hearing symphonies in wind across a ridge and arias in the screech of hawks and eagles, the huff of grizzlies and the pierce of a wolf call against the unblinking eye of the moon. He was Indian. The old man said it was his way and he'd always taken that for truth. His life had become horseback in solitude, lean-tos cut from spruce, fires in the night, mountain air that tasted sweet and pure as spring water, and trails too dim to see that he learned to follow high to places only cougars, marmots, and eagles knew. The old man had taught him most of what he knew but he was old and too cramped up for saddles now and the kid had come to the land alone for the better part of four years. Days, weeks sometimes. Alone. He'd never known lonely. If he put his head to it at all he couldn't work a definition for the word. It sat in him undefined and unnecessary like algebra; land and moon and water summing up the only equation that lent scope to his world, and he rode through it fleshed out and comfortable with the feel of the land around him like the refrain of an old hymn. It was what he knew. It was what he needed.

The horse stepped up and he let her have her head and she trotted through the trees toward the creek that cut a south-west swath along the belly of a ravine. She was a mountain horse. It was why he'd picked her from the other three they kept. Surefooted, dependable, not prone to spook. When they got to the creek she walked in and bent her head to drink and he sat and rolled a smoke and looked for deer sign. The sun was creeping over the lip of the mountain and it would soon be full morning in the hollow. It was a day's ride to the mill town at Parson's Gap and he figured to cut some time by going directly over the next ridge. There was a deer trail that snaked around it and he'd follow that and let the horse pick her pace. He'd ridden her there a dozen times and she knew the smell of cougar and bear so he was content to let her walk while he sat and smoked and watched the land.

When she'd taken her fill he backed her out of the creek and turned her north to the trailhead. She followed the trail easily, the memory of warm livery, oats and fresh straw, and the sour apples the kid brought her before bedding down beside her for the night urging her forward, and the kid sat in the pitch and sway and roll of her, smoking and singing in a rough, low voice, wondering about his father and the reason he'd been called.

2

THE TOWN SAT IN THE VEE OF A RIVER VALLEY. There was a steep flank of mountain on either side where the water rushed through and the mill sat a mile or so beyond, gathering the force of the flume. He could see the grey-white spume from the stacks before he crested the final ridge and when he topped it the town lay spread out along the edges of the river like a bruise. The horse snorted and shook her head at the sulphur smell. The kid blinked his eyes at it and kneed the horse forward to the downward trail. The trees were stunted and there were no varmints or scavengers except for crows and ravens that squawked at them as they passed. It was sad country and the kid had never liked coming here. The mill town kids were crude and laughed at him on the old horse and called him names when he passed. Sometimes they pitched stones at him. But he would just pull his hat brim down low over his eyes and hunch his shoulders against the plink of stones and the guttural scrabble of their voices. The last half-mile he had to follow the highway and the horse grew agitated at the rush of vehicles with drivers who hadn't the sense to slow or give a wider space when they passed. Some even honked. Horses on the road were seldom seen here and they were a curiosity. People stood on the steps of their houses and stared and he was aware of how he looked: the worn dungarees and boots, the faded mackinaw, the wide-brimmed hat and the old saddle, weather-beaten, the flank skirt cracked and scraped and scarred a hard brown like the body of an insect. He kept his face neutral. He rocked with the rhythm of the horse and let his shoulders roll some, both hands resting on the horn, the press of his knees calming the horse when she skittered at the cars or the screeching metallic sounds of town life.

The highway bellied out into a wide avenue that was the main street, and the kid turned down a side street a few blocks before he reached it. The houses were small, tar-papered or sided with crumbling wood, and most times there was sheeted plastic in the windows and dead automobiles in the twitch grass of the yards. There was woodsmoke and the greasy smell of cooking. Large dogs on chains raced out to bark and growl, and he had to ease the horse forward up the street. At the far end was the farm where he liveried the horse. It wasn't much. Five acres tucked against the sprawl of the town on one side and the jutted wall of mountain on the other. They had a pair of ponies, a jackass, a goat, and a few chickens that all bedded down in the same slumped, dilapidated barn. But the oats were good and they kept the straw fresh and they were half-breeds who'd known the old man for decades and they fed him and seemed to understand his quiet ways and let the kid be whenever he arrived. There was no one around so he unsaddled the horse and brushed her out and left her with oats and hay and made his way back down the street toward the heart of the town.

It was evening. Purple. The autumn chill was in the air and he could smell the frost coming and the rain that would follow sometime the next day. He could hear the clink and rattle of families settling in to their evening meals and there were kid sounds at the back of most of the houses and the dogs hunkered down near the front doors and raised their hackles and growled at him as he passed. His boots scrunched on the loose gravel of the asphalt. He rolled a smoke while he walked and traded solemn nods with men standing in their yards, smoking and drinking beer out of bottles. They were hard-looking men, grease-stained, callused with the lean, prowling hungry look of feral dogs, but his size and his tattered look let them take him for one of them and they let him pass without speaking. He smoked and squinted at the jutted angles of the town. When he got to the highway again he picked up his pace and strode purposefully to the main street, where the lights glimmered in the evening haze. He made his way lower, past the shops and mercantiles into the greyer, seedier area near the river where the grim bars and honkytonks were alive with the clatter of glasses, shouts, curses, laughter, and the smoke and sawdust smell that hovered just above the blood and piss and semen of the alleys and muddied parking lots. He wrinkled his nose at it and walked on harder, looking at no one and giving no sign of indecisiveness. There was a row of rooming houses farther down that backed onto the riverbank where mill workers and itinerant drunks and fugitives stayed and it was where he knew he'd find his father. The houses sat in the gathering dark, dim and unwelcoming, and when he came to a slatternly woman weaving drunkenly along the sidewalk he stepped to one side to let her by.

"Eldon Starlight? You know him?" he asked her.

"Got a smoke?" she said in return.

"Only rollies."

"Smoke's a smoke."

He took his makings from his pocket and twisted a smoke while she watched and licked at the corners of her lips. When he handed it to her she reached out a hand and leaned on his shoulder and the fumes off her were sharp and acidic. She motioned for a light and he sparked a match and held it up for her and she put a hand demurely on his and winked at him while she took the first draw. She kept her hand on his until he had to pull it away. She eyed him lazily while she smoked and he felt awkward.

"You're a big one, aren't you?" she said.

"Eldon Starlight?" he said again.

She laughed. "Twinkles? What do you want with that old lech?"

"I need to find him."

"Finding him ain't never hard, darlin'. Standing him more'n an hour's the trick."

"Do you know where he is?"

"If he ain't passed out drunk out back of Charlie's, he's second room on the right, third floor, third house down. But I'm way better company than old Twinkles and I like 'em young and big like you. Come on. Let old Shirl show you a good time."

"Thank you," he said and stepped back onto the sidewalk and turned to walk away.

"Suit yourself," she said. "Indian."

3

THE HOUSE LEANED BACK TOWARD THE SHORE so that in the encroaching dark it seemed to hover there as though deciding whether to continue hugging land or to simply shrug and surrender itself to the steel-grey muscle of the river. It was a three-storey clapboard and there were pieces of shingle strewn about the yard amid shattered windowpanes and boots and odd bits of clothing and yellowed newspapers that the wind pressed to the chicken-wire fence at its perimeter. There were men on the front verandah and as the kid climbed the steps that led to it they stopped their chatter and watched him. He tried the door but it was locked and when he turned, three of them stood up and faced him.

"Eldon Starlight," he said evenly.

"Who the hell are you?" the tallest one asked and spit tobacco juice at the kid's feet.

"Franklin," he said. "Starlight."

"You his kid?" the one beside the tall one asked. He had a lazy eye and it made the kid check over his shoulder.

"Yeah," the kid said.

"Never knew Twinkles had a kid," the tall one said.

"Neither'd Twinkles," a fat one said from behind them and they all laughed.

"Hell, kid, have a drink," the tall one said and motioned for him to lean against the verandah rail.

"No," the kid said. "Thanks, but no."

"Damn. Polite and he don't drink. Can't be Twinkles' kid," the fat one said, and they laughed again.

The kid watched while they passed a gallon jug of wine

around and when they'd all had a drink the fat one sat forward on the lawn chair he occupied and took a draw on his
smoke. He breathed it out in a long stream and scratched at
his chin with a big-knuckled hand.

"What brings you here, kid?" he asked.

"I'm aiming to see him."

"He ain't right."

"I heard."

"Not all of it, you didn't."

"Guess I'll see."

"I guess. But just so you know."

"I heard," the kid said.

The fat one rose and waddled to the door. He was tall but
equally rotund and the boards of the verandah sagged and
creaked with the weight of him. When the kid stepped to pass
he blocked the kid's view of the street. He had a sour smell of
old tobacco, stale whisky, and unwashed feet. The kid moved
back a step and the man grinned.

"You get used to it," he said.

"Don't expect to."

"Your pap's no better."

The fat one unlocked the door and pushed it open with
one wide arm and held it for the kid, who looked at him and
nodded. The man nodded back and when he eased the door
closed behind him he farted, loud and wet, and the men on the
verandah laughed and the kid strode quickly to the shabby
stairs across the small foyer. He stood there a moment and
looked around. It was drab. There were low lights in the ceil-
ings and they served only to add a level of shadow to the
murk of the decor. The walls were panelled a cheap laminate
brown and the threadbare carpets had faded from pumpkin

to a sad, mouldy orange and the newel of the staircase was split and cracked. He could smell cooking and hear the jump of fat in a fry pan. Spiderwebs. Dust. An old cat slunk out of the corner and eyed him warily, and when he turned to the stairs it hissed and arched its back and the kid shook his head at it and began to climb.

There were men sounds coming from every room. Belches, curses. The pale blue light of televisions seeped through the cracks of half-closed doors and it gave his movements a spooky, out-of-time feel. He could hear a man's raised voice. It was something addressed to a woman and the kid was embarrassed to hear it and when he came around the corner he tried to creep by but the door was open and the man who spoke turned to look at him. He kept rambling loudly. He stared straight at the kid and his eyes were crazed and the bush of his beard was mottled with tobacco and he had no teeth so the words were garbled some and crazy-sounding. As the kid eased past he saw into the room and there was no one else there. The man laughed suddenly, sharp like a bark, and he stood and shook his fist at the kid and stepped forward to slam the door.

He came to his father's room. The door was shut. Across the hall a tall, skinny man stood at a hotplate, turning baloney in a fry pan. He looked at the kid flatly and eased a foot up and pushed the door closed. The kid pressed an ear to his father's door. He could hear murmuring voices and for a moment he thought it was a television or a radio but there was a guttural laugh and then a woman's voice and the glassy thunk of a bottle set hard on the floor and the complaint of bed springs. He knocked. Silence. He heard whispers and scurried movements.

"Well, come in, dammit."

The kid turned the knob and eased the door open. The room was bare except for a dresser, a wooden chair, and the bed, where his father lay with a woman leaned against his chest. There were empty bottles lined along the dresser mirror. Clothes had been flung and were scattered every which way along with empty fast-food boxes and old newspapers. There wasn't a square foot of open floor in the entire room. The closet door dangled off its hinges and there were tools hung on nails and piled on the shelf. Saws, hammers, wrenches, a chainsaw, a rake and a shovel, and looped yards of electric cable. There was an old bicycle sitting up against the far wall partially disassembled with the wires and gears of it strewn around the back wheel and a rusted scythe with its hook bent up to the ceiling. The hot plate was crusted with grease and dribbles, and a coffee can overflowed with butts and ashes and a few jelly jars stuffed full of the same. A black-and-white television was tuned to a snowy channel. The man in the bed just stared at him and the woman eased her chin down and looked at the kid through the top of her eyes and batted her eyelashes.

"Well?" the man asked and raised a bottle to his mouth.

"I'm Franklin," the kid said.

"Jesus," was all he said and took another pull at the bottle. "Got big, didn't ya?"

His father's face was slack, the skin hanging off the bones like a loose tent, and there were lines and creases deep with shadow. There was stubble on his chin. His hair was weedy, gone to grey, and curled at his neckline, with bangs combed over one eye. He grinned and the teeth that remained were stained and crooked. When he raised an arm to wave him in it was rail-thin, the bones of it stuck out jarringly, the hand large with long, splayed fingers that told of the size he once owned, gone now to a desiccated boniness. But the eyes burned. They sat behind the twin fists of cheekbones hard and bright as marbles, and the kid was struck by the coyote amber of them, going to hazel but wild, intent, and suspicious. He stepped into the room, kicked a sweater out of the way, and shut the door behind him.

"The old man said I should come," he said.

"Grab a chair," his father said and pointed.

The kid pulled the chair away from the wall. He spun it and sat with his arms folded across the back of it, looking at his father and the woman.

"Drink?"

"Got no use for it."

"Smoke?"

"Got makin's."

"These are tailor-mades."

"Makin's smoke better."

His father laughed. It came out raspy and hoarse and he coughed a few times and the woman laid a hand on his chest and looked at him, worried and protective. The cough eased and his father leaned up on one elbow and pushed himself higher in the bed and looked at the kid.

"This here's Deirdre," he said, hooking a thumb toward the woman. "She's a whore."

The woman slapped playfully at him and blinked at the kid girlishly and it turned his stomach some. She pushed herself up in the bed to sit beside his father, smoothed down her lank blond hair and raised the bottle to her mouth, and the sheet tumbled down so that her breasts bobbed openly and the kid felt himself stiffen and blush.

"You could have some. She's okay with it."

"Thanks. No." the kid said.

"Go on. It's free."

"Not havin' to pay don't make it free."

"Suit yourself."

"I will."

They looked at each other and the woman eased the sheet up. They could hear the raving man down the hall and the sound of someone's radio playing an old country waltz. The room was directly over the verandah and he heard one of the men shout at someone passing in the street and a woman's voice let go a string of curses and the men laughed and hooted.

"Well, I'm here," the kid said.

"I can see ya."

"So? What is it you got to say?"

"I gotta have a whattaya call . . . agenda?"

He shook a cigarette loose from the pack behind his pillow and lit it and blew a series of smoke rings and then raised the bottle to his face and drank. The kid waited.

"Don't like me much, I guess," he said and set the bottle on the floor.

"Don't know you much is all," the kid said.

"I'm your dad."

The kid looked at him blandly. He took out his makings and rolled a smoke while his father and the woman watched. He lit up with a wooden match and when he blew it out he stuck it in one of the jelly jars filled with butts and ash. "Just a word to me," he said.

"We gotta talk, and I don't aim to do it here."

"Where then?"

"You hungry?"

"I could eat."

His father prodded the woman with an elbow and she shrugged and pushed the sheet back and slipped her legs over the side of the bed. She was thin but her breasts were full and bobbed when she moved and the kid kept his eyes on her. She caught him looking and winked. Then she stood and turned to face him and stretched full out and he took another long draw on the smoke. She bent to retrieve her clothes and began to dress. His father slid out of bed and the kid could see the gauntness of him, his buttocks like small lumps of dough and the rest of him all juts and pokes and seams of bone under sallow skin. He watched him dress and finished the smoke and the woman took another jolt out of the bottle and walked to the door.

"Later?" she asked.

"Not likely," his father said.

She looked at him and the kid thought she was going to say something more but she just nodded and opened the door and stepped out and shut it quietly behind her. He could hear her move down the hallway. The raving man stopped suddenly then started up again once she'd passed, and he could hear the clunk of her steps on the rickety stairs.

"That your woman?" the kid asked.

"Told you," his father said, poking at his hair with a comb. "She's a whore."

His father sat on the edge of the bed and pulled on a pair of work boots and laced them up halfway so that the tongues hung out and flapped. Then he picked up a tattered old denim jacket and swung it on, stood and wriggled his shoulders, and looked at the kid.

"Take ya to eat," he said. "My treat."

"Guess you're doing your father thing now."

"Not especially. It's a belly thing is all."

He tapped another cigarette loose from the pack on the bedside table and tucked it behind an ear then walked past the kid, opened the door, and stepped out into the hallway. The kid watched him walk away. He turned to look at the room, shook his head sadly, and walked into the hallway, pulling the door shut behind him. His father was a dim shadow at the head of the stairs. The kid followed him out into the street.

4

THE PLACE WAS A DANK HOVEL. It had the look of an old garage or warehouse, a low-slung one-storey joint that hadn't seen paint in years. There was a hand-painted sign under a lone spotlight on a rickety pole held in place by guy wires run to the roof. The sign said *Charlie's*. The windows were swing outs and one of them was held open by a broomstick. Sounds from a jukebox and the garble of voices and the clink of glasses, and when they stepped through the door the kid saw a plywood bar set up on old barrels and mismatched tables and chairs strewn haphazardly around the room. The lights were dim, giving the faces that turned to look them over a pall as if they were shrouded by shadow, and the talk lowered. As the kid followed his father across the room, the weight of their eyes on him was like the feeling of being watched by something unseen on a mountain trail. His father strode through the room, merely flicking a wrist in greeting to those who spoke to him, and opened a door at the far end and stepped out onto a deck. It was suspended over the dark push of the river by huge pilings and the kid could hear the hiss and gurgle of it from beneath the boards. There were propane heaters set around and there were knots of men at the tables. His father walked to an empty table close to the railing and hauled a chair back and sat looking out over the water. The kid shook his head and when his father still did not speak he took his makings out and began to twist a smoke. He drummed his fingers on the table. After a moment he lit up and took a draw and looked out at the river streaming past like a long black train. When he turned back he saw a tall, gangly man step through the door with a bottle on a tray and walk quickly to their table, set the bottle down and then stand and look at his father, who continued to look at the river.

"Twinkles," he said finally.

"I'm right here."

"You still owe."

"I know. I'm good for it."

"You ain't workin' no more."

"I'm still good for it."

The tall man looked at him and squinted and studied him a moment.

The kid smoked and looked away. "How much?" he asked.

"He owes thirty," the man said.

The kid put the smoke in the ashtray and dug in his pocket for the cash the old man had given him. He counted out forty dollars and handed them to the man, who looked at the bills as though they were foreign things.

"Change?" he asked.

"How much for the hooch?"

"You can have it for the ten."

"He wants to eat," his father said.

"All's we got left is the chicken and some beans."

"Put it on my tab."

"I don't know, Eldon."

"Hey, I made up what I owed."

"Yeah."

"Well?"

The man set the tray down and folded the money and tucked it in his pocket. He looked at the kid, who finished his smoke, ground it out on the deck, and stashed the butt in his chest pocket. "You want a drink with that?"

"Coffee," the kid said.

"And you?"

"I ate," his father said.

He nodded and walked back across the deck and the kid turned and looked at his father, who sat with his chin in one hand. "Your treat, huh?"

The kid smirked and put his feet up on the chair across from him. His father opened the bottle and raised it and took a couple of heavy swallows and set the bottle down and wiped at his mouth with the back of his hand. The plume from the stack downriver was like a ghostly geyser and the lights of the mill all orange and hazed like a carnival lot. On the far shore the town disappeared into the shadows thrown by the dim run of lights along the thin streets. The line of mountain was a black seam above it all.

The man returned with his coffee. The kid drank and waited, feeling angry and impatient. His father was silent. For a while there was only the garrulous talk of the men in the background, the high arch of a fiddle on the juke, and the swish of the river beneath them. The coffee was bitter and hot and he cradled the cup in his palms and watched his father.

"So how come they call you Twinkles?" he asked.

"It's bullshit."

"What?"

"Starlight. Twinkle, twinkle. You get it."

"Yeah, but you ain't exactly the twinkly sort."

"What am I then?"

"How in hell would I know? Cloudy, I guess."

His father shook his head and took another drink, smaller, more deliberate. "How I feel, I suppose."

"You fixin' to die?"

"Jesus. How'd you get so hard-assed?"

"Just asking a question."

The man brought the chicken and beans and a tortilla, and the kid dug into them and ate hungrily while his father watched him and nursed the bottle along. It was good chicken and he slopped up the beans with the tortilla and washed them down with the coffee. He sat back in his chair. His father stared at him with flat eyes and for a moment the kid thought he was stone drunk. They sat wordlessly and looked at the river.

"She cuts right through past the mill. Picks up speed and rolls out into the valley thirty miles or so downstream. You know it. Same valley leads to the old man's. You come up that way?" his father said and pointed at the line of mountain.

"I know it. I hunted that whole territory," the kid said.

"She's a good river. I been on her most of my life one way or another. Used to be in the old days we'd float log booms down from the falls. Mile long, some of them booms. Me and a pike pole walkin' the length of them, keepin' them movin' right down to here. Then after a couple days we'd head back up and do 'er all over again. Right to freeze-up. But that was years ago."

"You lumberjack?"

"Some. I liked it better on the water but you had to cut and fall in order to get out there. Got to be a boomer if you worked out well enough." He shook his head sadly. "Nowadays they use trucks. Takes the heart out of it."

"When was this?"

"Hell, I was young. Your age. I went to work when I was fourteen."

"So I guess you called me here to tell me that?"

His father sipped from the bottle. "You get right to it, don't you?"

"Got to. Winter's coming. Stuff needs doing."

"I got to ask you a favour."

"Seems to me you're the one who owes."

"I do. I know that. Sometimes though, you got to give to get."

"I already give forty."

"I ain't talking about money. Money's no use in this particular thing."

"What then?"

"I want you to head into the backcountry with me."

"You must be drunker than I thought."

"I want you to take me out into that territory you come through. The one you hunted all your life. There's a ridge back forty mile. Sits above a narrow valley with a high range behind it, facing east."

"I know it."

"I want you to take me there."

"Why would you want to go out there in your condition?"

"Because I need you to bury me there."

The kid sat with the coffee cup half raised to his mouth and he felt the urge to laugh and stand up and walk out and head back to the old farm. But his father looked at him earnestly and he could see pain in his eyes and something leaner, sorrow maybe, regret, or some ragged woe tattered by years. His father twirled the bottle slowly with a thumb and two fingers.

"You won't make it forty miles," the kid said.

"You didn't walk here, did you?"

"Well?"

"I'll ride your horse."

"So it's my walk then?"

"Jesus, kid. I'm dying. Where's your heart?"

He turned from his father and looked out across the slick black of the water.

"All right," his father said. "You won't do it."

The kid slapped at the table with one hand. He stood up and there was silence behind him as everyone stopped their talk to watch. He shook his head and rubbed at his chin with one hand.

His father sat leaned forward with his elbows on his knees and lit another smoke. "There's things need sayin'." He said it flatly, looking down at his shoes.

"Why? So you can feel better?"

"I was thinking about you."

"You never thought of me before."

"I did so."

"Yeah. Right." He reached out and took the bottle off the table and held it up and studied the level of it, sniffing at the top of it before setting it back down and kicking at his father's chair. His father raised his head slowly and peered at him sideways. The kid sat down.

"I need you to bury me facing east," he said. "Sitting up, in the warrior way."

"You ain't no warrior."

His father sat and sucked at the smoke between the pinched ends of his fingers then tossed it over the railing. He stood and reached out and took the bottle and raised it to his mouth and swallowed twice, hard, and then pitched the bottle over the railing too. He turned to the kid and he weaved some but put a hand down on the tabletop to steady himself and looked at his son with half-closed eyes. "I was once," he said. "Need to tell you about that. Need to tell you a lot of things."

"So you want to walk and talk about the good old days?"

"Weren't no good old days. But you need to hear still. It's all I got to give ya."

"Ain't never gonna be enough."

He looked at the kid and there was no more talk so he turned and made his way slowly across the deck and through the door into the barroom. The men at the other tables watched him go. They looked at the kid. He sat with his feet propped on the chair his father had just occupied and rolled a smoke. When he was finished he set it between his lips and held it there without lighting it, content to stare away across the water to the black hulk of the mountain. Then after a few minutes he stood up slowly and made his way to the door and walked through the bar without looking at anyone and out into the flat dark of the street. He looked up for the shape of his father making his way back to the house but he was nowhere to be seen. There were few people on the street. The kid stood there looking at the outline of his shadow spilling across the street. He could smell sulphur from the mill and the mouldy smell of cheap beer and he turned finally and followed the stars north through town, stopping to buy a few sour apples that he fed to the mare before bedding down beside her in the familiar dilapidated warmth of the barn.

5

HE COULD SEE THE MOON through the slats of the barn when he woke. It was early morning and it was in its descent but it hung in the sky like a glacier pouring down light with the sheen of melting ice. There were shadows everywhere. It was bright enough that he could see his way to the back door of the old barn and he got up and walked there to smoke. There were coyotes in the field. He could see the sleek shape of them trotting and bounding near the fence. Six of them. Cavorting. Celebrating moonlight. From where he stood leaning on the bottom half of the door he could see the huff of their breath. Clouds of it roiling then dissipating in the early morning air as they chased each other, and the kid thought of fog and the way it shrouded the land in the frosted wet of spring and autumn, the punch of ridge or scarp or mountain behind it sudden as a bear. They wheeled and dashed and now and then they yipped at each other and then stopped suddenly and looked at him. He cupped the smoke in his hand and turned his wrist so the lighted end of it pointed behind him. They waited. Silent. Still as the air around them. In the phosphorescent glow of the moon he thought he could see their eyes, dilating, peering hard at him with the ancient light of the wild in them, measuring and judging him in the dim distance. They lowered their heads, their snouts poking near the ground, and watched him. And then they began to dance, or at least that's how it seemed to him. One by one they began to weave sinuously back and forth, cutting between each other, snout to tail, a walk then a half-trot until one of them nipped at the tail of another and they exploded into a frenzy of playfulness, abandon, and a joy so sudden and pure that the kid smiled and leaned harder on the door to watch it. Then the largest one broke the dash, halted, raised its nose to the air, whirled, and loped to the trees. The others followed in a dark line. They vanished into the trees, winked out of view as though the woods had folded itself around them, cocooned them, the chrysalis impermeable, whole, wound of the fibres of time, and the kid wondered what shape they would bear when they emerged into the moonstruck glades.

It was cold and he shivered. There was some sacking hung on the near stall and he pulled it around his shoulders. It smelled of grain. The horse nickered behind him. He pushed the door open and stepped out into the barnyard. There was a scrim of frost on the rippled mud of it and his footsteps crunched some when he walked. When he got to the rail fence at the far end he straddled it and hung his boot heels on either side of the middle rail and looked around at the town and the mill and the mountains behind it that led to the valley above the river where his father wanted to go.

His father. The kid thought of him with the whore in the sad little room in the house that leaned toward the water. It was a ragged life. To die in it seemed more sorrowful than he could imagine. If he simply left him to die he could go back to the farm and work it and hope for the best. Nothing would be different. There was nothing else for him. Truth was, he wanted nothing else because that life was all he'd known and there was a comfort in the idea of farming. He knew the rhythms of it, could feel the arrival of the next thing long before it arrived, and he knew the feel of time around those eighty acres like he knew hunger, thirst, and the feel of coming weather on his skin. Memory for the kid kicked in with the smell of the barn and the old man teaching him to milk and plow and seed and pluck a chicken. His father had drifted in and out of that life randomly and the kid recalled the first sense of him as the thin prick of the sawn door frame in the kitchen on his shoulder, leaning there, watching him smoke and drink and talk with the old man, trading furtive glances with him and then staring down shyly at his boot tops. The voice of him gruff and garbled with drink. When he disappeared again he always left money in a jam jar behind the sink. "Your pap," the old man said whenever he doled out money from it, and for the longest time the kid had thought he meant the jar.

He learned his name was Starlight when he was seven. Even then the connection between them remained loose and untied and the kid remembered saying their names over and over to the darkness in the attic room where he slept. Eldon Starlight. Franklin Starlight. Four blunt syllables conjuring nothing. When he appeared the kid would watch him and whisper his name under his breath, waiting for a hook to emerge, a nail he could hang context on, but he remained a stranger on the fringes of his life. The old man was gruff about it, sometimes even seeming bitter to the kid, and he never spoke at length of it. He was content to provide as well as he could and he had.

It was the old man who had taught him to set snares, lay a nightline for fish, and read game sign. The old man had given him the land from the time he could remember and showed him how to approach it, honour it, he said, and the kid had sensed the import of those teachings and learned to listen and mimic well. When he was nine he'd gone out alone for the first time. Four days. He'd come back with smoked fish and a small deer and the old man had clapped him on the back and showed him how to dress venison and tan the hide. When he thought of the word *father* he could only ever imagine the old man.

He sat on the fence rail and rolled another smoke, looking at the spot where the coyotes had disappeared. The spirit of them still clung to the gap in the trees. But the kid could feel them in the splayed moonlight and for a time he wondered about journeys, about endings, about things left behind, questions that lurk forever in the dark of attic rooms, unspoken, unanswered, and when the smoke was done he crushed it out on the rail and cupped it in his palm while he walked back to the barn in the first pale, weak light of dawn.

6

THE FIRST THING HE REMEMBERED was the gun. He must have been three or four. It hung above the mantel of the stone fireplace and to him then, it seemed like it owned a silent form of magic. It seemed to hang suspended above everything, silent, calm, drawing all the light to it. It felt as though it rang with stories and adventures. He could sit for hours and just stare at it, waiting for the tales to fall.

Now and then the old man took it down and set it in the middle of the hard plank table and he and the kid would just look at it together.

"Can I?" he'd ask.

"Go on then," the old man would say, and the kid would reach both hands out and slide it slowly across the table so it lay lengthwise in front of him. He'd run his hands along the length of it. He'd come to love the feel of it on his palms. The slick, oiled blue-black of the barrel. The polished girth of the mount and the stock. The checkered and deliberate feel of the pistol grip. He'd poke the trigger guard with one finger, letting it swirl slowly around the bend and back before slipping it in and feeling the glassine curl of the trigger itself against the inside bend of his first knuckle.

He'd always look at the old man then, thrilled at all the magic he could feel alive in that curl of metal.

"What is she?" the old man would ask.

"She's a Lee-Enfield carbine," the kid would say.

"And what does she shoot?"

"She shoots 18-grain 30.30 bullets in a brass casing."

"Shoot at what?" the old man would press though he was always grinning.

"Bear, moose, elk, wolves. Anything bigger than a bobcat." It was the kid's stock answer.

"Why?" The old man would always lean his elbows on the table and cock one eyebrow at him.

The kid would purse his lips together, feigning deep concentration even though the both of them knew the old routine by heart.

"Because you can't tan a hide in pieces," he would say, and the old man would cackle like he always did when he laughed and slap a hand on the table. Then he let the kid hold the gun.

He knew the names of all the parts by the time he was four. He could break it down and reassemble it by the time he turned five and he became the gun cleaner and caretaker from that moment on. He knew how to oil the rifling in the barrel and how to bring the outside metal to a dull blue sheen. He took care to ensure that the trigger held just enough slickness to make it cool and reassuring to the touch. He rubbed the stock and grip with wood oil and used a light file on the checkering of the grip. He could handle it with his eyes closed.

"Man shoots he's gotta know what he's shootin' with," the old man said. "No good to hunt with a stranger. Ever."

"She's a tool," the kid said.

"Damn straight," the old man would say and tousle his hair. "And what do you know about tools, Frank?"

"They're only as good as the care you give them," he'd say proudly.

"Won't ever learn no better truth than that, Frank. See ya keep it."

He did. The old man got to trust the condition of the gun every time he took it down. But he always made sure the kid watched him check it out. When he was satisfied he would load the clip and shove it in the pocket of his orange hunting jacket and give it a firm pat. He never said a word. He didn't need to. The kid's eyes drank in every move.

When he was seven the old man taught him to shoot. At first he plinked away at cans with an old .22. He got so he could hit them from a kneeling position, flat on his belly, and standing with the gun braced against his hip.

"Sometimes you got no proper time to raise it," the old man said. "Gotta know how to fire on the rise. Save your life someday. You watch."

The kid shot targets for a year. The old man gradually increased the distance until he could hit a bleach bottle hung from a branch from two hundred yards out every time. He learned to shoot with the wind, how to calculate drift, to know how much a bullet would drop over a long stretch of ground and how the impact decreased at the same time.

"Gotta hit what you shoot at and you gotta drop it." The old man made him repeat that to himself over and over until it lived in his head like a nursery rhyme. "Ain't right to let nothing suffer."

"Gotta drop it." It became the mantra he spoke to himself at his school desk.

He never did take to school. In the beginning it terrified him. The beat-up old bus would pick him up and he'd be surrounded by yelling, screaming, frantic kids whose noise hurt his ears. Then they'd be made to sit in silent rows with their feet tucked together under the desk and their hands loosely folded on the top. The teachers talked too fast and they never repeated things like the old man did until he could cotton on to them, and he got lost easily.

He knew his numbers and his letters. The old man had taught him that. He knew bushels, pecks, pounds, and ounces from harvesting, sacking grain, and feeding stock. He knew to write lists of food and chores that needed doing and letters the old man made him write to the man who came around every now and then to drink in the kitchen and eye him whenever he walked through the room. He could count and figure and write better than the others, but the lessons made no sense to him. Nothing seemed built to help him plow five acres with a mule, help deliver a breeched calf, or harvest late fall spy apples, so he mostly let the words fall around him.

The school kids left him alone. He was the only Indian kid and they didn't trust him. He didn't hold out much trust for them either. They were mostly town kids who'd never gutted a deer or cut a dying heifer out of a tangle of barbed wire. They lived for games and play and talk, and the kid was used to being talked to and treated like a man. The edges of the schoolyard where he could get an eyeful of the trees poked up along the northeast ridge where he snared rabbits and shot squirrels became where he spent his time.

The teachers called him aloof and cold. They called him difficult. They sent letters home that the old man would read and then toss into the fire.

"No one's meaning you over there, are they?" he'd ask.

"No. They mostly let me be."

"Good. You'd tell me if they were?"

"I'd say."

"Good. Do your best at what you can, Frank. There's better and more important learning to be had out here on the land. That's one thing for sure. But some things you just gotta learn to stand."

"What I figure," the kid would say, "there ain't one of those little towheads would know how to square a half-hitch or get a hackamore on a green broke colt. But they make fun of me cuz I won't do the math or read out loud."

"How come you won't do none of that?"

"I don't know. I can get the numbers sorted around in my head without scratching around on paper, and I guess if a guy's to read he oughta be able to do it alone and quiet. Works best for me, least ways."

"Sounds right sensible to me," the old man said. "But the law says you gotta go until you're sixteen. Least ways, you got this place and we get out to where it's real as much as can, don't we?"

"Yeah," the kid said. "That's what saves my bacon."

When he could shoot as dependably with the carbine as with the .22 the old man let him start to hunt. They'd take horses and cross the field and plod up the ridge and by the time they were down the other side the land became what the old man called "real." To the kid, real meant quiet, open, and free before he learned to call it predictable and knowable. To him, it meant losing schools and rules and distractions and being able to focus and learn and see. To say he loved it was a word beyond him then but he came to know the feeling. It was opening your eyes on a misty early summer morning to see the sun as a smudge of pale orange above the teeth of the trees with the taste of coming rain in his mouth and the smell of camp coffee, rope, gun powder, and horses. It was the feel of the land at his back when he slept and the hearty, moist promise of it rising from everything. It was the feeling of the hackles rising slowly on the back of your neck when there was a bear yards away in the bush and the catch in the throat at the sudden explosion of an eagle from a tree. It was also the feel of water from a mountain spring. Ice like light splashed over your face. The old man brought him to all of that.

———

He taught him to track before he let him do anything else. "Any idiot can shoot a gun," he'd tell him. "But you track an animal long enough you get to know their thinkin', what they like, when they like it, and such. You don't hunt the animal. You hunt their sign."

He had to learn to walk all over again. The old man showed him how to move in a half-crouch that played pure hell on the top of his thighs. They burned after half a mile and the agony was fierce but he could feel stealth building in his stride. He learned how to curl his foot from the outside in when he planted it to avoid snapping twigs or crunching gravel. It meant that he walked pigeon-toed. The motion was difficult to master and he worked deliberately at it. He'd go out alone to the ridge and practise through the evenings until he could navigate the length of it and back soundlessly. He learned upwind from downwind and came to know how sound was amplified in the still, half-lit world of the forest. He learned caution. He learned patience. He learned guile. Together, he and the old man would creep along behind deer, keeping a parallel tack, and follow them in that half-crouch for miles.

Furtive was a word he learned then. The old man showed him how to slip between trees like a shadow. He taught him to move with exquisite slowness, almost not like moving at all, so that every inch of forward motion seemed to take a year. He learned to wrap himself in shadow, how to stoop and crawl between rocks and logs, how to hide himself in plain sight. He learned to stand or sit or lay in one position for hours. He could slow his breathing so that even in the chill air of winter the exhalations could be barely seen. He learned how to go inward, how to become whole in his stillness and forget the very nature of time.

Then he learned to read sign. Tracks were a story. That was the old man's thinking. Every movement left the story of a creature's passing when you learned to see it. The kid spent hours on his hands and knees touching the edges of paw prints with his finger to test the dryness of the earth. He learned their smell. He could determine how the spread of the print told exactly how the animal was moving. He knew a trot, a lope, a walk, the creeping, inching of a predator on the hunt, and the hunched and gathered fold of prey in shadow.

"See this trail," the old man said one day.

There was a dim line through the bracken.

"Yeah."

"See sign?"

"No."

"Are ya sure? Look closer."

He walked to a stump and sat and watched the kid study the ground. There was nothing discernible. When he closed his eyes and breathed the kid got a sense of something. He knelt. He pressed his face close to the earth and reached out with one finger and laid the nub of it on the moist surface of leaves turning to rot. Then he turned them over slowly. In the mud was a coyote print, barely visible but there nonetheless. He looked up at the old man.

"Coyote," he said.

"How old's the sign?"

"A day. But it rained last night. Could be two."

"Male or female?"

The kid squinted at the track. "Female," he said. "Not so heavy as a male. And the dirt's pushed forward some at the front. She was trotting. Likely on the hunt or coming back with something for the kits. The den'll be close."

"What colour you figure her to be?"

The kid looked shocked and the old man cackled and slapped at his thigh. They followed the dim sign to a hillock and spent a few hours watching the coyote kits play outside their den.

He shot his first deer when he was nine. He tracked the buck out of a marsh and upward through the talus onto a high ridge. There were times when the rock made it impossible to follow sign.

"You know him well enough," the old man said. "Go where you figure he'd go."

He found a slip of hoof in lichen at the edge of a table of rock leading into thin juniper. They wound through strewn boulders. He crept slowly with the rifle cradled across his chest. Finally, he turned his back to a rock and sat hunkered down on his haunches. He bolted a shell into the breech of the gun. Slowly. Silently. He looked across at the old man and nodded. Then he rose to a crouch and made his way around the boulder. They were at the edge of an alpine meadow. Nothing moved. The kid sat with a stump at his back, staring out across the wide expanse. Nothing stirred. Finally, a shadow eked out of the cover of a small copse of stunted pine. The buck was a juvenile but large. The kid didn't move. He barely breathed. When the buck turned into the wind and showed his flank he raised the rifle off his knees and pressed the butt into his shoulder. The shot clapped and echoed off the surrounding ridges and slopes. The buck dropped where he'd stood and the kid and the old man walked slowly across the meadow without speaking. For years he would recall the crackle of their footsteps through the dry underbrush and moss and the feel of the old man's hand between his shoulder blades.

It was a clean heart shot. The buck died instantly. The kid stood looking down at it and there were tears suddenly. He wept quietly and the old man stood by and waited. When he wiped at his nose with his sleeve the old man handed him a knife.

"Cut the throat, Frank," he said.

When the slash was made the old man drew a smear of blood with two fingers and turned the kid's face to him with the other hand. He made a pair of lines with the blood on each of his cheeks and another on his chin and a wavy line across his forehead. His face was calm and serious. "Them's your marks," he said.

The kid nodded solemnly. "Because I'm Indian," he said.

"Cuz I'm not," the old man said. "I can't teach you nothing about bein' who you are, Frank. All's I can do is show you to be a good person. A good man. You learn to be a good man, you'll be a good Injun too. Least ways, that's how I figure it works. Now you gotta give thanks."

"Thanks?"

"To the buck. He's gonna feed us for a good while, gonna give us a good hide to tan. So you pray and say thank you for his life on accounta he's takin' care of your life now. Our life. It's a big thing."

"How do I do that?"

The old man looked up at the sky. "I was never much for prayer. Least, not in the church way. But me, I figure everything's holy. So when I say somethin' I always just try'n feel what I feel and say whatever comes outta that. Always been good enough for me."

"I feel sad," the kid said.

"Yeah. I know. Speak outta that, Frank. What you say'll be true then."

The old man walked off and sat on a fallen log. The kid stood over the body of the buck and looked down at it. Then he knelt and put a hand on its shoulder. It was warm, the fur felt alive under his palm. He closed his eyes and let the sadness fall over him again. When the tears came he spoke.

"Thank you," he said. "I'm sorry about this. Whenever I come here, I'll think of you. I promise."

It was all he could think to say. After a time he stood and wiped snot off on his sleeve. He looked up into a mackerel sky easing toward sunset. The act of praying made him feel hollow and serene all at the same time. It was an odd feeling but he felt better for having done it. A wind rose out of the west. It would rain soon. They'd have to work fast to field dress the buck and haul it down the ridge to where they'd left the horses. He looked at the old man sitting on the downed log staring up into the same sculpted sky. He followed the angle of his gaze and watched the sky again. Blue. He thought he understood what that meant now.

The gun became his when he turned eleven. By then he'd dropped moose and elk and black bear. He could track all of them through any kind of terrain and territory and the shots he took were always planned, sure, and deliberate. He learned the value of ammunition. He never wasted a shot. He tracked and waited and bided his time until the animal offered the best possible target. He never rushed. The old man taught him that a hunt was a process. There was a scale and a tempo to it that the land and the animal determined. A man, or a kid, could set themselves into that rhythm and follow it. When he did the kid found that time didn't matter. What mattered was the process. He learned to pray before he went out and he learned to pray when he returned with game. Framed like that, a hunt became a ceremony. That was the old man's word.

"Got to come to know that things get taken care of, Frank," he said. "Me, I don't know if I ever got cozy with the word 'God,' but I know something's makin' sense out of all of this. Man's gotta trust that somehow. So I figure, what the heck? Even if I'm wrong, there's worse ways to live than stopping to thank the mystery for the mystery."

He liked that. When he stood out on the land he could feel it. It lay in the sense of being hollow and serene like he had felt after he shot the buck. It was in the sure heft of the gun in the crook of his arm and the knowledge that he could take what he needed and use it. Most of all, it was in the process of tracking game, letting himself slip out of the bounds of what he knew of earth, and outward into something larger, more complex and simple all at once. He had no word for that. Asked to explain it, he wouldn't have been able to, but he understood how it felt against his ribs when he breathed night air filled with the tang of spruce gum and rich, wet spoil of bog. That particular magic that existed beyond words, beyond time, schools, plans, lofty thinking, and someone else's idea of what mattered. The kid went to the land. It was all he needed. The gun anchored him there. It was how he came to understand the value of living things, by his ability to remove them. Taking life was a solemn thing. Life was the centre of the mystery. The gun was his measure. His hand on the velvet flank of the deer. A cry born of a loss he slowly came to understand was part of him forever.

7

"OKAY," HE SAID. "But I gotta know what the deal is."

His father sat on the edge of the bed, half dressed and the bony feet of him stuck out between cast-off clothing and junk, stark and pale as dead fish. He was smoking and he held it between the tips of fingers that were yellow brown and quivering. Deirdre sat beside him.

"What deal?" his father asked.

"How do you know you're getting ready to die?"

"The liver," he said. "She's shot. All kinds of crap making its way into my body now."

"From drinking, I suppose."

"Yeah."

He looked at his father sombrely and felt his anger rise. "But you don't *know* it's the end."

"I feel it coming on now. Some days I'm good for nothing. Today's one of the good ones. I shake a lot. Sweat then cold. Sometimes both at the same time."

His father reached under the bed and pulled out a bottle and twisted the cap off and drank. He closed his eyes and breathed out heavy and lay back on the mattress with his head against Deirdre's thigh. The woman looked at the kid and licked her lips and he could see the struggle for expression in the glassy booziness of her eyes.

"And you think I'm the one knows how to take care of you at the end." He looked over at the woman. "You know what he's askin'?"

"Yeah," she said.

"You all right with it?"

"He's an Indian."

"That says it all for you, I suppose."

"We all got a right to go out the way we want," she said and smoothed the hair off his father's brow and traced the lines of his face with one finger. The blue nail polish was chipped and broken and when she raised the hand back up to her own face it trembled and she reached for the bottle in his father's fist. She drank and regarded the kid.

There were no words in him and he stood and looked at them and pinched his lips together grimly. He raised a hand as if to let it lead him to words but all he could do was curl it into a fist and shake it in the air. Then he turned and walked out the door and slammed it behind him. He strode down the hallway and stopped at the head of the stairs. He wanted fresh air. He wanted the street and the feeling of escape that would come from walking away. He paused and looked around him at the dilapidated ruin of the house. The handrail wobbled in his grip. He closed his eyes and wished for the old man's counsel and the familiar air of the farm. But all he could hear was the sound of his heart hammering in his chest so that he sat on the stairs and put his head in his hands and rocked slowly back and forth until he felt it pass. Then he stood and turned and put one foot on the stair above. "Damn," he muttered and walked back to the room.

They were laying on the bed now, his father with a ragged shirt draped over him unbuttoned and hanging off his frame.

"I ain't packed for this. I'm gonna need some things," he said. "Rope, snare wire, fishing line, hooks, matches, a hatchet, and one of them folding pick axes and shovel, a pack. The forty I give out was most of what I had."

"Deirdre," his father said.

She rolled over on to her side and reached down beside the bed and came up with a cracked old leather bag. She rummaged around in it and brought out a clump of bills. She held it out toward the kid.

"There's enough there," she said.

"Jesus," he shook his head and looked toward his father.

"Bring me back a bottle for now and a few for the trip," his father said. "It don't matter much now."

He looked at the kid and waved him off. The kid buttoned his mackinaw and when he looked up they were both watching him.

"What?" he asked.

"She said you favour me."

"Is that a fact?"

"Around the eyes and how your mouth sits," she said and gave a small grin.

The kid let his gaze sweep around the room; the gathering of tools, worn and broken and unused for years. "You sure you're ready for this? We still ain't made a move yet."

"I'm sure."

He stared at his feet a moment then nodded without looking up. "I'll bring the horse," he said.

He strode to the door and swung it open and turned and looked back at them. His father lay with his eyes closed with his cheek against the woman. She was propped up against the wall on three thin pillows, swathed in cheap sheets and a pilled wool blanket. Her hands were reaching down, cradling his face in her palms, and her expression reminded the kid of the Madonna and he stood and watched a moment as a solitary tear slid from one eye and travelled slowly down her face, hung on the cliff of her chin, and then dropped onto his father's brow. She smoothed it into his skin with one finger and when she looked up at the kid she raised the finger to her mouth and licked it and he nodded solemnly to her and stepped out into the hallway and eased the door closed behind him.

He led the horse up out of the dinginess of the river edge and on through the merchant strip. His father rode sloppily, fighting to find the rhythm of the horse with both hands clutched around the saddle horn. The horse neighed and shook her head around at the rough weight and the kid had to keep a tight hand on the halter. It was mid-morning and the shops were busy with the regular flow of housewives, delivery people, and rural folk in town for supplies. People stopped and stared openly. His father kept his head down, more out of a desire to sit the horse, the kid thought, than any discomfort at the gaze of the townsfolk. The pack was cumbersome and he'd have to reload it once they were out of town and he shrugged and tried to settle it better and each time he did the horse kicked up some. The scrape and rattle of hoofs on the pavement drew more looks and the kid did his best to stay focused on the road. He didn't like attention. He'd always done his business here quickly, never straying or altering from the list in his mind, never speaking more than what was due and moving as quietly and as efficiently as he did on the trail. Now he kept his eyes straight ahead and pulled firmly on the halter. He felt ashamed, as though everyone knew the nature of his journey, could discern from the look of him that his father would not return, and he kept his eyes on the road and walked.

Once they were beyond the main street the walking was easier and they made better time. Still, the motor traffic unsettled the horse and when she shimmied his father grumbled and cussed and leaned back in the saddle and swayed.

"Just sit the damn horse," he said.

"Tryin'," his father said.

"Not hardly." He found the dim trail that led down from the mountain and once he walked the horse on to it he could feel her relax. There was the crunch and shuttle of gravel under her hoofs and even with the taint of the mill the air was cleaner and the kid inhaled deeply and set his shoulders into the walk up out of the river valley. When the grade sharpened his father leaned forward in the saddle and the kid could smell the fetid breath of him again, all booze and tobacco and a rotted high smell like a dead thing. He turned up his nose at it and pulled the horse harder up the grade. His father grunted at the effort of holding on to the saddle horn. When they crested the ridge and eased out onto the flat the kid was sweating and he stopped the horse and wiped at his brow with the sleeve of his coat. Then he wrestled the pack from his back and reached for the canteen draped off the saddle. While he drank, his father sat upright in the saddle, looking down at the town and the roiling of the mill stacks against the green wall of mountain and the perpendicular push of the sky.

"Lived here a long time," he said.

"Yeah?" the kid said, sloshing a handful of water across his face.

"I'll miss it."

"What's there to miss?"

"You get known somewhere, it hangs on you."

The kid leaned the pack against a log and began to sort it out for balance. His father had only brought an extra set of clothes and he'd bought himself a sweater and a pair of dungarees and socks with the money the woman had given him. He settled the clothes in the main compartment and arranged the bush things and the booze in the side pockets. Then he used some of the rope to lash the breakdown pick and shovel and hatchet to the sides. When he was satisfied he lifted the pack with one hand and tried it for heft and balance. It sat right in his hand and he clipped the hasps closed and set it back against the log.

"We got no food," his father said.

"Don't need food."

"Plan on starvin'?"

"Plan on gettin' us what we need."

"Don't got a gun."

"Don't need no gun either."

"You're the boss, I guess."

"That's right." The kid kicked at the dirt and then took another swig from the canteen. His father hauled a bottle out from inside his coat and tilted it up and drank a few hard swallows then cupped a hand over his mouth and his chest heaved some.

"You wanna be takin' it easy on that," the kid said.

"It's just for the sick. Calms me down."

"If you can't sit the damn horse, we ain't going nowhere."

He handed the bottle down and the kid stuck it in the pack. When he swung it up onto his back his father nudged the horse with his heels and she stepped forward farther onto the shale and gravel of the flat overlooking the river valley. He leaned forward so his forearms rested on the horn and swept his gaze along the serpentine wind of the river and over the jut of the town before settling on the stained edge of the sullen and downtrodden neighbourhood they'd left that morning. He nodded and raised a hand to it, purse-lipped and solemn.

"Mean that much to you?" the kid asked.

"There's memories."

"Seems kinda grim."

"Yeah. Still."

"I guess."

The kid reached for the halter and turned the horse, and his father looked back over his shoulder while they walked to the trees, and when the view winked out he raised his chin and looked up at the sky and sighed so that the kid looked up and studied him. There was a redness in his eyes. He pulled a smoke out of the pack in his pocket and lit up and he swayed some so he pressed with his knees to steady himself and sat deeper in the saddle. The horse nickered. The kid looked forward on the trail and led them deeper into the woods and soon they could no longer hear the logging trucks on the highway and the world became the shadow and dip and roll of alpine country and they walked solemnly without speaking.

He was strong from the farm work and used to the terrain so he walked them along at a brisk pace. By late afternoon when the sun slanted down behind the western peaks and the shadows deepened in the ravine where they walked, they'd covered five or six miles by the kid's reckoning. They'd been following a stream for the last few hours and the trail was good. It was the top of the free-range land and the summer trek of cattle along the stream had beaten down the brush and tangle and only the scuttle of rocks made the going rough but they were smallish and the horse never complained. They'd stopped twice to water. Both times his father had asked for the bottle and taken a few swallows. He rode slumped in the saddle for the most part and a few times the kid had checked to see if he was still there, slapping at his shin until he'd grunted and shifted his shoulders about. When they came to a place where the stream eddied out into a wide pool with a shelf of flat at its edge the kid pulled the horse up and helped his father down. He sat him on a rock and tended to the horse. Then, while his father smoked, he made a fire ring from shore rocks and gathered twigs from the fall of nearby trees and fashioned a twig bundle and set it in the ring of stones and put a match to it. The bundle flared and burned hot and bright and he added limbs and branches and had a blazing fire in minutes.

"Pretty good trick," his father said.

He took the fishing line from the pack and tied it to a sapling he propped in the rocks at the shore and he turned stones until he found a grub then baited a hook with it and set the line adrift on the rippling current at the head of the pool. While he was gathering wood for the fire the sapling twitched. The trout was fat and he cleaned it in three quick slices of the hunting knife at his belt and flayed it and pierced it through on a forked stick and stuck it over the fire before rerigging the line and setting it out again. He had another fish in minutes. They ate them right off the sticks, pulling the meat from the skin and flicking the bones into the fire. His father asked for the bottle once he'd eaten, and the kid handed it to him without a word and marched off back into the woods again.

When he returned he had five stout saplings and an armful of spruce boughs. He shaved the saplings and used the strips of bark to bind them into a lean-to frame and piled the spruce boughs on before laying an armful more on the floor of it. Then he piled logs behind the fire so the heat would radiate toward the lean-to and stoked it so it was hot and helped his father into it and sat him down on the spruce boughs. He was weak and his upper arm was thin in the kid's grip. He groaned and shifted about, trying to get comfortable, and once he'd settled he asked for the bottle again and the kid retrieved it and sat beside him and rolled a smoke.

"Where'd ya learn all this?" his father asked.

"What the old man didn't teach me I taught myself."

"Spent a lot of time out here, I guess."

"Enough."

"Me, I never did." He stared at the fire and took a small sip from the bottle then nestled it in the boughs at his feet. "We lived in a tent for the most part when I was a kid. Out here. Places like it. But there weren't ever time to fish. We worked as soon as we could walk. I toted firewood around on a wagon. Had to scavenge it. Didn't have no axe. Busted it all up by hand and sold it to the people around us."

"Oh yeah?" the kid said and prodded at the fire with a stick.

"Indians. Half-breeds. Some whites were with us every now and then. Mostly breeds and Indians though. In the Peace Country. Way up north of here. Our people just followed the work but most places wouldn't hire a skin or a breed. Not regular, least ways. Get a day here, a day there sometimes, but there was never nothing fixed. So I scavenged wood. It's all I learned to hunt when I was kid."

His father shook a smoke out of the pack and lit up and smoked a moment. "Your grandparents were both half-breeds. We weren't Métis like the French Indians are called. We were just half-breeds. Ojibway. Mixed with Scot. McJibs. That's what they called us. No one wanted us around. Not the whites. Not the Indians. So your grandparents and them like them just followed the work and tried to make out the best they could. We camped in tents or squatted on scrubland no one wanted or in deserted cabins and sheds and such. Never no proper home.

"When we got to the Peace it was all we could do to survive. Some of the men remembered how to do all the stuff you been doin' but there weren't no horses and there weren't no time to take the chance on bringin' down a moose or an elk. So they learned how to forget about it. Just hung around the mills waiting for work. Most times it never come."

The kid stood up and laid some more logs on the fire and stirred the embers around to stoke it higher. It was full dark. The horse stomped her hoofs in the bush behind the lean-to and there was the rustle of a varmint in the underbrush somewhere back of them. The creek was a glimmering silver ribbon and the kid walked over and set four hooks on a long line and baited them and anchored the line to a stone and cast it out into the current. Then he walked out of the fire's glow and stood on a boulder looking out over the creek and the bush behind it and on up to the ragged break of the mountain against the sky.

"So how come no one thought about just going out onto the land?" he asked without looking at his father.

His father lay on one side, leaning on his forearm and staring at the ground. "You get beat up good enough you don't breathe right," he said.

"Meaning what?"

"I don't know. All's I do know is that I was ten before we made it into a town and then it was learnin' all about how to make my way through that."

The kid stepped off the boulder and walked back to squat by the fire. "You paint a sad picture," he said. "Figure you're the only one who ever got dealt a lame hand in life?"

"No. That's not what I'm saying."

"Sounds like it to me. I got dealt from the bottom of the deck myself, you know."

"Shit. All's I'm tryin' to say is that we never had the time for learnin' about how to get by out here. None of us did. White man things was what we needed to learn if we was gonna eat regular. Indian stuff just kinda got left behind on accounta we were busy gettin' by in that world."

"So I don't get what we're doin' out here then."

His father raised the bottle and drank slowly. He set it down and scrunched around trying to get comfortable and then lit a smoke and sat staring at the fire for a while. He closed his eyes. The kid could feel him gathering himself, pulling whatever energy he had left from the day up from the depths of him and when he spoke again it was quiet so the kid had to lean forward to hear him.

"I owe," he said.

"Yeah, I heard that before."

"I'm tired, Frank."

"Jesus."

"What?"

"That's the first time you ever called me by my name."

His father arranged his legs under him clumsily and when he found balance he leaned back and caught himself on one arm and looked at the kid and reached out with his other hand and squeezed his arm. Then he eased back on to the spruce boughs and wrapped his coat around him and closed his eyes. He was asleep in minutes. The kid watched him, studying his face and trying to see beyond what he thought he knew of the man, the history that was etched there, the stories, the travels, and after a while all he could see were gaunt lines and hollows and the sag and fall of skin and muscle and the bone beneath it all. When his father's breathing deepened the kid draped his mackinaw over him and walked out to check the horse and gather some bigger wood for the fire. In the forest the night sky was aglitter with the icy blue of stars and he stood in the middle of a copse of trees and arched his neck and watched them. Then he stooped and prowled around for wood he wouldn't need to chop and thought about his father scavenging breakable wood and trundling it about for the few cents it would bring, the potatoes, carrots, or onions it would add to the pot, maybe even a rabbit if he were lucky, and he had an idea of him as a small kid, and when he stood finally with his arms full and made his way back to the camp he understood that he bore more than wood in his arms.

8

HE REMEMBERED THE FIRST TIME HE SAW HIM. He must have been five, near on to six. It was dusk. Summer. The hens were roosting and he was tacking up an extra skein of wire at the base of the hutch. There'd been a fox or a weasel taking hens. They'd lost three already and the old man was angered by it. So the kid had asked how they could fix it. It was a small task and the old man wasn't prone to babying. Instead, he listened when the kid asked questions and he took time to show him how to do things. Then, rather than hover over his shoulder, he left the kid to whichever chore he'd shown interest in. If he needed a hand or the chore needed fixing once he was done, the old man would help him through it so he could learn. But for the jobs themselves, he was left to work. So the kid was hunkered down at the base of the hen hutch busy with arranging the wire. He'd dug down a good foot or so and set the wire in the ground before covering it and getting to the task of tacking staples around the upper section to the wood frame. He liked the hens. He liked their bobbing, pecking scurry and the old lady sort of attitude they took about their roosts. He liked eggs too, so it didn't feel like a chore to him.

He was aware of the man before he saw him. When he turned his head there was the shadowed outline of a man in the doorway. The kid never moved. He squinted against the light and then turned back to the hutch.

"Varmint?" the man said.

"Yeah. Got three hens already," the kid said.

"Shame. You could shoot it."

"Have to be up all night waitin'."

"Suppose. You all right there?"

"I just got to tack up this wire."

"See you up to the house then."

The kid focused on the frame and tapped in a staple. When he turned his head again the man was gone. When he had the wire up he headed for the house with his tools.

He heard them as soon as he entered. Man talk. Deep, rumbled voices that had no pitch or sway, just a long rollout of words that left him knowing that what they discussed had weight to it. The kid put the smaller tools on the metal toolbox by the back door and hung the wire snips and the hammer on hooks set in a peg board nailed to the mudroom wall. He banged the hammer some when he hung it and then stomped his feet on the rubber mat to let them know he was there and the talk dropped off then started in again as he hung his jacket.

They sat at the kitchen table. The old man eyed him as he walked to the refrigerator. He was pouring whisky into mugs. When the kid turned with a glass of milk the old man nodded to him and he pulled a chair up to the table and sat.

"This here's Eldon," the old man told him.

"Sir," the kid said and nodded. He spat on his hand, slid it along the thigh of his pants to dry it and then reached it out across the table.

Eldon shook hands with him. "You get that wire hung good?"

"That varmint'll let me know how good I done."

Eldon laughed. "Ain't that a fact," he said. "Them varmints are a smart bunch."

"Not near as smart as me."

The old man reached out and rubbed his hair. The kid beamed

at him. The three of them sat through a moment of silence and the kid looked back and forth at the men and sipped at his milk.

"You look up Seth Minor like I told ya?" the old man asked.

Eldon swallowed some of the whisky and sat back in his chair with his hands folded around the mug. They were pale and the kid could see the blue veins clearly like tiny rivers through his skin. He fished a smoke out of the chest pocket of his shirt and fumbled with a lighter. When he got it going he took a draw and then exhaled across the table and the kid had to wave the cloud of smoke away from his face. Eldon coughed and shot back another hit of the whisky. "I did," he said finally. "It never amounted to much. Seasonal is all."

"It's a season," the old man said. "You get four seasonals, you get a year."

"Sure. Easy enough for you to say. Ain't much call for bush-trained men no more. The tree toppers and the trucks took away the work."

"They still got call for fallers."

"Had to pawn the saw," Eldon said and coughed again.

The old man shook his head and took a sip from his mug. "Man don't put his tools in hock," he said.

Eldon stared hard at him. The kid could see red veins in his eyes and a pale yellow cloud behind them. "Yeah, well, seasonal jobs'll put you places you didn't plan on."

"Gonna blame it on the work, are ya?"

"Shit luck," Eldon said. "All's I'm saying."

"We don't cuss around here." The old man tilted his head toward the kid.

Eldon flicked a look at him too. "Cuss'll say it plain sometimes."

"Plain says it plain around here."

"Yeah. Okay. Your house and all," Eldon said. He tipped back his mug and swallowed and then held it out to the old man, who shook his head, sighed, and plopped a shot into it. Eldon tilted his head at it and the old man poured more. "But it's all gonna pan out. Got me on at the mill regular. Got in a couple months already and I figure the goose is hanging pretty high."

"That goose's been hung before," the old man said.

"Different friggin' goose," Eldon said and laughed. "Frig's no cuss word, is it?"

"Not so's I'd notice, I suppose."

"Good friggin' thing then," Eldon said. His face was ruddy now and he smiled more. He looked at the kid and winked.

The old man got up and began to rattle around at the stove and the kid and Eldon took turns looking at each other without speaking. There was the smell of stew, peppery and tangy with garlic and onions, and the old man set biscuits to warm in the oven. Eldon reached over and snuck the bottle across the table while the kid watched and poured himself a large dollop. He held a finger to his lips and winked again and the kid wanted to say something, but he didn't. He just sat there and watched while Eldon drank off more of the whisky and settled back in his chair and flopped one leg over the other and smoked and exhaled clouds at the ceiling.

They ate. The men mostly talked about the farm. When he was finished the kid gathered all the plates and cleared the table. Eldon was the only one with the whisky now. The old man sipped at black tea. The kid washed the dishes and set everything back in the cupboard. He caught Eldon staring at him every now and then but there were never any words. The looks felt odd, like there were words hung off them, but

Eldon never said a thing to him. When he was finished he said good night and went to his bedroom, where he coloured in a book until he was tired enough to get into bed. He heard the rumble of their talk. He thought he heard a sob and the old man's voice rise some then it got quieter but he could still hear them talking.

"Who is he?" the kid asked while they were milking in the morning. Eldon slept on the couch near the woodstove. The kid had looked at him when he got up. His arms and legs were flung wide and his head was tilted back with his mouth wide open.

The old man pulled at the cow's teats and the kid watched his shoulders work. "Someone I known years ago," he said without looking back at him. "Different fella now but I knew him good at one time. Least I thought I did."

"He smells funny," the kid said.

"He's been rinsed through pretty good."

"With that whisky?" the kid asked.

"Yes, sir. Some men take to it. I never did."

"Why not? Does it do bad things?"

The old man looked at him over his shoulder. "Keeps varmints away," he said.

"How so?"

"Savvy what a varmint is?"

"Yeah," the kid said. "Pests. Things you don't want around."

"Well, whisky keeps things away that some people don't want around neither. Like dreams, recollections, wishes, other people sometimes." The old man turned on the stool and set the milk pail down on the floor between his feet. "Things get busted sometimes. When they happen in the world you can fix 'em most times. But when they happen inside a person they're harder to mend. Eldon got broke up pretty bad inside," he said.

The old man shook his head and wiped at his face with one hand. "It's a tough thing. Hard to watch. Hard to hear. But folks need hearing out sometimes, Frank. That's why I let him come here."

"He seems sad."

"Pretty much. Sad's not a bad thing unless it gets a hold of you and won't let go."

"He sleeps funny," the kid said.

"Chasin' varmints, I suppose," the old man said.

He was gone by the time they finished the chores. All that remained was the smell of old booze, stale tobacco smoke, and a sheaf of bills in a glass jar on the stove. The old man stood in the doorway staring at it, rubbing at his chin whiskers.

It was almost a year before he saw him again. He was herding cows back from the open range beyond the ridge. When they broke through the trees at the field's edge there was a dull blur of orange at the head of the lane. The closer he got the more the blur took on the shape of an old pickup. The cows took to the scent of home and trotted toward the barn. The lot of them aimed for the open gate that led to the back paddock. He rode in slow and walked the horse past the truck.

She was a weather-beaten old Merc that was a few thousand miles beyond her better days. She was slung low on her springs and the windshield was starred with cracks. The front bumper was wired on. There was a rag stuffed in where the gas cap should have been. When the kid rode by he saw a clutter of tools flung into the bed: a rusted chainsaw, pry bars, falling wedges, a bow saw, several axes and mauls, and a scattered heap of shovels. A pair of fuzzy dice dangled from the rear-view mirror.

After he'd stabled the horse he walked through the house. There wasn't anyone there. There was a whisky bottle and a single glass on the kitchen table. Tobacco stench hung in the air. He went to the barn and walked the fence line around it. He found the tracks near the gate that opened out onto the tractor path leading to the woodlot where the old man chopped and stored their winter fuel. It was less than a quarter-mile and he heard no sounds of sawing or cutting. As he walked he listened and halfway there he could hear shouting.

"Stubborn old son of a bitch!" It was Eldon's voice.

"Shut up! Just shut the hell up!" The old man's voice, harder and louder than he'd ever heard.

When he cleared the last bend he saw them. They were sat apart from each other, leaning on stacked cords of wood. Both of them were heaving for breath. The kid could tell by the spill of the earth at their feet that there had been a scuffle, maybe even a full-on fight. There was a spot of blood at the corner of Eldon's mouth, and the old man looked winded and half spent. When they saw him they both put their heads down and stared at the ground. The kid walked silently to a round of fir they used for a chopping block and sat down on it, not saying a word. He looked back and forth at them and it took a minute before they raised their heads to look back at him.

"Tell him," Eldon said.

"Not my place to tell him. It's yours," the old man said.

"I don't know that I got it in me."

"You come here all full of beans for it."

"Yeah, well."

"Yeah, well, nothin'. He's here now."

The kid was puzzled and there was a spear of anxiety in him at their words. Eldon put his hands on his knees and let out a breath. He hadn't shaved. He looked as broke down as the truck. He took something metal from his pocket, screwed the top off, and drank. He swiped the back of his hand across his lips and stood up, tucking the thing back into the pocket of his faded dungarees. He wavered but caught his balance, and put one hand on a hip and looked over at the kid.

"Got something needs tellin'," he said.

The kid looked at the old man, who leaned back on the stacked lengths of wood and waved him over. The kid crossed to him and sat beside him. The old man put an arm around his shoulders and the kid peered up at him, wary at the sudden weight of the moment.

"What?" he asked.

"Hear the man," the old man said.

The kid turned to Eldon.

"I'm your pap," he said.

The kid looked again at the old man.

"I said I'm your father."

"What's he saying?" he asked.

"Sayin' what he needs to say. Or thinks as much anyhow."

"Is it true?"

"Ask him."

Eldon had caught his full breath now and he had a cigarette he twiddled between his fingers.

"Is it true?" the kid asked him.

"Truest thing I ever said," Eldon answered.

"That can't be true," the kid said. He stared at the old man wide-eyed. "I thought you were my dad."

"I'm raisin' you. Teachin' you. There's a diff'rence," the old man said. "But I love you. That's a straight fact."

"How come then? How come he's my father?"

"Gonna have to ask him, Frank. It ain't mine for the tellin'. Certain things when they're true gotta come right from them that knows them as true."

"How come?" he asked.

Eldon peered at him, then struck a wooden match and lit the cigarette. "Don't know as I can say right now," he said. "It's complicated."

"What's complicated mean?" the kid asked.

"It means he ain't got it all organized in his head," the old man said.

"Then why say?" the kid asked.

The old man tousled his hair. "That's what the scrap was about," he said.

"I don't even know you," the kid said.

Eldon scratched his head. He took another long drag on the smoke. They could hear the nattering of ravens in the trees. When he looked over at the kid again his face was taut-looking. "That's why I said it."

"I don't understand."

"Me neither rightly."

"Then why *say*?" He stood and moved a few steps away from the old man. He put his hands on his hips and stared at Eldon.

"Jesus," Eldon said. "You got him talkin' like a man."

The old man smirked. "Someone got to," he said.

Eldon ground the smoke out on the logs. He flicked it across the open space with one finger. The old man eyed him sternly and Eldon strode over and retrieved the butt and put it in his pocket. He looked at the two of them sheepishly. "Thing is," he said slowly. "I don't know why I come. Except somethin' told me I needed to. Hell, the truth is, I don't know why I hadta say it neither. Just kinda felt like I did. Savvy?"

"No," the kid said.

"Damn," Eldon said. "This is tough business."

"You called it," the old man said.

"Shit," Eldon said. "Sorry. About the cussin', I mean. I'm way too sober for this."

"You know how to fix that. Always did."

"Yeah," Eldon said and stared at the ground. He traced a half-circle back and forth with the toe of his boot. Back and forth. Back and forth. His lips were pinched together and his shoulders slumped. The kid felt sorry for him. He'd never seen anyone trapped by their own words before. It looked like tough business like he'd said.

"It's all right," the kid said quietly.

Eldon looked up at him and the kid could see that his eyes looked wet. His hands shook as he rubbed at his chin. He looked ready to bolt. He took a huge breath and looked up at the sky. He exhaled loudly and when he looked back at the kid and the old man he looked desolate. It scared the kid some and he edged closer to the old man. "How come this is such a rough go?" Eldon asked.

The old man stood up. "Truth ain't never easy. Especially one you had hung up in you a long time. I give ya points for gumption though."

Eldon closed his eyes and lowered his head. "Thing is," he said, "I don't know where to go from here. It's out. It's there. But I plumb don't know what to do. Maybe this was for shit."

The kid looked up at the old man, who stepped over and put a hand on his shoulder. They both studied Eldon, who stood straighter and set his lips into a grim line.

"I gotta think on this," Eldon said. "I gotta go."

"To where?" the old man asked. "It's out. You said yourself. Can't go nowhere without the truth of it followin' you around. You owe now."

"Owe what?"

"Time. You lost seven years of it."

"I can't change that."

"No. But you can make the years coming different."

"How?"

"Gonna have to work that out for yourself. Me? I'd put the plug in the jug and sort it out quick."

Eldon looked at the kid. His face seemed to waver like the shimmy the wind makes on the face of a pond. The kid just looked back at him calmly. "He just needed to know, is all," Eldon said and fumbled about for another smoke.

The kid switched looks back and forth from the old man to Eldon. He needed one of them to tell him what to do. He could hear the cows bawling in the paddock and the hard, flat clap of a rifle shot echoing off the ridge. Eldon fidgeted. Then he pulled out the whisky and tipped it up and drank. When he pulled it away from his mouth he studied it as though surprised at the emptiness. Then he stood and tucked it back into his pocket. "Sorry," Eldon said. "I shoulda thought this through." He looked at the old man, who just shook his head sadly. Then he stared at the ground and puffed out his cheeks. When he looked up the kid could see how spooked he was. "Sorry," he said again and stomped off.

All they could do was watch him go.

"My father," the kid said.

"Yessir," the old man said.

"He never said nothin' about my mother," the kid said.

He watched as the old man's face clouded. "Comes a time for it I'll tell ya but for now it's up to him," he said.

"Why?"

"Because it's a father's thing to do. It's him who owes ya that. Not me."

"Maybe he'll be too scared to talk about that."

The old man scowled. "Could be yer right there," he said.

9

IN THE MORNING HE WAS FEVERISH. The kid could see the yellow cast of him and when he offered up the bottle his father waved it away and struggled to a sitting position and lit a smoke. He pushed the kid's hand away from his brow and stared at the ground.

"What do I do?" the kid asked.

"Nothing. Liver's shutting down."

"Can you eat?"

"I can try."

He checked the nightline and there were three trout that he cleaned and flayed and placed over the fire on sticks. When they were finished he handed one of the sticks to his father and he picked at the flesh and tried a few mouthfuls and then handed the stick back and took a drink from the bottle. The kid ate the fish. He walked out to where the horse was tied and brushed her out and saddled her. Then he walked her close to the lean-to and left her there and began cleaning up the camp and reloading the pack. It was sunny but crisp and his father kept the mackinaw pulled around him. The kid kicked out the fire and then killed it with a canteen full of water and handfuls of sand from the creekbed. Then he disassembled the lean-to and laid the boughs and saplings in the trees and helped his father up onto the horse.

"Why do that?" his father asked.

"Respect. Gotta leave it the way you found it," he said.

"Can't ever leave nothing the way you found it."

"You'd be the one to know that, I suppose."

"What're you sayin'?"

The kid stared up at him. He could feel words churning in his gut, like fish fighting their way upstream. None broke the surface. He brushed the horse's neck and stared at her brown orb of an eye. "Nothin', I guess," was all he said.

He shouldered the pack then grabbed the halter and walked the horse out of the camp and down the trail that led north and west along the creek. His father struggled to sit the horse and settled for clutching the saddle horn two-handed again.

"Try and feel her step," the kid said. "You have to move with her."

"Ojibways weren't horse Injuns."

"Still. Better if you read her step. Don't tire out that way."

"I'll tire out anyhow."

The creek was boisterous from rain in the higher elevations and it drowned out the sound of the land. The kid kept an eye on the trees. Cougars were known in these parts and they bore no fear of man. There were tracks in the mud of the trailside: deer, raccoons, skunks, rabbits, and one sudden, bold, clear print of a bobcat. He looked up at his father to point it out to him but he was slumped in the saddle with his chin bumping his chest and he called to him. His father raised a hand limply from the saddle horn then let if fall. He was weaker. There was a different odour coming off him now, something like old leaves mouldering on the forest floor, and the kid wondered if the moment was close by. The thought raised a lump in his throat and he gritted his teeth and mouthed a silent curse at himself for it. He punched his thigh and scowled. He walked the horse more carefully up the pitch of the trail. His father's head lolled and he moaned now and then and the kid wondered about binding his hands to the pommel and his feet to the stirrups.

The trail left the stream after three or four miles and began a long, meandering climb around the jut of ridge. The trees were farther apart here, the bed of soil a mere four inches thick, and he could see the roots of them pushed across the skin of the mountain like veins. They climbed steadily for the rest of the morning and when the sun had reached its zenith he looked for a level place to stop. They came to a clump of pines with one thick root poked out of the grass and gravel and he took the horse into it and helped his father down and set him with his back against the root until he was comfortable. Then he strode off and returned in a short time with mushrooms and greens and berries that he crushed up and fashioned into a paste. He gathered a clump of it on a stick of alder and held it out to his father.

"You don't want me to eat that?"

"It eats better than it looks."

"It'd want to." He took a mouthful and washed it down with water from the canteen and looked at the kid with surprise. "Don't taste bad."

"Sometimes I'll put some pine resin in with it if I got a pot and a fire. Makes a good soup. Lots of good stuff in there."

"Old man?"

"Yeah. At first he brung me out all the time when I was small. Showed me plants and how to gather them. Everything a guy would need is here if you want it and know how to look for it, he said. You gotta spend time gatherin' what you need. What you need to keep you strong. He called it a medicine walk."

"Hand us that crock."

The kid reached across to the pack and rooted around for the bottle. His father drank in small sips and peered out through the trees at the territory they were in. The kid rolled them each a smoke and they lit up and sat silently. Now and then his father would close his eyes and let his head fall forward and then push it up again with one hand. Then he leaned his head back against the root of the tree and closed his eyes and the kid could hear him breathing. It was ragged and forced at first and his hand clenched and unclenched at his side and he put the other to his belly and groaned. Gradually he eased and his breathing grew shallower and quieter. His mouth hung open and he huffed and clawed around at his pocket for the smokes. The kid leaned over and dug out the pack and shook one out and held it to his lips and lit it for him. His father smoked without using his hands and kept his eyes closed. The kid scuffed around at the gravel with the alder stick.

'There's a place just up this face worth seeing," the kid said. His father only grunted.

"I been goin' there a long time. It changes. Maybe because I got older. Got more sense now. I don't know. It's just special," the kid said. "There's signs up there. Symbols. Painted right into the rock. When the old man took me there the first time he said it was sacred because no one can ever figure out how come the paintings never faded. They been there a powerful long time."

"I hearda places like that. Never been to them. Never seen them."

"Seems like maybe you should see it now."

"We gotta climb to it."

"The horse can get you most of the way. I'll lug you the best I can up the rest."

"Sounds like a lotta work for a few paintings."

"Lotta times, I guess, you never know what you need until you lay eyes on it."

"You got to be a philosopher," his father said.

The kid looked at him and shook his head. "Not so much. I mean, out here things just come all on their own sometimes. Thoughts, ideas, stuff I never really had a head for."

"I never had much of a head for anything. My back got me through."

"That and the hooch," the kid said and nodded toward the bottle.

His father glared at him. He tipped the bottle up and swallowed. He coughed and gagged a bit. He held a hand up to his mouth and closed his eyes. When the urge to retch passed he leaned back against the root and eyed the kid who lowered his gaze. "Don't judge me," he said.

"Ain't," the kid said.

"What is it you're doin' then?"

"Just watchin' is all."

"Watching what?"

The kid stood up and pitched the stick into the fire. "Guess I'll tell you when I got that figured. Right now, I'm just watching."

His father took a feeble sip of the whisky. The kid kicked dirt over the fire and stamped it out then walked to the horse, snugged up the tack, and led her back to where his father lay. His father struggled to his feet. The kid took his arm to help him up onto the horse. His hand encircled the whole bicep. He had to reach out and grab his father by the belt to hoist him up into the stirrup. He stood with his foot in it and caught his breath before kicking his other leg over to sit in the saddle.

There was a narrow path that led around boulders and between trees that eased upward with the flank of the cliff at their right. The forest thinned out. There were large gaps between trees. The ground was a mass of pine needles, roots, and rocks. Here and there a small copse of aspens or birches lent a dappled look to the slant of the path and the horse nickered at it. The kid patted her neck. His father looked around and clutched the saddle horn for balance and they walked easily for a while until the trail canted upward sharply. It pressed tight to the cliff. They began a tenuous, snaking climb. His father had to lean forward in the saddle and the horse fought for purchase in the talus and gravel.

The trail bellied out onto a small ledge. The trees were stunted. Only junipers seemed to flourish and they spread wide right up to the edge of the cliff. The trail became barely visible along the cliff face. "We're gonna leave her here," the kid said. "It's about eighty feet more."

"Might as well be eighty miles," his father said. "Way I feel anyways."

"I'll get you there. Everyone should see something like this."

The kid tied the horse to a small tree and his father was able to walk on his own for a dozen yards. Then the trail tilted up and the footing grew less stable. The kid moved behind him and put a hand in his belt and the other between his shoulder blades. His father grumbled but the kid pushed on. They stopped now and then so his father could catch his breath. The kid looked out over the valley below them and waited. When he was ready his father huffed and the kid propelled him steadily upward. Eventually they reached a ledge about ten feet long and four feet wide. The wall of the cliff was flat. The kid eased his father down close to the edge. It took a moment for his breathing to settle and when he finally raised his eyes to look at the cliff face his mouth draped open.

"Damn, Frank," he said.

The kid sat down beside him and they both stared up at the wall of rock. There were symbols painted in a dull red, black, and a stark greyish white. There were birds, oddly shaped animals, what appeared to be horses and bison, horned beings, stars, and assorted lines and shapes. The drawings stretched a full twenty feet up and covered the entire wall. They studied them without speaking for a long time.

"Take me up to it," his father said quietly.

The kid stood and helped him stand. Together they shuffled to the face of the cliff. His father reached out and put his hand on the rock. Then he slid it over and covered a small dog-like shape and raised his head to look up at the array.

"What do they signify?" Eldon asked.

"I don't know. Near as I can figure they're stories. I reckon some are about travelling. That's how they feel to me. Others are about what someone seen in their life. The old man doesn't think anyone ever figured them out."

"Ain't a powerful lotta good if ya can't figure 'em out."

The kid shrugged. "I sorta think you gotta let a mystery be a mystery for it to give you anything. You ever learn any Indian stuff?"

His father lowered his gaze. He turned his back to the wall and slid down to sit. He brushed a hand over his forehead and closed his eyes to heave a deep breath. "Nah," he said finally. "Most of the time I was just tryin' to survive. Belly fulla beans beats a head fulla thinkin'. Stories never seemed likely to keep a guy goin'. Savvy?"

"I guess," the kid said. "Me, I always wanted to know more about where I come from." The kid took out his makings and rolled them each a smoke. They lit up and smoked quietly for a minute or two. "I could come and sit here for hours. I spent three days here once when I was thirteen. Sorta thought if I spent enough time studying them drawings I could figure out what they were supposed to tell me."

"They ever?"

An eagle drifted over the valley. There was a yap of coyotes from somewhere below and the snap of a limb as something big moved through the trees above them. "Not really, I guess. Nothin' real, least ways," the kid said after a while. "But it seemed to me no one came here no more. Like they forgot it was here. That made me sad. So I kept comin' so there'd at least be someone even if I didn't know how to read 'em or get what it was they were tryin' to say. At least there was someone."

His father just looked at him.

"I can't reckon someone dying," the kid said. "Scares me some to think of it. Don't exactly know how to face it. Don't know what I'm s'posedta do when it happens. So I don't know how come I brung ya here. Mighta just been for me."

His father slipped the whisky out of his coat pocket and dribbled a little of it into his mouth and sat there looking out across the wide expanse of space that hung over the valley. "Mighta," he said.

10

THEY MADE THE BOTTOM OF THE CLIFF by mid-afternoon. His father was weaker. By the stream the kid helped him off the horse and washed his face with handfuls of cold water, then held a cup out for him to drink. His father sipped at it and when he swallowed there was an audible clack in his throat. Then he coughed. The kid sat him back against a rock. He closed his eyes and leaned his head back and the kid listened to the sounds of the land around them. The breeze sent leaves fluttering and the rush of the water was like a low whistle underneath that. The horse whinnied. The kid put his hand to his father's head and felt the heat of him. Then he stood and faced the west and put his face up and closed his eyes. There was rain coming.

"Got to get you inside," the kid said. "Rain and cold ain't good for you."

"You got a cave in mind?" his father asked. He opened one eye and studied him.

"There's a deserted old trapper's cabin a few miles off. It's off our route some but not by much."

"Got a bed?"

"There's a cot is all."

"I could stand a bed."

When he'd rested the kid pushed him up into the saddle again and they walked along the stream for a mile or so. Then the kid led the horse west. There was a meagre trail that was overgrown with bracken but he knew where he was headed. His father looked up every now and then but didn't speak. They soon broke through the trees into a wide marsh. The grasses were high and bent in the breeze that was stiffer now and cold. The footing was boggy and the horse's hooves made loud sucking sounds. The kid clomped through looking for tufts of grass to aid his steps. There was a wide pond with a beaver dam in the middle. At the far end the spruce and fir began again and the ground was firmer and dry. The horse seemed to know where she was headed and picked up her pace some. His father grasped the saddle horn and swayed before he caught the rhythm of her step and settled into a looser sway. They walked into a clearing where there was dilapidated cabin gone grey with age and an open shed canted to one side. There was a feeble curl of smoke from the chimney.

The horse nickered at the smell of hay and the door to the cabin opened. A woman stepped out. She cradled a shotgun in the crook of her arms. She was short and burly and she wore men's clothes. Even her boots were a man's and when she walked her step was deliberate and heavy. She had the wide, squat face of a Native woman but her skin was fair and her eyes under the wide, battered brim of her hat were a pale blue. She stepped off the porch and stood mutely, her eyes flicking back and forth between them. The hands that held the shotgun were grimed with dirt, hard-looking, dry, and she flexed them while she fixed her flat stare on them.

"He sick?" she asked, swinging her gaze to the kid. Her voice was gruff and rattled out like she hadn't used it in while.

"Yes," the kid said. "My father."

"What's he got. The fever?"

"No, ma'am. He's drink sick. He's dying."

"Drink sick? Well, least it ain't catchy. Rain's comin' and I don't imagine you fancy a night out in it. Feels like a good soak on its way."

"Appreciate a place on your floor, that's true," the kid said.

"Well, fetch him in then. There's hay and the well's back of the shed. I got stew and I do a pretty good biscuit. If he's drink sick, some cedar tea will help his fever."

"Thank you, ma'am. My name's Franklin Starlight. This here's my dad. Eldon."

"Becka Charlie," she said. "Proper name's Rebecca but no one much latched on to the Ree part. Been Becka all my life."

"Ma'am." The kid touched the brim of his hat.

"Becka," she said.

"All right."

She set the shotgun down on the rail of the porch and helped him get his father down. Together they walked him into the small cabin. The kid looked around. It was different from the empty, mice-ridden place he'd seen the last time he'd been there. There was one window with three panes smashed out and covered with thin, scraped hide so the light was yellowish and eerie. The cot was set in the back corner. There was a pair of chairs cut out of blocks of cedar and a rough table made from a sawn log with four crossed saplings for legs. The fireplace was stone and mud with a wide hearth that held a hornet's nest, a stuffed owl, a bible, and a rattle made of deer hide and antler. Dishes and pots were piled on a board set across a large pail and her clothes were hung on nails in the wall: suspenders, dungarees, wool socks, flannel work shirts, and a rain slicker. She had a broom fashioned out of a length of cedar branch and the floor bore the signs of regular sweeping.

"She's rough but she holds the warmth of the fire," Becka said. "I done the roof last summer so she's dry. Chinked the walls fresh. You're welcome to make yourself at home."

They sat his father down on one of the block chairs and Becka tended to the fire. When it was roaring good she set a cast iron tea kettle on a tripod next to the flames. The kid left them to see to the horse.

The mare had already walked to the shed and was eating hay. The kid fetched a pail of water from the well and set it down for her and then stashed the saddle and the blanket on hooks nailed to the shed's remaining wall. Then he brushed her out. When he was finished he walked around the cabin. There was a privy set fifty feet back in the trees. A rough garden that hadn't been there on his last visit, with a tangle of plants turned hard brown by frost, sat in a small clearing threatened by a spill of blackberry bush and wild rose. Back of the garden in the shade of a clutch of cedars was a grave marked by a wooden cross. The cross was new.

When he got back to the cabin his father was wrapped in a blanket. The fire blazed a fine yellow. There was a steaming cup set on the remaining chair and he flopped his coat over the back of it and took the cup in his hands. The heat of the tin felt good on his palms. He inhaled the scent of the tea. Pine gum with a touch of mint. The kind he'd make himself out on the land. It offered more heat and he drank it slowly.

The woman hauled an empty pail over close to the fire. She overturned it and sat on its bottom. Her feet were broad and flat as paddles in the wool socks. She had them pulled up over the bottoms of her faded work pants, and the tails of the coarse shirt hung over her hips and made her look shorter and squatter in the flicker of firelight. The kid thought she looked like a gnome and he grinned at his sally.

"Grin like a gopher, you," Becka said. "How old are ya?"

"Sixteen," the kid said. "Be seventeen pretty soon."

"Big'un."

"I guess. Never really thought about it."

"He's bad, huh?" Becka hooked a thumb at his father, who had nodded off. He was folded in the crude chair like a rag doll.

"His liver's shot. He ain't got long."

"Funny thing about drink," Becka said. "Comes a time ya gotta drink to stay alive at the same time it's killin' ya. Never took to it, me. My father did though."

"That who's in the grave yonder?" the kid said.

She turned her head to squint at him. He could feel the force of her studying him. He raised the cup and drank in order to break the look. "Cut right to it, don't ya?" she said.

"Got raised to speak my piece and to ask direct. Saves a lot of time and wonderin'."

She snickered. It sounded spooky in the glimmer. "That it does," she said. "Come from him, that kind of reason?"

"No. I wasn't raised by him."

"Well, whoever give that give ya good sense."

They sat drinking tea. Beyond the crackle of the fire it was quiet. He could hear the wind through the trees. Behind it there was the patter of rain on leaves and limbs and it grew louder as it neared like a wave of surf across the land. When it hit the cabin it spattered and drummed on the roof and Becka laid another log on the fire. His father snored. The kid put a hand to his forehead. It was cooler but clammy still.

"He took some cedar tea?" he asked.

"Drank a whole mug."

"Works good."

"She's an old cure but a good'un."

"You know cures?"

"Some. My dad was Chilcotin. My mother was Scotch. They both had heads fulla the old ways. I got raised up in it. Held on to a great bunch of it all these years. Never know when it'll come to serve ya."

The kid nodded. He drank the last of the tea and set the cup lightly on the floor at his feet. The rain was heavy, falling in sheets he could see when he looked out the single pane of the window. He turned to the fire and stretched his legs out in front of him. The warmth fell over him like a blanket and he was asleep before he knew it.

He woke to the smell of fresh biscuits. The rain had slacked off to a steady patter on the shingles. He was alone in front of the fire that had been banked to an orange mound that threw a steady push of heat into the cabin. He yawned and stretched and when he stood and turned to the table by the window, his father sat looking at him, his eyes in the firelight glistening like marbles. He was still wrapped in the blanket with a pair of the woman's wool socks on his feet. He nodded and turned to lean his forearms on the table and watch the woman stirring an iron pot at the opposite end of the table. There was a pan of biscuits beside it.

"Coulda slept for hours," the kid said. He carried the trunk chair over to the table and sat.

"Shoulda," Becka said. "I'da kept this warm for ya."

"Just as well I'm up anyway."

"She eats better hot, that's for true."

"Fetch us that hooch, Frank."

The kid turned. His father was staring at him. His eyes were empty. His face was haggard and everything seemed to fall downward, held in place by the nub of his chin. "Why'nt you just have some more tea?" the kid asked.

"Why'nt you quit shin-kickin' me and fetch me that hooch?"

"You done good today is all's I'm sayin'."

"Day's still on."

The kid shrugged and walked to where he'd set the pack and rustled around for a bottle. He could feel his father's eyes on him. When he turned with it in his hand his father's mouth had draped open and his eyes were lit with orange from the fire. He looked like a spectre. He handed him the bottle. His father's hands shook when he grabbed it and the kid had to twist the cap off for him and pour a slug of it into his cup.

"Can't let a drunk push you around," Becka said. "They run with power like that."

"He ain't drunk right now," the kid said.

"He wants to be. It works out to be the same in the end."

"How do you get to come to call me out?" his father said. There was fight in his voice.

"You're in my home, that's how I come to it."

"This ain't your home. You're squattin' is all."

"This was my grandfather's way back when," Becka said. "It come to my daddy and when I brung him here to die it come to me, you wanna know the truth of it."

His father could only look at her. He lifted the cup and swallowed what was left of the whisky. "Sorry," he mumbled.

Becka busied herself with plates and utensils and while she rattled around the kid sat staring out the window at the rain. "Sure could eat," he said after a while. "I want to thank for you for your kindness."

"Reason people got a door is welcome," Becka said. "Besides, I been without company a while now. It's good to talk to something other than the ravens and the trees."

She ladled the stew into bowls and slid them down the table toward the kid. He put a bowl in front of his father but all he did was stare at it. The stew was rich and strong with the smell of wild meat and the kid felt the enormity of his hunger. When she'd trundled over a length of wood to sit on and served herself he dug in with his spoon. His father took a biscuit, dipped it into his bowl, and then chewed it slowly. His head was down and he stared at a spot on the table. Becka ate lustily. She bent over her bowl and spooned stew into her mouth with a bite of biscuit. She smacked and gobbled and the kid smiled at her enthusiasm. He threw off decorum too and ate with the energy of his hunger. His father just poked at his food. He slopped whisky into his cup and drank slowly.

He and the woman ate three bowls of the stew apiece and finished off the biscuits. Then Becka served them a cup of tepid tea and while the kid sipped at his she ladled the last of the stew onto a plate with the remnants of a biscuit. She spooned his father's bowl onto it and headed for the door.

"Dog?" Eldon asked.

"Usedta have one named Curly but he died. This is for the spirits," she said.

"Spirits? What kinda witchcraft you practise anyhow?"

She turned at the open door and crooked her head and looked at him. "Ancestors," she said. "Grandmothers, grandfathers, our people who gone before. The trees, the animals, the birds. Them spirits. If that's witchcraft to you, I feel sorry for ya."

"Seems like kinda a waste of good food."

"Not eatin' it is a waste of food."

"I'm sick," he said.

"Might not be so sick if ya ate."

"I got no belly for it."

"Seems to me ya got no belly for a lot of things."

He managed a dull sneer. Then he tilted the cup and drained it and set it back on the table, eying her hard all the while. She only shook her head and walked out the door.

"She's tough," the kid said.

"She's a bitter old washed-out bitch."

"Took us in outta the rain."

"Yeah. So she'd have someone to sermon to."

"I never heard no sermon. Just someone talkin' straight."

"Straight outta the loony bin's my thinkin'."

His father fumbled about for a smoke and the kid rolled two from his makings. When he was done he helped his father out the door and onto the porch. There was a bench and a willow sapling chair. He set him in the chair and lit his smoke and took a seat on the bench just as Becka strode around the corner of the cabin. She sat beside the kid and he felt the bench sag with her weight. She took an old pipe from her pocket and crossed one leg over the other and lit up. The three of them smoked in silence. The rain slapped down and then seemed to break suddenly to become a light shower and down into a fine mist with fog rolling in from the trees.

"She'll clear off by morning," Becka said. "Be muddy but you'll travel all right."

"The horse is a real mudder," the kid said. "She's a mountain horse."

"Looks like a good mare. Where ya headed?"

"West."

Becka nodded. She smoked her pipe and levelled her gaze at Eldon, who sat motionless in the willow chair. The smoke billowed around her face. Her gaze was intent and serious and the kid could almost feel her thinking.

"I wouldn'ta expected it from you," she said.

"What?" His father gave her a bored look and then stared back at the floor of the porch.

"The warrior way," she said quietly. "Givin' yourself back to the land. I wouldn't have thought you had any of that teachin' in you. That's what this is, right? He's takin' you somewhere west of here so you can get buried in the warrior way?"

The kid was shocked. "How'd you know that?" he asked.

She kept her gaze on his father. "Not hard to figure. He's on his way out and there's nothin' west of here for miles and miles and where there is somethin' he won't make it. He don't savvy spirit talk. So I know he ain't been schooled in traditional ways. But he's a sorry sumbuck, that's plain. So now he figures that goin' out in some kinda honourable fashion is gonna fetch him some peace way yonder. 'Cept it ain't likely to."

"You read all that in a few hours?"

"Like I said, mister. It ain't hard to figure."

"You don't know the half of it."

"I ain't the one that needs to, I suppose."

His father looked up at the kid. He wondered if it was an effect of the light but the kid could see him soften. Then he pursed his lips and lowered his head again.

"I could use me more of that fire," he said finally. He looked square at Becka now. "If you don't mind I wouldn't mind to pay back a little of what I owe."

"I don't follow," she said.

He looked at the kid. "For him. I got some story that's needed telling for a long time."

She nodded. Together they helped him into the cabin and sat him in the trunk chair in front of the fire. He asked for more whisky and she poured him some. While he sipped at it they arranged their seats close to him. The fire wavered in the hot and orange coals. The sheet of it pressed out into the darkened space of the cabin in waves. It took him minutes before he started to talk.

11

IT WAS THE WAR that brought him to the world. He was eleven when his father went to fight it and he found that sudden absence jarring, like a tooth that falls out when you chew. It could sit in your palm and be seen as a tooth but its place was gone and there was only a hole. He'd never heard of Europe, Germans, or Hitler. They were only sounds to him, and the only meaning he found for them was the gap in his life when his father sauntered off to meet the train. The war was the knowledge that things could be taken away.

"Send his pay home," his mother said. "It's what he says. Like that's a good enough reason to fight."

His father became envelopes. He became the sporadic ones his mother picked up from the general delivery box or the ones she gave him to lick before she sent them off to Belgium, France, and Italy. He became the taste of glue. They were set down in a shack on a sugar beet farm in Taber, Alberta. His mother cooked and sewed and helped with chores in the out-buildings. The pay wasn't much but the job put a roof over their heads. He went to work in the fields. Most days he followed along behind the machine that slung the beets into a wagon, picking up strays and lugging them in a sack tied to his waist. The little they could spare went into a cigar box his mother kept below the floorboards beneath her bed. The bed they shared.

His father became the scratch of a pencil nub on paper in the wavered light of a candle. He became the faraway look in his mother's eyes as she wrote, staring into the candle flame for minutes at a time. He became the long act of waiting. He became the flash of him, white as a bone and clenched in his mother's hand. The words she read, moving her lips, her finger tracing them across paper crumpled and creased from being composed against a root or stump or the broad back of a fellow hunched in a foxhole in places with strange names she couldn't pronounce. He became the sound of those words read to him in the flickering light. Then he became the taste of beef, the feel of new shirts against his skin, and new stout shoes on his feet. He was in the tiny wads of bills that some-times arrived with the letters that became a slingshot for him, a pale blue dress with white polka dots and a kerchief to match for his mother.

"For the train," she said to him. "For when he comes home."

The war was the knowledge that things could be missed.

His father became weeks of worry. The tiny lines that broke out overnight across his mother's brow, at the edge of her eyes, the back of her hands, and the steady, downward droop of her mouth. Her back huddled in the doorway look-ing out across the stretch of land, smoke from a cigarette around her like a rain cloud bearing the tears she would never let him see. He became silence. Nights of it. Mornings stretched to their limit by it. Days chinked with it like mud and straw stuffed into the gaps between boards to keep a chill wind from whistling through. The silence lived in her face, moved in her step and her hands when she touched him. It became the outline he could see walking the fields and meadows in the glimmering light of evening. His father. Grinning. Waving. Free of whatever terrors he lived with. Silence became his lullaby and it served him until one day a man stood in the doorway and his mother collapsed on the floor, sobbing, wailing, punching the rough boards, entrenched in a grief so deep and sudden it scared him and he had to run, chasing the vague outline of his father across the fields and hollering as loud as he could, spitting snot, and blood from where he'd bitten through his lip. The war became the knowl-edge that life can strip you raw, that some holes are never filled, some gaps not chinked, some chill winds relentless in their pitch and yowl.

His mother was lessened by the loss of his father. He could see that. He could feel it. She took to dancing in the polka-dot dress. Twirling, sashaying, dipping, and spinning to music he couldn't hear, her arms clenched about herself. Other times the blank look on her face, one hand reaching out to a space that would never be filled, the fingers curling slowly, the hand drawn back to her face to cup her mouth and chin. The absence like the space between words. "You're the man now," she said softly one night. He didn't even know she knew he was there, half hidden behind the door jamb, watching, remembering. She swept a wisp of hair back from her brow and he liked the smallness of the gesture. It made her girl-like. She was small in the dress. He wanted to protect her.

So work became his war. He turned thirteen and he became serious. Grave. He bent to the work that came to him with an expression that appeared cold, angry perhaps, and he attacked it with what some took as vengeance. But it was just his way. He worked like a grown man, like how his father worked.

They travelled in a battered caravan of rusted trucks and broken cars held together with wire and poor welds, stacked and stuffed with tools and gear, furniture and possessions. They followed rumours of work. They slept by day and drove at night in order to arrive at a place when the light was breaking and put in a full day's work from the get-go. They were fruit pickers, wood cutters, tree planters, fish gutters, trench diggers, stall muckers, and the lucky few with a skill set were itinerant masons, carpenters, and welders. For the most part they were lucky to get on anywhere and they took whatever they could get if it meant full bellies.

"There's those that would try to take advantage of us now," his mother told him. "We got to pay our own way."

They wound back and forth across the mountain ranges to the flatlands and back again. They found dams and earth-works and paving crews and one summer the whole lot of them worked a railroad section, levelling track and clearing bush. There were trailers to live in and food was run in regular by train. There was nowhere to spend wages and they came out of it with full pockets and high hopes. He was almost fourteen. His growth had hit, and he gained six inches over the course of the winter. He towered over his mother and the work had made him thicker so that he had the look of a man. He could haul a chainsaw through thick brush to buck dead-fall. He could slam a tamping bar under railroad ties for hours to pack the gravel in. He was strong. Purposeful. He earned his keep. Every payday he would hand the full packet to his mother without a word. She'd look at him and nod and he would take that as his measure and be proud.

No one bothered them about school. They were transient and never in one place long enough to garner attention or else tucked away in a work camp far from truant officers or social workers. He got educated in the ins and outs of machinery and tools. He learned to read moving parts and the sound of engines so he could fix things before they broke. He learned the geometry of framing and the science of planting and harvest and by the time he was full-on four-teen he understood the mathematics of earned money. There were books too. His mother read to him every night and he came to love the sound of her voice in the flicker of firelight or candle and the worlds spun into being by Dickens, Twain, and Robert Louis Stevenson. He never found a facility with words himself. It didn't matter. He was a worker. The more they travelled the more he absorbed and he became a jack of all trades, fluent in the language of workers and the unspoken dialect of sweat and strain.

Jimmy Weaseltail became his best friend. His only friend. Jimmy's father's roots were Blood tribe and his mother was a skinny, long-haired woman named Spence from a small town in Ontario. Jimmy was their only son. He had four sisters and he was the eldest. The other kids had dolls and toys and care-free hours to spend at play. But Jimmy's dad had been crippled in a construction accident and there was no one else but him to take up the load. They worked together. The two of them tackled everything they could and if a foreman or a lead hand doubted their abilities in the beginning, they were convinced and sold on their grit, gumption, and utility by the end of the job. They pushed each other. They found the ebb and flow of their energies and their skills and a natural rhythm of work that made them a seamless unit. The pair of them trundled wheelbarrows, staggered under bundles of cedar shakes, dug post holes, mucked stalls, and forked hay. They could outwork grown men and on most jobs were elevated to harder, more challenging work that paid bigger money. That it was some-times dangerous did not concern them. Or slow them down. Instead, they'd grin and get down to it, each of them driven by the presence of the other. The men around them spoke of the whoops of laughter that came from them even as earth, wood, steel, and rock flew or was crushed or stacked or hauled on shoulders frightening in their strength for two so young. They were working men. It was all they knew.

"What's fired together is wired together," Jimmy would say.

"Joined by sweat and muscle," he'd reply.

"Forged by steel."

"Welded by grit."

"Screwed by circumstance."

It became their running joke.

Jimmy liked to hear his mother read too. The three of them would sit together and the words would join them. His mother's voice. His friend: open-mouthed and gazing at her in wonder, agog at the way words filled space. The smell of grease, oil, wood, dirt, and stone that clung to them like a cloud, wafted to the ceiling on candlelight and words. This was the stuff of his childhood. These were the recollections he stored within himself. The toil and the drudge and the relentless job-to-job trek, lost in the magic of that; the spill of words from a page and the feeling of togetherness in what-ever meagre shelter they could afford or were provided. His idea of family forever locked in the shared embrace of story.

"You think when I'm old enough I could marry your mom?" Jimmy asked him one day.

He laughed. "You crazy? She'd never have a runt like you."

"I work bigger."

"Takes more'n that."

"Oh, yeah. Like what?"

"I dunno. I guess ya kinda gotta be like them guys in the stories."

"White guys?"

"No. Heroes."

"Like your dad?"

He remembered looking at the sky. It was a hard blue like his mother's eyes when she looked at him like she was reading a book. He felt the sting of tears, the salt of them, their taste at the back of his throat. "Yeah," he said. "Like that."

Summer. 1948. They wound their way from Alberta to the Yukon and then south, downward into the Nechako Valley. Half the men got hired on with a logging company. While the men felled and bucked, he and Jimmy became boomers, working flotillas of logs and corralling them into booms for the long float downriver to the sawmill at Parson's Gap. They were nimble and quick and the work became a game. They used the pike poles like cudgels and swung and bashed at each other, fighting for balance on the roll of the logs. They never bought into the danger. Never gave a moment's thought to the current beneath the logs, the weight of them that could crush a man in a single bob or block his reach for air. They loved the river. The silvered serpentine look of it. The smell. They loved the feel of open space around them, the trees, rocks, and lines of vertiginous cliff and ridge that framed the river valley. The sky hung above it all rich as a promise, and days were spiked with the energy of labour and the thrill of the boom.

Lester Jenks. He was the boom foreman. He was a New Brunswicker, raised in logging camps and lumberjacking full-time by the time he was their age. He liked their bravado, the aplomb they brought to the art of the boom, and he encouraged their play and rambunctiousness.

"A cautious man'll die out here," he told them. "You need to be playful as an otter and sturdy as a bear. That's what'll save your skin in this job."

Jenks taught them to log roll. He showed them the foot-work that would keep a log spinning in the froth and yet allow them to work it, manoeuvre it, herd it into the boom, and rest it lightly against the outside logs. When they fell he laughed. When they cussed and clambered out, water peeling off them like sheets of light, he slapped them hard on the back and showed them one more time. Jenks was fast. He was a tall, athletic, heavy man but light on his feet, agile, and completely fearless. The look on his face when he worked the log was one-half childish delight and one-half jubilation like a demon cajoling souls, and the faster he spun a log beneath his feet the more crazed and flushed his face became. They learned to mimic him.

Together he and Jimmy would spin a timber in the flow. They'd stand a few yards from each end and run. The log would slip in the water and twirl slowly at first until they picked up speed and then it would spew froth out behind it as they ran. Then they'd exchange a look and reverse it. They'd catch the log lightly with the hobs of their boots, slow it, coax it to a roll, and then run again and spin it the other way while Jenks watched and applauded their skill. It became a dance they did, another entrance into manhood burgeoning at the edges of the boom. The two of them set out against the river. The logs at their feet. The bob of them. The airy feel of suspension. Weightless. Then the impossible release of gravity as they ran and spun the log, churning the water and moving it forward and backward, locked in rhythm, eyeing each other, daring each other, the current, the flow, the muscle of the river forgotten until all that existed was the speed and the pitch and bob of logs in the water and the feel of them free, unencumbered and uncontained.

"Where'd you get the moxie?" Jenks asked one day over lunch.

"My dad rodeo-ed," Jimmy said. "Bulls. Didn't pay none so he quit."

"You?" Jenks asked him.

"Don't know," he said. "It's the action. The thrill to it."

"Like the feel of danger, do ya?"

"Don't feel dangerous."

"What's it feel then?"

He thought for a moment. "Free, I guess. Like I'm doin' what I gotta do and there ain't nothin' much to stop me."

"Said like a true daredevil. I can trust a man like that," Jenks said.

They spent a long time talking. Jenks knew the ins and outs of logging and he shared adventures from camps from Nova Scotia to northern Quebec. He'd wandered west on a whim one year and came to love the rugged interior mountains. There was work from Vancouver Island to the northern border to Alaska but he favoured the Nechako. He'd never been much to settle but found a cabin to his liking and a truck he'd come to love.

"And a passable dog," he said with a laugh. "Fellas been known to make a home with less, I figure."

So he told Jenks about the caravan, about the winding road that led to jobs, the things he'd done for money, and then he told him about his father, the war, and about his mother.

"She's where I got so strong," he said. "When my dad died she just got even more gumption. I use that. The sight of her. It keeps me going."

He told him about the feeling of words spun out of the darkness and how the sound of her voice reading to them became someone painting images in the light of candles on the walls or firelight on the branches of trees. He told him how her voice held his world together.

"I could use me some of that," Jenks said.

At first it was shared meals in the cookhouse where his mother worked. Jenks listened to their talk and marvelled at how easy it came out of them. Then stews and soups and plates carried over to the shack they called home. The candles, the talk eased and made merrier by the flow of wine and beer that Jenks seemed never in shortage of. He watched his mother's face change in the light of the man's attention. She became girlish; shy, then bursting out into soft blooms of laughter, one hand covering her mouth. Jenks himself grew more animated, sparkling in her company, the rough and manly jokes making Jimmy and him gape at the daring it took to say them in front of a woman. She never complained. Instead, she came to share his boisterous energy and they rollicked in the wash of the tales she spun of camps and fields and tough men and tougher women. Later, when the words from the books quieted them down, her face composed itself into lines and edges gilded by the soft yellow candlelight, framed in the rapture of magic spells cast by faceless men in a long ago time, and they were hushed and dazzled, made into children again, and each of the three of them loved her for her acts of conjuring, shifting nights into days of adventure, daring, and mystery. The words compelling in the textures she wove them in. The dreams made real by the shifts of tone, emphasis, and the long, almost painful pauses she held them with, restrained and breathless, until released into the flow of the tale again. He watched Jenks reach one callused finger out to touch the back of her hand one night and the edges of her lips curled into a small smile while she read.

———

Stories were his wound. When he came to think of them it wasn't for the glimmer of worlds spun out of darkness and firelight, it was for the sudden holes life can sometimes fall into. Their cabin at the logging camp became Jenks' second home. He rarely left. At first he was just there in the mornings, curled up by the fire in a sleeping bag. Then he was at his mother's side, walking through the bush or along the edge of the stream. Then he was the lump beside her in her bed.

"Thought she loved your dad," Jimmy said.

He spat in the dirt and rubbed at it with the toe of his boot. "Me too," he said.

"So what's this then?"

"Maybe she's lonesome."

"Lonesome's one thing. Shackin' up's another."

He lit up a smoke. They'd both taken to tobacco and he lit another off the end of his and handed it to Jimmy. They stood in the trees, eying the cabin where his mother and Jenks slept through the mid-morning haze.

Jenks became a demanding boss. There was a tougher edge to his voice and he separated himself from them. There were harsh orders and he rode them hard and insisted on a deliberate approach to the booming. There was no room for play. But they took his words without complaint. They felt the line he drew between them and shrugged him off and set to work. They understood that. The need to bend your back to things. The need to get a job done for the job's sake. They'd been raised with it. But it didn't make the change any more likeable.

"Frickin' thinks he owns us now," Jimmy said.

"Big man now, I guess," he said. "Probably never had no woman before."

"Not like your mom, least ways."

"Straight fact," he said.

He saw the first bruise after a month.

She walked out of the bedroom ramrod straight. She walked to the counter and clattered some dishes into a pile in a ten-gallon pail and splashed water and soap over them. It was morning. He watched her and when she turned to look at him the bruise sat in a ring around her throat. Purple. Like small blooms. He stood up slowly and he could feel his guts compress. She watched him and her mouth hung open. Her eyes were vacant and dull, a murky sheen on them like black ice.

"What the fuck?" he said. He'd never used man-talk in front of her before.

"Eldon." She said it like a whisper. She held a hand up, palm outward as though warding him off.

He could feel his thighs shaking. There was a spike in his vision, the clarity of the morning sudden and sharp. He swallowed and took a step toward her and she put a hand on his shoulder. It was cool. He stared at it, the lines and follicles etched clearly against the small clumps of knuckles.

"I'm okay. I said things I shouldn't."

"He hurt you." He couldn't say anything beyond the obvious.

"I ran off at the mouth." She looked down at her feet.

"About what?"

"It doesn't matter." She looked up at him and her face was grim. "It's over."

He looked down at her face. There was wet at her eyes and

he felt a part of himself crumble and ache. The shaking in his legs stopped and he stood there firm and held her to him. She breathed against his chest.

"Don't like it," he said.

"I know," she said. "But we're past it."

He sat in the dimness and stared at Jenks when she read to them that night. The big man did not turn his head. He stared down at a spot between his mother's feet and tapped a finger slowly on the floor. There was the small curl of a smile at his lips. She read a long time and he got up now and again and tended to the fire, banked it low so it would burn long, and every time he crawled by Jenks the man would only nod. He felt himself madden. There were words that needed saying and Jenks wasn't speaking to him. He hated him for that.

Within a week there were more bruises. They were on her shoulders and arms and back. He saw them through the half-open door to the bathroom. She faced the mirror and traced one hand down her cheek and stared at her reflection. She cupped her face in her palms and closed her eyes and he could see her fight against the tears. When he stepped toward the door she gave a startled look and eased the towel up over her shoulders and closed the door. He stood in the vacant space. He had one hand up and stretched toward the door. All he could feel was distance.

That night she read stories. But he couldn't get beyond watching Jenks sit there mute and solid as a boulder. He sat and stared at him and clenched and unclenched his fists, and when his mother caught his eye she stared at him while she read and he wanted to hit her too.

"Fucker punched her," he said to Jimmy later. They were smoking in the dark behind the shack.

"I didn't see no marks."

"He hits her where no one can see."

"She don't say nothin'?"

"No. That's a pisser. She pretends it's nothing."

"Whattaya gonna do?"

"Can't know. I wanna crack him. Kick his ass. Sumthin'. Anything."

"He's our boss."

"I know. Don't mean we gotta take no shit. There or here. Especially here."

They smoked their cigarettes down to the butt and lit two more off them and ground the first out under their boots. It was full dark. Moonless. An owl. Ravens. The sound of a truck gearing down for the hill that led to the highway into town. He took a draw and held it, felt the smoke churn in his lungs, then let it out with his head tilted back, straight up toward the stars.

"Happens again or worse, somethin's gonna give," he said. He flicked his smoke out into the air and they watched it arc like a falling star and land in the gravel and roll.

"I'm in," Jimmy said.

Four nights later he stood in the trees. Neither he nor Jimmy could stomach the idea of sitting with Jenks while she read now and while Jimmy excused himself politely, he'd taken to walking out after he'd eaten. But he never went far. He found a place in a copse of trees that provided a good vantage point and he stood there and watched the cabin. Now he saw the lights in the cabin flicker before he heard the sounds, and when he drew close enough to discern them they rumbled and crashed like logs in a flume. He heard the slap of an open palm on skin, and the crash of silverware, and when he broke from the trees Jimmy was suddenly beside him.

They ran in huge leaping bounds. She was screaming openly now and they could hear them slam into walls. They cleared the front step together and strode through the door into the pale yellow light of the shack. Jenks was bent over her with one hand at her throat and the other drawn back behind his shoulder ready to slam it into her. She could see them over that shoulder and her eyes were wide and filled with horror. Jenks turned his head, and when he saw them he let her go. She slid to the floor in a heap and let her head fall onto her arms while Jenks turned to face them. He stepped forward slowly. The bulk of him eating up the narrow space between them.

"You want some, pissants?" A thin line of spittle draped from his lips. He raised his fists.

"Not us who needs the beatin'," Jimmy said.

"You two couldn't beat a rug."

"Step up and see, asshole," Jimmy said.

He moved beside Jimmy and they squared to face Jenks, who smiled and spread his legs wide. Then the smile vanished slowly from his face and he stood clenching and unclenching his fists, urging them toward him. Taunting. When he moved they stepped apart. He grinned again. He was big and they could hear the floorboards creak beneath his weight and he juggled his fists. His mother crawled across the floor to the shelter of the space beneath the frail table and it cut him deeply to see her reduced to scuttling like a rodent.

"She don't need none of you," Eldon said.

Jenks smiled. "What she need she gets," he said. "Know that if you were man enough. Kid."

"My dad woulda killed you."

"Yer dad ain't here."

"We're here," Jimmy said, taking a step forward.

"Then come ahead. Don't let fear or common sense hold ya back."

He could barely breathe. The roof of his mouth was dry and he fought to swallow. When he put his hands up the tightness in his shoulders made his arms tremble and when Jenks saw it he laughed and swung a long, wide punch at him. He ducked it. He could feel the whoosh of it in the air but he never saw the kick coming. It caught him in the belly and all the air went out of him and he fell to the floor, the rough wood of the floorboards at his cheek, the sharp, bitter taste of puke at his throat, and he closed his eyes.

Then he heard a dull whack like an axe handle on a sandbag and the cabin shook as a body hit the floor. He flicked his eyes open and Jenks lay beside him. They lay there eyeball to eyeball and he saw the man's amazement when he raised fingers to his face and they were dripping with blood. He rubbed them on his cheek and his hand trailed down the lines of his face and fell and his big knuckles clunked to the floor and his eyes slammed shut and he didn't move again.

He rolled onto his back and stared up at Jimmy. There was a hunting knife and a short, stout club in his hands.

"What the fuck, Jimmy?"

"I been waitin' for this," Jimmy said. "Waited the son of a bitch out is what I done."

They heard his mother scream. They turned and she crawled out from under the table and scrabbled across the floor to where Jenks lay and put her hands on his face.

"Don't worry. He's out," Jimmy said. "I done it. I took care of it."

"You killed him," she said. When she looked up she was crying.

"Woulda done more if I coulda."

"You killed him," she said again.

Jenks moaned and clutched at his side and blood seeped between his fingers. His mother scuttled closer and lifted his head and sat with it cradled in her lap. When she looked up at them again she was dry-eyed.

"You can't say he didn't deserve this and more," he said, stepping up to stand beside Jimmy.

"You don't know him."

"Don't care to."

She put a knuckle to her forehead and closed her eyes. Then she shook her head as if to clear it and when she spoke it was harder. "You can't stay here. You gotta run now. If he don't sic the law on you the company will. He's a foreman. You attacked him. They'll jail you both."

"Be worth it so folks know what a shit heel he is," Jimmy said.

Jenks moaned again and his eyes fluttered open. They circled and spun and then came to rest and he stared at them, mute and vacant. "You'd best pack, Eldon," she said.

"You'd choose him over me?" he said, his breathing rough and ragged.

"I'm not choosing. I'm telling you how it has to be."

He stood up. He held his hand out and stared at it and stared at her. He wanted to slap her. He forced the hand down to his side. Jimmy eyed him. He glared at his mother and grimaced and he could feel the muscles in his face quiver at the hard set of his jaw. He felt his throat constricted and aching.

"I ain't asking. I'm telling," she said.

He crossed the room in quick strides and pulled a rucksack from the closet and flung a few clothes into it. He went to the cupboard and pulled down the mason jar with his wages in it. "Ain't gonna need this," he said to her. "Got you a man to provide now. Only now there ain't gonna be no one to help you when he does it again. But that's yer choice, isn't it?"

"Go now, Eldon, if you know what's good for you. The both of you. Just go!"

He crossed the room and flung open the door. "Jimmy," he said. He draped the rucksack over one shoulder.

Jimmy heaved a deep breath and looked square at her. "Hope he makes it," he said. "But you tell him to watch his back. He won't never, ever know where I'm gonna be."

When Jimmy joined him at the door his cheeks were wet and he wiped at them with the edge of his fists. They stepped out onto the porch and turned and looked back at her. She lay Jenks' head softly on the floor. Then she stood, smoothed the front of the smock dress, and regarded them blandly. "You best go," she said. "I'm gonna fetch help."

He glared at her then took the knife from Jimmy's hand. He drove the knife into the jamb of the door. The shack shook under the impact and they turned and walked away into the night, the thrum of the knife quivering.

12

"DID YOU GO BACK?" THE KID ASKED.

"No."

"Not ever?"

"No." His father pulled the blanket tighter around himself and stared at the fire. He was trembling. The lines on his face were deeper, the shadow and the flicker of the flames making it look pocked, scarred, and ravaged. "Wanted to. Sometimes I even kinda headed that way. But we was proud. Both of us. Jimmy and me.

"We followed the work wherever it led. Lost ourselves in money, good times, the feel of men around us, the toughness of them. We wanted that. To be tough. Not bugged by nothin' even though we were."

"Your mother?" Becka asked. "You never wanted to find out how she made out?"

His father gazed at the kid meekly. There was a depth to his eyes the kid had never seen, a woe, a bleak space all the light seemed to seep into and fade, and it embarrassed him and he looked away. His father picked up the mug of whisky and held it in both hands, spun it slowly in his palms then set it down on the floor again. He put his head back and stared at the ceiling. "Didn't know how to try," he said. "Never cottoned on to whether she wanted me gone or saved."

"You're sure she was makin' a choice?" Becka asked.

"Felt like it right then," he said. "Felt like I was no account and it pissed me off. Made walkin' away easier, but the anger cooled after a time. Then it was just guilt an' shame over leavin' her alone with that bastard. Got to be so it ate at me bad. I dealt with it the only way I knew how."

He looked at the kid. But the kid wouldn't meet his eye, and he put a hand to his forehead and ran his palm across the top of his head. "Love an' shame never mix," he said. "One's always gonna be runnin' roughshod over the other. Lovin' her. Feelin' guilt an' shame then gettin' angry as hell at myself. I never could figger what to do and then there was a whole pile of years gone by an' I give up on it."

"You chicken-shitted me out of a grandmother," the kid said quietly, staring at his feet.

"Wasn't no chicken shit," Eldon said quietly. "You think leavin' was easy and then stayin' gone?"

"What would you call it then?" The kid looked up at him and glared. "You run off with yer tail between yer legs like a whipped pup."

His father picked up the whisky again and held it to his lips. He closed his eyes. He sighed and set the mug down on the floor again without drinking. "Hurt is all," he said. "Big bad hurt."

"You coulda made a choice too."

"Them were tough years, Frank. Losin' my father. Workin' my ass off tryin' to take his place. Didn't never get to be no kid. Not proper, least ways."

"I never got to be no kid neither."

"At least you was taken care of."

The kid laughed. It was bitter and hollow and his legs were bouncing up and down. He rose and marched to the fire and stirred it around with a poker, causing embers and ash to fly around in clouds. He arranged the logs and then arranged them again. Then he set the poker against the hearth and stared into the burst of orange flames he'd created. When he spoke again he stayed looking into the fire. "You think that's all there is to it. Bein' taken care of? Goin' to school and bein' picked on because you don't know who the fuck you are, bein' called Injun, wagon-burner, squaw-hopper, Tonto?"

"Just like me," Eldon said.

"I ain't nothin' like you," the kid said.

"Some parts, maybe."

"No parts. I never been no chicken shit."

The kid walked back and sat on the chair and slumped down into it, facing the fire. He put his elbows on his knees and jammed his fists up under his chin, closing his eyes. "I get it," he said finally.

"Do you?"

"Yeah," he said. "I get that you were scared to go to jail. But you never done it. Jimmy did. Jimmy did what you shoulda done. So I get it. Maybe you didn't wanna face your shame about that."

"I'da had to give up Jimmy to the law if I stayed."

"He wasn't family."

"He was all I had."

The kid looked at his father. He felt tears coming. "You had her," he said, his voice breaking. "You had a mother."

His father met his look and they stared at each other. The kid shook his head to clear his eyes and his father looked away. There was only the crackle of the flames.

"Besides, Jenks' friends woulda half killed me if I'd stuck around," his father said finally.

The kid turned away. His face was set hard and grim in the flicker of the flames. "Gettin' half killed once's gotta be better'n bein' half alive forever."

When he didn't say anything further his father stared at him wide-eyed. Then he leaned down and took up the mug, his hands shaking crazily, and he drank all of it off in one huge gulp.

"Yeah," the kid said, nodding. "Yeah."

The kid lay under a thin blanket close to the fire and heard rain dripping from the eaves over top of his father's ragged snores. The dampness deepened the chill and he shivered some and hitched himself closer to the hearth and laid another couple logs onto the embers and then laid back down and drew the blanket tight around him. Eldon lay on the floor a few feet off. The kid watched him for a moment or two and saw him shiver and shake. He got up and put his blanket over him. The fresh logs flared and there was a wild sear of heat and he had to back off a few inches. Becka came and set a kettle close to the flames and sat down beside him. They watched the fire without speaking. They heard Eldon moan and shift about behind them.

"He's worse," the kid said. "Just in the last day or so."

"What he done was brave. You know that, huh?"

"Done what?"

"Tellin' you. That took some grit."

"I don't think it'd take much grit to tell what ya already know."

"Maybe. But it sat in his gut a long time. Most'll just give stuff like that over to time. Figure enough of it passes things'll change. Try to forget it. Like forgettin's a cure unto itself. It ain't. You never forget stuff that cuts that deep."

"A story like that woulda been good to hear before now, knowin' nothin' about where I come from an' all."

"You didn't grow up with him."

"No."

"Them that raised you then, they never said nothin' about your mother?"

"I asked once. But I was told it was a father's job to do, tellin' me about her."

"He never come out with it?"

"Whenever I seen him he was mostly always drunk or drinkin' an' he never did make much sense. I got raised good. Never wanted for nothin' an' I got no gripe with any of that."

"Except that they never said nothin' about your mother."

The kid stared at his father's sleeping form. Becka rose and poured water from the kettle into a teapot and the kid smelled mint. She poured each of them a cup and the kid set his between his feet. "I'd look at women in town sometimes or at gatherin's we'd go to wonderin' if she was one of them or if maybe she'd been walkin' by me ev'ry day an' I never knew."

He stopped and picked up the cup and stared at it wrapped in his hands. "I get that some things take some workin' up to. But he could die tonight fer all I know."

"He won't."

His father moaned and the kid regarded him. "He don't seem much of a warrior to me." He sipped at the tea.

"Who's to say how much of anythin' we are?" Becka said. "Seems to me the truth of us is where it can't be seen. Comes to dyin', I guess we all got a right to what we believe."

"I can't know what he believes. He talks a lot, but I still got no sense of him. So far it's all been stories."

She only nodded. "It's all we are in the end. Our stories." She stood and put a hand on his shoulder and gave it a pat. Then she poured some more of the tea in his cup and padded off to the cot, where he heard her rustle about some and then everything was silent.

In the morning she warmed up porridge with water from a tin she kept in the rain barrel and cut up berries to sweeten it. The kid ate but all his father could do was finger the rim of his bowl. He picked a berry or two out and sat there moving them around in his mouth. When he was finished the kid gathered their few supplies and carried them out to the shed where he watered the horse, brushed and saddled her. Becka walked his father out. He could tell by the look of him in the daylight that he was weaker. He had a deeper yellow cast and he shook with the effort of walking. It took both of them to help him up onto the horse, and the heat from his skin was powerful. The kid took rope from his pack and cut it into three lengths. Together he and Becka tied his father's feet to the stirrups and his hands to the pommel. Then they walked off a few yards and Becka put a hand on the kid's shoulder.

"Give him some of this when he needs it," Becka said. She handed him a rough hide tied up into a bundle.

"What is it?" the kid asked.

"Ain't no medicine I know can help him perfect. But I made this up for my own father when he was near the end. It'll soothe him when it counts."

"Thanks."

"Don't thank me yet. When he gets too weak to even take in booze he's gonna be sicker. Booze sick. Hard and ugly. He's a lifer. Been drinkin' all his life and stoppin' sudden ain't no good idea. It ain't gonna be no pretty picture. You won't be up to thankin' me much when that happens."

"What can I do when that comes about?"

"Can't know. The bad news is he's gonna be a terrible handful. The good news is, on toppa what he's got goin' now, it ain't gonna last long. But give him some of this when the worst of it is on him."

The kid kicked at the dirt. "I guess I better get to it then. But I do mean to thank ya."

"Ain't done nothin' no one else would do no different," she said. "I was glad of the company."

"Me too."

"You could stop by when you're on your way home."

The kid could only nod solemnly.

He tied the sack of medicine and their supplies behind the saddle and led the mare out of the shed. It was cool and damp and he could feel the chill of winter on the breeze. He hauled a deep breath into him and stood looking at the trees along the ridge to the west, undulating and serpentine, and found himself wishing suddenly for home. When he looked down Becka had disappeared back into the shack. The bulk of his father slumped in the saddle and the cloud of the horse's breath was all that framed the day in front of him and he walked the horse across the rough yard and into the trees.

13

THE WALKING WAS DELIBERATE. The horse seemed to sense the dire situation and he let go of the reins and she was content to plod along behind him. After the rain the land was a gumbo of smells. Pitch and bog, the tang of spruce, and the dank, rancid smell of wet bear tracing the weave of the creek to his left. He drew it all into him, closed his eyes a few paces and held it, let it fill him. The night and his father's story had drained him and he needed the feel of the land at his feet and the sounds of it to quell the clamour in his head. His father. He thought about what Becka had said and worked at finding some pattern to the shards and pieces of history he'd been allowed to carry now. They jangled and knocked around inside him. It felt like jamming the wrong piece into a picture puzzle. Like frustration alone could make it fit the pattern. He cast a look back over his shoulder at his father, who seemed to be asleep, but he'd mumble when the horse's step over a rock or a root made him lurch in the saddle. When the kid looked back at the thin trail they followed he felt worn and makeshift as the trail itself. He had no idea what was about to happen. He didn't know if he could carry out what they'd set about to get done. He looked back over his shoulder at his father again. The sky was clearing and the sun splattered light against the green-black boughs of the trees and the birds came alive with it and he lost himself in the feel of the land shrugging itself into wakefulness.

He never saw the bear until the horse snorted and reared. They'd come around a long bend in the trail that followed the creek and he hadn't paid attention to the change in the direction of the wind. He cursed himself for his carelessness. The bear appeared suddenly. It was a boar grizzly and it stood on its hind legs on the rocks by the creek that ran about twenty yards away. The bear itself hadn't heard them over the rush of the creek.

The horse clattered on the rocks of the trail and the kid scrambled back and flailed about for the reins that had come loose in his hurry. The mare was sunk back on her hind quarters as the bear roared and his father swayed dangerously, unable to centre his weight. The kid found the reins and braced against the yank and pull of the mare. He walked toward her and she shied and shimmied. He could hear the bear huffing behind them.

"What the fuck?" his father said and pulled at the ropes that bound his hands to the pommel.

"Be quiet," the kid said. "We got a bear here."

"Jesus."

Eldon settled in the saddle as much as he could and the stable weight made the mare easier to manage and the kid was able to grab hold of the halter and she calmed some but twitched nervously. When he could handle her he walked her off to a copse of birch and tied her and loosed the ropes that bound his father and helped him off the horse. He laid him in moss beneath the birches. He could hear the bear prowling slowly along the creek, cuffing at stones and growling low in the throat.

"Whattaya think yer doin'?" his father croaked.

"Can't run," the kid said. He slung the pack from his back and dropped it on the ground beside the tree. "Gotta face him."

"Are you nuts?"

"Gonna have to be."

"He'll kill ya."

"If I'm scared shit he could."

"You ain't?"

"Yeah. But he don't gotta know that."

He hobbled the horse with the rope from his father's foot and secured the halter tie to the birch. Then he walked out toward the bear. It stood swinging its head back and forth ten yards up the trail. He hadn't wanted to turn them away from it. He knew that retreat with their backs toward the bear was to show fear. Now the only way was forward. He held his hands out wide and tried to make himself appear as large as he could. He stood up on his toes and opened his eyes and mouth wide and growled. The bear lowered its head and stared at him through the top of its eyes. It swayed its head and shoulders. There was a rumble from its throat. He could see that it was a juvenile, maybe in its first year away from its mother. The boar hadn't grown the grizzly hump at the shoulders and it had yet to fill out its massive size. Still, it was dangerous. It seemed to want to hold the trail and the bend in the creek. The kid took a slow step forward and spread his arms out wide again and growled with the stride. The bear lurched to its hind feet. It stood there all seven feet of it and bellowed. He could hear the horse shy and buck some in the trees. He took another slow, measured pace forward. The bear roared again. It echoed back to him through the trees and he heard the horse's ragged whinny.

He moved again. The bear shook its head and there was a spray of spittle. There were only eight paces between them now. The bear dropped to the ground and cuffed at the trail with both fore paws. There was a sudden trench in the dirt. The kid slid forward another step and held the outstretched posture. He could smell the high, bitter scent of the bear. He growled and drew in as big a breath as he could until he thought his ribs would crack. The bear shifted left and right. He took another step. He could see right into the boar's eyes and the bear held the look and raised its snout to sniff. The kid's heart seemed to clang in his chest but he moved forward in another sliding step and the bear kept up the lateral shifting, and when the kid let the breath out and began striding forward and raising his arms outward again the bear broke. It turned and trotted off a few yards, then it raised its snout and sniffed again. The kid held his pose. The bear growled its discontent. Then it turned and walked off slowly, looking back over its shoulder every few paces and the kid didn't move an inch. When it reached another bend in the trail the boar broke into a trot and then a full gallop when it reached the trees, and the kid could hear the snap and break of branches as it took off up a ridge until the clatter of stones was all that remained of its presence.

Silence. It draped over everything. When the kid finally allowed a breath the world kicked into gear all around him and he heard the croak of a raven in the trees and the splash of a fish in the ripple of rapids at the creek. He slumped. He closed his eyes and drew deep draughts of air until he could taste it again. Then he turned and walked back to the copse of birch.

The horse was still spooked and shied at his approach. The smell of the bear remained sharp and sour on the wind. He stood and spoke to the mare and rubbed her and when she calmed he stepped around her and walked to where his father lay on his belly. He groaned when the kid eased him onto his back.

"You don't look too good" he said.

"Feel booze sick," Eldon said. "And a godawful lotta pain."

The kid rose and got the medicine sack Becka had given him. There were four glass jars of liquid. He lifted one out.

The medicine looked mossy and slick against the glass and when he opened it the smell was fungal, peaty with rot. He held his father's head in his palm and held the jar to his lips.

"What's this?" Eldon asked.

"Becka stuff. She said it'd help you when it counted."

"Counts now."

"Okay then."

He drank a few gulps. His face twisted but he held it down. "Tastes like shit," he said, wiping at his mouth.

"Figure you choked back worse in your time."

"Some. Not like this. It's like drinking swamp."

"We'll rest here. If ya can't ride no more I'll make camp."

His father put his head back against the trunk of the birch and closed his eyes. The kid could hear him moan.

"Tell me if I can do anything," he said.

"What's in this stuff?" Eldon asked.

"Can't know. Becka called it medicine."

"Heats up the belly. Get kinda light in the head too. Kinda woozy."

"That's good then."

"Yeah. Don't feel no booze sick no more. Just kinda like a head fulla cotton. Ask you somethin'?"

"Go on."

"How'd ya know what to do?"

The kid shrugged. "Out here you do what ya need to do when ya need to do it is all."

"Still, that was a fuckin' grizzly."

"Juvenile. Not full grown. Likely confused the hell outta him."

"Took some balls is all I'm sayin'."

"Seems to me that everything takes nuts."

"The old man teach ya to move through fear?"

The kid sat and crossed his legs. He peeled a twig off the birch and picked at his teeth with it. There was a stiffer breeze now and the trees swayed and creaked. When he raised his head to look at his father, his father had a grave, sombre look. He considered his words before he spoke. "Can't no one bring ya to that. Some things you just gotta get to on yer own."

His father stared at him passively. There was a droop to his head and it slipped down in a hard nod but he lifted it back up and stared at the kid again. "Medicine, huh?" he slurred.

"Yeah," the kid said.

"Works good," his father said. His eyes closed and his head dropped sideways and the kid reached over and straightened it and laid it back against the birch. He kept a hand to his cheek. It was warm and flushed but less hot to the touch than it had been at first light. He kept it there. Then he rose and began to make camp.

It was late afternoon when his father woke. The kid had the camp set, and there was a fire of birch logs that threw great heat and his father rolled onto his side to face it. His eyes were clearer. He seemed calm, and when he lifted a hand to his face to wipe the sleep away there was no shake to it and he held it out in front of him and stared at it. The kid handed him a cup of water and he drank thirstily. Then he lay on his back again and stared at the sky through the limbs of the birch.

"The old man told me that everything we need is out here. Trick is learnin' how to find it and use it."

"You savvy?"

"Some. I can treat a cut. But I could never doctor nobody."

"You figure on maybe tryin' to get to learn it."

"Don't know what I figure," the kid said. "All's I know most times is how to shake out what's in front of me."

"That's lots sometimes."

The kid rose and strode into the trees and returned with an armload of wood. He set a few pieces on the blaze and they watched as it took and the heat surged out again. His father moaned. "How you doin'?" he asked.

"Not worth a shit, really."

"Could you eat?"

"Don't reckon."

"You want some of that hooch?"

Eldon cranked his neck and scrunched his eyes tight trying to settle on the spruce boughs the kid had laid under him while he slept. "No," he said.

His father shifted about and stared at the fire. He was quiet a long time. The kid could hear the creek over the snap of the fire and the rustle of the frail breeze in the trees. He waited. When his father spoke again it was in a whisper and he had to lean close to hear him. "Gotta shake out what's in front of me," he said.

"Amen," the kid said.

"Do me a favour?"

"Sure."

"Pour it out. The hooch. Pour it out. Get rid of it."

"You sure?" the kid asked.

"No. I ain't. But if it ain't around I can't reach for it and I wanna go out clean. Or as least as close as I can. I can get through on that Becka juice."

"You need some now?"

"Yeah," his father said. He took the jar the kid held out

and sipped at it. Then he handed it back and settled on the boughs and closed his eyes. The kid could tell when the medicine hit because his father's breath got deeper and slower. "Tell me a story," he said dreamily.

"What kinda story?" the kid asked.

"Any kind. Any kind at all."

He was asleep in minutes while the kid scratched about in the dirt with a stick trying to recall a tale. He sat a long time and watched his father sleep. Then he got up to feed and water the horse and to rinse his face in the creek. When he came back to the fire the sun had sunk below the line of the western ridge and the world was shushed into the purple-grey of early evening and there was only the fire, the trees, and the bent form of his father sleeping. He eased the booze bottles out of the pack. Then he stood with them clutched in his hands, watching his father sleep. He turned and walked slowly to the creek and stood on the smooth stones at the bank holding the bottles, the water silvered in the hushed light.

14

HE WAS NINE THE FIRST TIME he and the old man rode horses to the mill town. The old man roused him early and they'd saddled them in the pale yellow dust of the sun. The barn seemingly filled with it. It was late spring and the last of the winter chill hung in the air. The horses were excited and they snorted great clouds of breath and he watched them billow and fade and when the old man walked his horse to the back door he followed, glad to be out in the flare of morning. They rode across the field and into the trees before the old man spoke.

"He called for ya," he said. "Got a letter in the post last time I was to town."

"Eldon?" the kid asked.

"Yeah. Says he wants to see ya. Don't know why. But we'll be busy as a bugger in a few weeks and there won't be no time fer ya to go. Now's best."

"Good thing you know where to go."

"Mill town. Parson's Gap, she's called. We never been there. Never had no call for it. Till now, least ways."

"What does he do there?"

The old man laughed and kicked his horse up to a trot. The kid urged the mare up and they trotted side by side. "He does a lot of things. Kinda sets his own pace through the world. I kinda admire the fact he's made it this far along."

"What am I supposed to do when I get there?" the kid asked.

"Visit, I expect."

"How's that done?"

The old man snorted. "Damned if I know. I was never much cut out for it. You sit and talk, maybe go fer a walk and talk some more. Always seemed to me to be an occasion for chatter is all."

They crossed a creek and the old man led the way up a ridge. He relaxed in the saddle and let the horse pick its way and the kid did the same. They rode that way until they had crested the ridge and started down the other side. "What are we gonna visit about?"

"He wants to know ya."

"We met already."

"I mean, that he wants to know ya like a father knows a son."

"And how's that?"

The old man rubbed at the back of his neck. "Can't say, really. Me, I was raised to the work. Bustin' sod, plowin', handlin' stock, stone boatin', that sort of thing when I was smaller'n small. That's what my dad and I done. Weren't time for talk. Not much, least ways.

"But now and again we'd fish. Head off to a spot he knew and we'd sit there all day long sometimes and just fish. Every now and then he'd tell me somethin', about himself, about where he come from, some of his adventures. An' because they were so rare, I held on to them. Every word. Like I could say 'em back to you right now like they come to me. I guess ya get to know a father like that."

The old man kicked his horse into a canter. The kid rode easily beside him and they let the horses have their head through the lighter bush and on into the scrub of a mountain meadow.

They made Parson's Gap by early evening. The Métis friends of the old man helped them bunk down in the barn and when the horses were tended to they ate together. The kid enjoyed their talk. They laughed a lot and the old man seemed in high spirits. The food was good and hearty and tasted of woodsmoke from the wood burner they used for a stove. He liked it. Later, the old man and he sat on the rail fence and watched the moon rise. They slept beside the stall where the horses were put. He drifted off with the smell of horse and dung and straw at his nose and he thought he'd never had such a comfortable bed.

In the morning they walked through the town. The kid was fascinated by the knots of people moving along the sidewalks. The town near the farm was smaller, without industry, and most of the people were farm folk who never had much time for town but for supplies, the post, and snatches of gossip at the mercantile. He could smell the mill here. It was everywhere. The high, astringent pinch of it. The town seemed to be encircled by ridges, the flanks of them dimpled with thin trees, and the rockface was grey, veined, with running splotches of dull orange where iron talus had spilled. The sky was a cap of grey. Where the streets slid down to the river, the houses were bigger, older, sturdier, and he liked the set of them, proud like roosters, with wide sidewalks and sculpted trim. The verandahs looked perfect for sitting.

"Does he live in one of these?" the kid asked.

"Not likely," the old man said. "Got me a street number here on the envelope. Said it's closer to the mill."

The land flattened out into a wide flood plain. The mill stood at the far end, sullen, industrial, dirty, and the clang and rumble of it hurt his ears. The houses were smaller here, unkempt, and there were skeleton frames of old cars and trucks strewn in yards and empty lots. Dogs slunk by with their heads down and growled at them as they passed. He could smell grease and cabbage and fish and here and there the foul air of untended latrines. Laundry hung out on lines above sullied kids' toys in yards more dirt than sod. The streets were rough, cracked, with potholes, and the edges of the sidewalks crumbled and the slumped power lines seemed so low he felt as though he could reach up and touch them. They came to an intersection and the old man peered at the envelope in his hand and then gazed off down the street to their right.

"This is her," he said. "Stepney Street. Now we got to find number nineteen."

There was nothing to distinguish the street from the one they turned off of. There were no trees. There were runs of ragged hedges and the occasional hump of flowerbeds laying untilled and grim with withered weeds. Number nineteen was clapboard, whitewashed, with a crumbling chimney and a gate hung by wire to rotted and canted wooden posts that were all that remained of a fence. They walked around it into the yard and they could hear the sounds of yelling and the crash of a bottle against the wall. Then a woman's voice high in the morning air. "I ain't cleanin' that no how." Another bottle smashed against the wall followed by wild laughter.

"This is her," the old man said. "Room three."

There was a small sun porch with a busted sofa where a man slept, his head flung back, gape-mouthed, and he had no teeth. The old man put a hand between the kid's shoulder blades. They stepped through a door that had once held glass but was now just the frame. The main floor was divided into rooms with a dim hallway marked by peeling wallpaper. A stairway led to the second floor. The first door had no number but the next one had a number two hung upside down and held by a pin. Number three beside it was where the ruckus was coming from. It sounded like wrestling: feet lurching about, the slide and crash of furniture, grunting and moans. The old man knocked.

"Christ, Henry, just bring that fresh hooch in here."

The old man opened the door. His father and a woman reeled about the room in a parody of dance to static-ridden music from a radio on a table. It was the only piece of furniture that wasn't spilled over or pushed into a corner. "What this?" the old man asked.

"Foxtrot," his father said over his shoulder.

"Who's the kid?" the woman asked. He let her go and she tumbled against the table and the radio crashed to the floor.

"Oh shit," he said, turning to face them in the open door. "Didn't expect you."

"You wrote," the old man said. He had a hand on the kid's shoulder.

"Yeah, but I didn't mean . . ."

"Mean what? For me to bring him?"

"No. I mean, yeah, just . . ."

"Just what?"

"Just wasn't thinkin' it was gonna be today."

"Today is a lot diff'rent than other days, you're sayin'?"

"Well, yeah. I'm paid. I'm just lettin' off a little steam is all." He fumbled two chairs upright and slid them over toward the door with a foot. He lost his balance and reeled and bumped into the woman, who was busy trying to right the table. They both fell. They laughed and then he clambered to his feet and stood there rubbing at his head with one hand, eying the kid and the old man and grimacing. "Fuck," he said. "Shoulda wrote and said when you were gonna get here."

"It wouldn'ta been no diff'rent. No matter what you say."

"Hey, I had plans."

"Yeah?" the old man said. "Like what?"

"We was gonna go eat somewheres. Maybe picnic out somewheres too. Buy him somethin' nice."

"Tell him that."

His father looked at the kid. He seemed to have trouble focusing. He scratched at his head and grabbed the back of one of the chairs and spun it and sat down hard. He shook his head to clear it and mopped his face with the palm of his hand. The back of it was grimy and the fingernails were rimmed with black. "Well, shit, kid. I dunno. I kinda thought we'd just find out what you wanted to do most. Wanda here's a friend. We're kickin' up our heels some. Work hard, play hard, you know?"

The kid stared at him. The room was quiet but for street sounds and the dull clump of footfalls on the second floor. His father was flustered and he hitched about in the chair and the kid watched him eye the bottles on the counter. He sweat. His eyes were webbed with red and the kid could see the yellow pall of tobacco on his fingertips. "You're supposed to try to get to know me like a father knows a son," he said quietly.

"Jesus. I know that. Think I didn't want that? Think I'da asked you here if I didn't wanna get to that?"

"You lied. All you wanna do is drink and dance and break stuff."

"Wanted to see ya, was the point of it all."

"Well, you seen me."

"I'm your dad."

The kid shook his head. "Ain't got one. Never had one. Wouldn't know what it's supposed to mean 'cept what you show."

"Hey, I'm workin' at the mine now. I got money. I could give you some. You could get you somethin' nice."

The kid looked up at the old man. There was a stern cast to his face and he eased the kid back through the door and stood facing his father, who looked up with his mouth hung open. He seemed dumbstruck and simple. "He's got no call for your money. He come here wantin' some of you. Not yer money. Any fool can give cash."

"Sorry."

"Tell *him* that."

"I'm sorry, kid."

The kid only stared. The old man turned his head and regarded him a moment and then put his hand on the door. "Wait for me outside, Frank," he said.

The kid turned and walked down the dank hallway and through the busted door and out into the yard. A fat tomcat sat cleaning his paws on the sun-warmed walk. He could hear raised voices. He felt awkward as though there was something expected of him that he had no idea of. It made him feel sad and he wanted to cry but he didn't know why. So he shifted his feet and kicked at loose pebbles of cement. Some of it rattled by the cat and he sprang to his feet and rolled his girth down the walk and down the street. The kid held a breath in his cheeks and stared back at the house.

After a while the old man came out and stood beside him. "Sorry you had to see that," he said.

"He's just lettin' off steam is what he said."

"I mean I'm sorry you had to see him like that."

"Drunk."

"Yeah. It ain't proper."

"What's proper mean?"

"It means ya come to kids clean. Not slopped-out drunk. I apologize for bringin' ya so you had to see that."

"So there's not gonna be no stories, no picnic, nothin'."

"Not this time, no. But I spied an ice cream joint on our

way through town. How's about you'n me treat ourselves to a big dish of that?"

"Okay. But you know what?"

"What?" the old man asked.

"We're both kinda at the same spot, him'n me."

"Is that a fact?"

"Well, he don't know nothin' about bein' a father and I don't know nothin' about bein' a son. Kinda makes us even, I figure."

The old man pinched his lips together solemnly and then leaned down and put both hands on the kid's shoulders. He looked at him openly and the kid felt uncomfortable. "You know everythin' there is to know 'bout bein' a son. Trust me on that."

The kid nodded. When the old man straightened and took a step down the sidewalk the kid stood there and stared at the house. It seemed to sag like it was tired, as though it had borne weight for far too long and needed to slump to the ground. There were cracks in all the windows. Shingles had come loose and blown away in the wind. Down the one side was a tangle of lilacs, un-pruned and ramshackle, old and uncared for, scraping against the side of the house, and there was only one bloom. It sat high at the point farthest from the house. A small dab of colour. It made the house more sullen, bleaker, and the kid wanted to pluck it and carry it somewhere where it would not feel alone, save it maybe, in a jar in the sunlight, and he felt the tears come until the old man walked back and put his arm around him and they made their way back to the barn where they'd left the horses.

———

He didn't go again until the next year. It was his birthday. The old man rode along but stayed at the farm with his friends and the kid walked to his father's place alone. There had been no letters, till the one recently asking for him to come. Whenever he thought about him he felt sad and remembered the drunken dance he'd done with the woman named Wanda and the dumbstruck look on his face when the old man had faced him down. His father was like a photograph that had been in the light too long. He was a stranger. But the kid felt a tie to him and there was a dull ache when he thought of him so he didn't lend much time to those thoughts. Still, there were fathers around the school, families, and the talk of them, and he was embarrassed at his lack. It made him more of an outsider. The old man taught him the word "guardian." It meant protector. It meant that as long as the old man was around there was nothing for him to be afraid of. It meant he was safe and cared for. But it didn't mean "father." The definition of that word was left to his observation. The men he saw around the school were quiet in the way of country folk but bearing a strength and resiliency he could see in the way they walked and held themselves. He never saw them drunk. He never saw them in a light that was less than predictable and he came to believe that fathers were made of trustworthy stuff, heroic in quiet ways, strong, made up of a thousand small details. He wondered if time was what held them in place long enough to get to know those details. So when he was asked to share a birthday with his father he was gladdened and went eagerly.

"See here," the old man said, showing him the words on the page of the letter. "He says that he promises to be straight. Says ten is a mighty important age and he wants to be with ya."

"You figure he means it?"

"As much as he can, I guess."

"Kinda wonder how much that is."

"Can't know. Up to you."

He was suddenly big for his age. Heavier, bulkier than the skinny kids at school. The work around the farm gave him a rugged, tensile strength that showed in his walk and the slope of his shoulders. He didn't look ten. When he walked through the town people studied him for a stranger and he kept his head high and walked purposefully. His father had moved and the kid found the street a few blocks away from where he'd last seen him. It was a brighter neighbourhood. The homes were neat and groomed and he liked the way the lawns framed for the verandahs and porches and the grand three-storey cliffs of them. The smells of paint, mown grass, and baking hung in the soft, unmoving air of morning. His father's place was at the far end of the wide street.

At first it struck the kid that maybe he had the number wrong. The house was painted a pale orange with blue trim. There was a truck in the driveway. There were flowerboxes hung along the length of the verandah and there was a swing rocker and deep wooden deck chairs. The main door was open. Through the outside screen door he could see people moving and heard the sound of laughter. He looked at the paper in his hand and then opened the gate and walked down the walk toward the front steps. A tall woman with white hair and blue eyes answered his knock.

"You'd be Frank, wouldn't you?" she asked.

"Ma'am," the kid said.

"I'm Jenna. Your father is so excited you were coming I swear he bathed twice."

"That's good, ma'am. It's my birthday."

"I know, and we are so glad to have you. Come in. I'll call your father."

The house was cool. The wooden floors gleamed with waxing and there were thick carpets everywhere. The kid had never seen plants indoors but the front room was filled with them. The furniture was pillowed and sturdy. He sat on the edge of a sofa and put his hand down and rubbed at the material. The place seemed to shine with care. Several men drifted down the hallway and then back and up the stairs where the woman had gone. They looked at the kid quizzically. They were big, muscled men in work socks, flannel shirts, and jeans. None of them said a word.

His father walked down the stairs behind Jenna. She was smiling when she entered the room and went to a chair beside the sofa and sat. His father stood in the doorway leaning against the jamb. He'd shaved and scrubbed his face ruddy. He wore jeans and a white shirt. He had his hands folded in front of him and the nails were trimmed. His hair was freshly cut and slicked back and when he looked at the kid he had a surprised look as though he were unused to appearing like that. The kid smiled.

"You ride them horses here again?" his father asked.

"Yeah. It's what we like best."

"Long ride."

"Yeah. But good."

"This here's Jenna. She's my landlady."

"What's that?"

"Means I'm a roomer. Me an' all the other guys work at the mill and rent out rooms here. She cooks for us, bags us lunches. It's a good go."

"I've packed a whopping picnic for you two," Jenna said. "It's such a grand day you'll have a wonderful time."

"What are we doin'?" the kid asked.

"Expect you'll have to open yer gift in order to know," his father said.

"You got me a gift?"

"It's yer birthday isn't it?"

"Yeah but . . ."

"But nothing. Birthdays are for presents and if you go into the kitchen it's on the table waitin' fer ya."

The kid rose and the three of them walked down the hallway to the kitchen that was flooded with sunlight. There was a long, skinny package on the table wrapped in bright paper and tied with a ribbon. He stood a few feet away and stared at it.

"Go on," his father said.

He sat and pulled the package to him and stared at it. Then he cast a look at his father and Jenna and eased a thumb into the seam. He parted the paper gently.

"Go on," his father said. "Just rip it."

He tore the paper off. It was a fishing rod. It was a two-piece rod with a reel and a small tin box of flies. He'd never used a rod and reel. The old man had taught him to bush fish with a hand line or trot lines baited and set out at night. He held the rod in his hands and looked at it as though it were a magical thing. He ran a palm along its length and felt its smoothness.

"You know how to fly-fish?" his father asked.

"No," the kid said.

"Well, ya will by the end of today. There's some big trout where we're goin'. The rig is all set up with line in the reel. All's ya gotta do is learn to throw it out there."

"You know how?"

"Well, I ain't exactly the best fisher but I can toss a fly out, yeah."

"Thanks."

"Hey, I figure every kid should fish with his old man."

Jenna had baked a small cake and they had a piece each. She packed the remainder in wax paper and set it in a wicker basket on the counter. She handed it to his father. "Take care with the truck," she said.

"I will."

She kept her hand on the handle of the basket and looked sternly at his father. "I mean it now, Eldon. You take care. No foolishness. Not today."

"I hear ya," he said. "It's my kid's birthday. God."

He turned to the kid. "No hooch, kid. Not today. Promise. All right?"

"Sure," the kid said.

His father looked pointedly at Jenna. She held the look a moment longer then let go of the basket. His father rattled keys in his pocket and grinned at the kid. "Burnin' daylight, young'un," he said. He walked down the hallway and the kid wiped cake crumbs off his face with the napkin Jenna had set by his plate. He thanked her. She smiled and put a hand on his head and looked at him steadily. Her eyes were so clear the kid felt as though he were falling into them.

"Go," she said. "Have the best day."

His father was waiting by the truck. It was red with black fenders and wooden slats on both sides of the bed. The kid climbed into the passenger side and set the rod between his knees. His father sat down behind the wheel and gripped it with both hands, staring out the windshield at Jenna, who stood with her hands on her hips at the top of the verandah stairs. He waved weakly. She only stared. He put the key in the ignition and the truck fired up right away and he slipped it into gear and backed slowly out of the driveway and drove carefully down the street. "Old worrywart," he said.

"She seems nice," the kid said.

"Battle-axe is what she is." The kid turned to him. "Means she's more bother'n good."

"She give ya her truck."

"Don't mean she's not a snoop and a stool pigeon."

His father threw him a look. He drove slowly until he turned the corner and then he stepped on the gas, worked the clutch fast, and the truck revved and spun gravel. His father whooped and slammed a palm on the steering wheel. He reached over and gave the kid a playful shake. Then he shifted gears and sped up as they passed the mill. They hit the edge of town and he worked the gears hard and they rounded a long, sweeping curve and were off.

He felt the pull of the country. The road his father drove was single lane and it wound its way up around the foot of a low mountain before it cut between twin rock columns at the head of a wide alpine meadow. There was a creek there, water glinting like a winking eye. The creek was narrow, bordered by small red willows and thickets of dogwood and thrusts of twitch grass and bramble. Rocks glistened with the sheen of spray tumbled into the air by small rapids that slunk into shallow pools of gravel and stone. Ridges ambled casually to the west and the meadow seemed held in place by them. There was a trio of birches set close to the rut of the road that bent and snaked its way to the creek. His father drove with both hands while the truck bucked and swayed and careened along the dip and jut of it, laughing now and smiling at the kid, who held on to the frame of the open window with both hands. He parked beside the trees.

When the kid alit he could smell the fecund bog of the meadow, the seep of it just below the grasses. There were hints of cedar on the breeze. The sun splayed across his face and he closed his eyes against it and he could hear the creek jostle its way through the outcrops of rock at it shore and from somewhere to the east a steer bawled and the song of redwing blackbirds rose all around him.

His father assembled the rods, explaining as he went. The kid watched as he set the reels in the reel seats, tightened the screws that held them in place, and then threaded the line through the eyelets and tied on tiny brown flies. He grinned at him. "Trick is to not use strength," he said. "The whole deal is about bein' graceful. Savvy?"

"Not really," the kid said.

"Don't know a whole lot about it neither except for this. You kinda wave insteada throwin'. I'll show ya." He laid one rod down in the carpet of moss and coarse grass away from the trees and walked the end of the line out a dozen yards. "Ya gotta let the rod do all the work," he said. "She'll bend and pick up tension and when yer ready you lay the line out smooth."

He walked back to where the kid stood and picked up the rod. He held the tip out in front of him and gripped the handle with his thumb laid out along the length of it. Then he slowly raised his forearm at the elbow and lifted it almost ninety degrees. The line was pulled off the grass. It peeled toward them in an arc and the kid ducked but it sailed past his father's head in a deep U-shape and when it straightened he pushed the arm forward again and the line followed. He let it flow out and brought the rod tip down gently and the line straightened, held in the air a fraction of a second, and landed in the grass.

"Easy," his father said. "Well, easy enough, anyhow. You wanna try?"

The kid took the rod in his hands. His father stood behind him and he could feel the length of his body along the back of him. His warmth. The smell of soap and tobacco. He took the kid's forearm and raised it. The line caught. "One, two, three," he counted in his ear. "Tick, tick, tick," he said. "Think about the face of a clock." Then he pushed the kid's forearm forward and held it when it hit the ten o'clock position. The line floated out and settled on the grass. "Do it like that. Easy. Gentle and count it out like I did and push her forward again."

"By myself."

"Hell yeah. I'm gonna set up the picnic."

While his father set out a blanket and the stuff in the basket in the shade, the kid worked the line. It was hard at first. He wanted to force it but when he did the line cracked like a whip behind his ear. "Easy there, jimbo. You'll knot the line," his father said.

It took a while before he could mimic his father's delivery. He looked at him now and then as his father lay on the blanket, sipping from a thermos. He launched a dozen perfect casts.

"All right then," his father said. "Got a feel for it? The rhythm?"

"Yeah." The kid smiled.

"Good. Now let's hit them pools."

They carried their rods and strode across the meadow. His father pointed downstream where the creek widened and picked up speed before sweeping into a wide curve that bellied into a long pool. He motioned with his hand and the kid followed him and they skirted the length of the pool. "Gotta get the sun in front of ya so ya don't throw no shadow. Spooks 'em."

They walked in a semicircle and approached the pool quietly, bent at the waist. When they could see the surface of the water, his father motioned him down to kneel in the grass. He raised his arm and followed the length of the pool with a finger. "See where the current comes in and follows through her?"

"Yeah."

"That's what ya gotta work. Go down to them rocks where it's shallow and cast up into the current. Watch your fly and pull the line in with your free hand. Slow. Let it ride the current."

"Where's the line go?"

"Let her drop at your feet. She'll float in the water. When ya get a hit raise the rod up and tighten the line. Keep the line tight and reel the bugger in."

"That's it? What if I lose him?"

"Then ya lose him. Only way to learn this is to learn it."

"Where you gonna fish?"

"I'm gonna head down to the next pool. If ya break off a fly, come down and I'll show ya how to tie on another."

"How do I get the line out. Can't walk it out on the water."

"Be a trick if ya could. Here. Lemme show ya."

Once he knew how to get the line out and cast his father walked away. The kid stripped line off his reel to prepare and turned his head and watched his father walk along the side of the stream. He seemed different here. There was nothing of the shambled man he'd first seen at the farm. This man seemed assured, confident. Happy almost. He heard him whistle as he walked, then he leapt across the creek on rocks and turned to walk the opposite bank, the thermos hooked to his belt and bumping along as he strode forward. The kid turned to the pool and made his first cast.

He bellied the line on the water. But the tension of it coming back off the surface helped him get a feel for the next cast and it landed straighter but with a light slap. He focused on being easy. His attention was rooted to the act of casting and he never noticed time slipping away. When he was finally able to make soft casts and watch the fly settle into the current and drift, it was mid-afternoon. The sun was arched toward the west and the shadows thrown by the willows were longer. He felt cool. He was hungry. He dipped his hand into the stream and drank then splashed some on his face and neck. He looked downstream to where his father had disappeared but could see no motion. So he stretched and returned to the process of casting.

The first thing he heard was his name being yelled. It was rough and frantic and he dropped the rod on the bank and clambered up it. His father was splashing through the water with a large trout cradled in his hands. He fought to hold the fish and he stumbled, reeled, and the kid thought he'd fall but his forward motion kept him upright.

"Hoo hoo!" he yelled. "Got me the granddaddy of 'em all."

He made it as far as the end of the pool the kid had fished before he fell. His foot slipped on a rock and he crashed headlong and the fish flew out of his arms, turning a lazy circle before landing on its flank in the shallows. The kid watched it right itself and then flash its tail hard and disappear into the trench where the current ran faster. His father fought for footing then fell again. The kid leapt off the bank and waded to him and caught one flailing hand. He tugged on it. He could feel his father's weight and he braced his feet against the rocks and held fast. It took his father several minutes to right himself. The kid helped him to the bank, where he collapsed, and the kid could smell the rank cut of whisky on his breath.

"Son of a bitch!" Eldon said. "That sucker went three pounds or I'm fucked."

"Drunk is what you are," the kid said.

"Hell, it's your birthday, kid. A little celebratin' is all I done."

"Shoulda known when I seen the thermos."

"Yeah well, lost the damn fish but we still got a picnic. Let's do 'er up."

The kid shook his head and went to retrieve the rod. His father scrambled up the bank. He tripped at the top and almost fell backwards into the stream but the kid caught his shirt tail. "Where's your rod?" he asked.

"Last I seen she was headed west."

"You lost it?"

"Fish too. Don't forget that."

The kid stomped off toward the trees where the truck was parked. His father weaved along behind him and he could hear him stop and unscrew the thermos cap. He spun around and watched him drink. His Adam's apple bobbed crazily. He lowered the thermos and looked at it puzzled and turned it upside down and shook it. "Fuck," he said. The kid walked hard to the trees and sat beside the basket. His father tottered right by and went to the truck and rooted around under the seat. He stepped away with a small bottle. There was the leer of a smile on his face.

"Figure to drink that too?" the kid asked.

His father tumbled down onto the blanket. "Waste not, want not. Ain't that the rule?"

"Yer already wasted."

"Got you a mouth, don'tcha?"

The kid shook his head. His father reached across to the basket and yanked out a sandwich wrapped in wax paper. He set about to eat it. The kid watched while he crammed in a huge mouthful and chewed at it savagely. Crumbs and bits of meat and slices of cheese tumbled out and he smacked his lips, breathing hard and wiping at his mouth with the back of his hand. He swallowed. Then he tipped the bottle and gulped. The kid got up and walked to the truck. The keys were still in the ignition and he turned them and the motor caught and he sat there, staring out the windshield at his father.

His father struggled to his feet and ran toward him. He lost his balance and careered forward. He barely managed to catch himself with outstretched hands on the hood of the truck. "Fuck ya doon?" he asked.

"Get in or walk," the kid said.

"What?"

"You heard me."

"You can't friggin' drive."

"Been drivin' tractor since I was eight. This truck ain't no account. Get in."

"What about the picnic?"

The kid slapped a hand on the wheel. Then he got out and walked angrily to the blanket and tossed everything together in a heap and walked to the truck and laid it in the bed. "Get in," he said again.

"Fuck'd ya do that for?" his father asked, fighting to climb into the passenger seat.

The kid glared at him. His hands were shaking. He felt hot. "Waste not, want not," he said.

His father slammed the door closed. The smell of whisky was high in the air. The kid rolled down his window and backed the truck into the grass and then pulled out into the rut of the road. He took it slow, but the truck still bucked along. His father held one hand out on the dashboard and gripped the door handle with the other. His head swung back and forth. When they got to the gravel road the kid turned back the way they came and his father settled into his seat. "Happy birthday," he slurred.

The kid let out a breath long and slow and focused on the road. His father passed out halfway back to town. He drove slow and carefully and found his way back through town to the rooming house and parked in the driveway. It was full evening. Jenna and two men had been strolling along the sidewalk and the kid went to them and handed her the keys. The two men walked to the truck and hauled his father out, bracing him between them and dragging him to the house and up the stairs while the kid stared at his feet.

"Got a paper and something to write with?" he asked.

"Yes," Jenna said. "Come in and I'll get it."

"Rather be out here, ma'am."

"All right," she said and went into the house. She came back a moment later with a sheet of paper and a pen. She gave it to him and he took it and leaned on the hood of the truck and wrote. When he was finished he handed it to her and turned and walked away.

You lied to me! was all it said in big childlike letters.

———

He didn't see his father again until he was twelve. Those two years passed without a word. At first he felt disappointed when a birthday came and went without a present or a card. But as the months went by he learned to forget about expectation. For a time he could allow the notion of having a father somewhere in the world gradually slip away and he was comfortable in his life on the farm. He didn't mark time by occasions. He marked it by the seasons like a farmer and when the letter came inviting him to visit his father again, he wanted to shrug it off. It was the old man who talked him into going.

He made the journey to Parson's Gap alone for the first time. What he would always remember about it were the hours spent on horseback and the feel of the open country all around him. When he'd arrived in town his father was with a woman. He wasn't drunk but he was drinking. They had supper at a diner downtown and then his father and the woman had left him. They'd gone off and left him with a radio for company and headed down to the mill workers' bar. He'd fallen asleep in the rocking chair his father kept as the only furniture in his room except the single bed and a battered fridge. Sometime in the early morning they lurched in and fell onto the bed. He sat huddled under a thin blanket in the chair, a shadow among shadows, barely able to breathe. They thrashed around and there were moans and curses and a sound like growling and the bed banged against the wall and he could feel the floor shake. He could see the moon of his father's buttocks rising and falling and the soles of the woman's feet like the flats of white paddles kicking against the current of the air, the room dense with the smell of them: liquor, cigarettes, sweat. It didn't last long. Her arms gyrated wildly in the air and she hit him on the back and shoulders.

They finished in a paroxysm of curses, wet kisses, and laughter before his father rolled to the side and flipped on the light. He didn't see him at first but the woman did. A thatch of hair tumbled over her eyes and she brushed it away and bit her lip. She elbowed his father. He turned with a crock of whisky in his hand. They both stared at him. The kid swallowed hard, his heart hammering in his chest and wanting to flee into the night. But he stayed where he was. Waiting.

"Jesus," his father said.

The woman cupped a breast and leered at him. He turned his head. There was a long silence before he heard the scrape of a match and then a breathy exhale. When he looked his father was handing the smoke to the woman, who continued to look at him with one forearm propping the bulge of her breasts.

"Son of a bitch," his father said. "Sorry," he said to the woman.

"I kinda like it," she said.

"Well, I kinda like that ya like it." They laughed and both took a hard slug of the whisky. His father smoked and squinted at him. The kid looked away toward the window.

The woman whispered something in his father's ear and gave the lobe a lick and he turned and flipped off the light and the kid could hear them rustle about. Then the light came on again. "Chevy says she wants to see ya watchin'," he said. He was grinning crazily. The woman smiled through blackened teeth. He pulled the blanket up over his face and they laughed and there was the sound of wrestling and few light slaps and then the wet slop of drunken kisses. He stood. They didn't notice. He gathered his shoes and crept to the door and turned and all he saw was a tangle of flesh so he stepped out the door and walked out of the rooming house and down the street to get the horse. He rode out of town in darkness. It was supposed to be a camping trip.

The letters about Christmas began the following September. He'd had no word from him since the night of the tryst. The letters outlined the turkey, the feast he would bring, the midnight expedition to get the tree on snowshoes to haul it back on a toboggan. They gave vague clues about presents. He wrote about gathering around the woodstove in the old man's house and singing old carols and listening to the cold snap the roof timbers. Each letter held something more and the kid felt himself grow excited despite himself.

The old man and he never gave much energy to Christmas. There was always a gift or two, but they leaned toward the practical: a hunting knife, snare wire, a new halter for the horse, a saddle blanket and such. He splurged on a turkey though and store-bought pies and a jar of sweets. For the kid, Christmas was all about the quiet, and the biggest part of it was the long hike the old man and he always took while the turkey roasted. They'd head off in a different direction or angle every year. They snowshoed in for two hours, built a fire, and drank strong tea, and in that cold and barren-feeling world, the kid came to know Christmas as a time when the land and its emptiness were perfect. Now and again the old man would tell him a story. But it was the thrill of the silence they walked through he loved the most. The land sleeping. The hushed atmosphere where even sound was absorbed and realized in the great white sanctity of winter. That was Christmas to his mind.

"Don't be gettin' all crazy in the head about this," the old man said.

"Right," the kid said but he couldn't hold back the excitement that built up in him with each of the letters. The promises were lavish. He would come on the bus and they would celebrate. The kid let himself stoke the fire in him and when they went to meet the bus in town two days before Christmas, his father wasn't on it. They waited for the next one. He could taste the salt of tears in his throat and he cursed himself for weakness. But not until that next bus turned the corner at the edge of the parking lot and he and the old man stood there watching it leave did he let it out of him.

"Son of a bitch!" he said and kicked at a chunk of ice.

The old man stood and watched him. The kid stomped around in a circle and hammered his fists into his thighs and he could feel the rage. He felt his jaw quivering with the need to cry, to wail, to scream. He raised his fists in the air and fell to his knees in the snow.

"Frank," the old man said. "Frank. Shoulda never let him near ya."

"Ain't pissed at him," the kid said. "Pissed at *me*."

"Ya done what anyone'd done," the old man said.

The kid sat back, still on his knees in the snow. "After what I seen?"

"Can't hold it against yourself for bein' a kid."

"I fuckin' know better and I ain't a kid."

"Ya got a heart is all. No shame in that."

"Feels busted up and sore right now."

"But ya got to move through it."

"Why?"

"Ain't no choice," The old man raised the kid's chin with

one hand. They knelt there in the snow and muck, the wet seeping into their pants. "Y'all right?" he asked.

The kid wiped at his nose with a sleeve. "I will be," he said. "Yeah. Ya will. I know that."

By the time they got back to the farm he was beyond it, ready for the return to his predictable life, the feel of the woodstove heat on his face comforting and real.

15

HE WOKE IN THE EERIE HALF-LIGHT OF PRE-DAWN. There was mist rising off the creek and when he roused he startled a deer come to drink at the far shore. The sky was a dim grey cut with a pale blue. The day would be warm. The stones he'd fallen asleep on had stiffened his back and it took long minutes of stretching to work the kinks out. He walked to the stream and knelt on the gravel and dipped his hands in to splash on his face and neck. Then he drank. He held the last mouthful in his cheeks and rinsed his mouth and spat on the stones and rose and walked back to where he'd left his father. He was sleeping. It didn't seem that he had moved all night and when he put a hand to his brow he found it hot. He covered him with his own blanket from the pack. Becka had put a small sack of supplies in there without his knowing and he was surprised to open it and find bacon, bannock, and beans. He cut the top off the beans with his knife and laid the bacon on the flopped over lid and set it by the edge of the fire once it got going. Then he sat on a rock and rolled a smoke. His father stirred at the smell of the food.

"God," he said. "Smells mighty good."

"Figure you could eat now?" the kid asked.

"Some. Got some water?"

The kid rose and handed him a cup and he drank slowly. His lips looked dry and cracked and he rubbed some of the water along them. The kid handed him the last of the smoke. "How you feel?" he asked.

His father bent his back and grimaced and put a hand to the right side of his belly. "Not good," he said. "How much more of that stuff we got?"

"It'll hold long as you don't gulp it. Ya gotta drink it slow. Measure it out. Save it. It ain't hooch."

"Speakin' of hooch. Did ya dump it?"

"You said."

"Damn."

"I never chucked all of it," the kid said.

His father stared at him blandly. Then he scratched at his whiskers and lay on his back looking up at the sky. The kid went to the fire and turned the can with a forked stick. The bacon sizzled and spat grease. When it was ready he used a pair of sticks to move the can onto the grass and sat and waited while it cooled. He hung the bacon off one of the sticks and carried it to where his father lay. He held it out to him and he took a strip and stuck it in his mouth. He worked the bacon around in his mouth and then spat it out. "Can't do it," he said.

"Try the beans."

"A little, I guess."

The kid knelt and put some of the beans on the tip of the knife and held it out. His father licked them off. He leaned back against the tree and closed his eyes. The kid shook him and fed him more of the beans. He was hotter now. The kid could feel the heat thrown off him like a wave so he walked to the creek and soaked his extra shirt and used it as a compress on his father's head. He ate some of the beans himself. When he was finished he broke camp, saddled the horse, and kicked dirt and sand onto the fire and danced on it to make sure it was out.

"You take a lot of care, don'tcha?" his father asked. His voice was a croak.

The kid nodded. "Got to. When you're out here alone there's no one on your back trail."

"I left a lot of back trail in my time," his father said.

The kid kept stomping down on the remains of the fire. "Musta been lonely."

His father took the wet shirt off his forehead and touched it to each cheek. He sipped some water from the canteen and when he spoke his voice was clearer. "I can't reckon lonesome. Seems to me a man makes a choice somewhere along the line that he don't need no wingers or others walkin' with him. I know I did."

"Seems a good choice to me," the kid said. "Reason I come to know things out here so good is on accounta feelin' better alone."

"Figure we're a pair of oddballs?"

The kid stopped stamping the fire and stepped out onto the grass. He kicked the residue of ash from his boots and took his time rolling a smoke. He handed the smoke down to his father and lit it for him. He busied himself rolling another for himself. He felt his father watching him but didn't raise his eye from his hands.

"I held words better in my head than speakin' 'em mosta my life," his father said. "They never come out arranged the way I wanted. But I could listen good. Always was partial to a good story. Places I went there was always someone with a whopper or a tall tale and I liked hearin' them. Went lotsa places, met lotsa men, but never had no chit chat, no banter, could never lay 'em out all loud and hilarious like other men I come to know. Guess I kinda envied them that."

The kid smoked and stared at the play of sunlight on the waffled surface of the creek. "The old man always said people waste a lot air talkin' about nothin'. I grew partial to that notion."

"Still'n all, I wish I'da come out with more," his father said. "More of what I seen, where I gone. Gettin' to this point a fella sees the lack, I guess."

"Call it a lack, not talkin'?"

"Feels like it. Ain't gonna be no one to speak for me when this is all said and done."

His father smoked and crushed the butt against the trunk of a tree. He looked up at the kid, who watched him, and he tucked the dead butt into his pocket. He exhaled long and slow and raised his head to the sky. Shadows fell on his face and the branches pushed by the breeze made it appear to move, to shift, to alter, and the kid felt hollow watching life dance across his dying father's face.

"Stories get told one word at a time," he said quietly. "Somethin' your grandmother said. Stories get told one word at a time. Maybe she was talkin' about life. I didn't have the ears to hear it though."

The kid waited for more. His father let his head drop, his chin nearly resting on his collarbone. His eyes blinked and he closed them finally and lay there, breathing deeply, and the kid thought he had passed out but he opened his eyes and turned to him. They regarded each other without speaking.

After a while, the kid helped him onto the horse and he could feel the bones in his back and ribs. He tied his feet and hands and his father hung his head and stared at the ground. He horse shimmied and he swayed in the saddle. The kid shouldered the pack and whistled and the horse started to walk.

They followed the creek another two miles and then cut to the north up a swayback ridge. The kid could see bear and deer scat and the tracks of skunks and weasels. The bush was thin, mostly big ponderosa pines and spruce and fir. There were large, open stretches strewn with rocks and they walked through splatters of holly strung along the edge of the trail. His father was unconscious. The horse seemed to sense the fragile nature of her load and walked lightly and they made slow time going up the ridge and when they crested it, the day had swung to noon.

He found a glade. There was deep moss in the shadow and he stopped the horse and untied his father and helped him down. He was soaked. It felt as though he were burning from the inside out, and the kid laid him on the moss with the pack under his head and roused him and got him to drink some of the medicine. It dribbled at the corner of his mouth. He slumped back with his head on the pack. The kid walked off and paced among the trees. His father lay with his eyes closed.

"You sleepin'?" the kid asked.

"Can't," his father said. "She's a harder fight now." His voice was frail and shaky. "How far we got to go?"

"I looked out off the edge of the ridge. We put in some good time we can make it by evenin' if yer up to it."

"No choice."

"All right."

When they'd rested he got his father back on the horse and led her down the far side of the ridge into the cut of a narrow valley. He remembered it. It was one of his favourite places to trap. There were small streams that wound their way down the sides of the mountains on either side and there were small meadows and bogs where fur-bearers came to drink. He told his father about his forays here. Now and then his father grunted and he took it for encouragement.

"Come here when it got too noisy in my head," he said. "When the old man got too old for the ride he let me make the trip alone and I got to prefer that. Never was afraid. Never seemed to be a place for fear. When ya come to know a thing ya come to know its feel. I know this place by feel nowadays."

"You're a good man," his father croaked suddenly. "The old man done good turnin' ya loose out here. He know how good ya are out here?"

"He knows."

His father slumped back down in the saddle and the kid led the horse along in silence. When they rounded the turn at the foot of the mountain the kid could see the ridge his father sought. They walked steadily. By early evening they were at the foot of it and the kid tightened the ropes at his father's feet for the climb. His breath was ragged and weak and the kid could feel the heat of him. Still, he shivered. He could only manage to wet his lips from the canteen the kid held up. The trail looped up and around the base of the ridge and it was easy walking and the horse stepped lazily along, the sway of her gentle as if she understood the depth of her mission. He led her along and the evening was bright and crisp and there was birdsong everywhere. The backside of the ridge was thick with fir, and as they climbed higher and more easterly the slope relinquished itself to pine and saplings of aspen and birch and patches of wild rose and sudden juts of mountain ash and juniper.

His father groaned now and then and the kid stopped the horse to check on him but he made no other sound. They walked through the early part of the evening and when they crested the ridge the kid walked the horse to the rim and looked out over the valley. A river plowed through the belly of it. It was turquoise from the melt of the glacier higher up that was the source of the flow and there was a wide flood plain that was heavily stoned at its edge, giving way to scrub pine and thickets of cedar and then the slender thrust of maples, red willows, and clumps and pokes of mountain grass and autumn wildflowers. He watched a doe deer and fawn step gingerly out of the reeds at the river's edge. A black bear waddled out of the bush a mile or so farther downriver. From where they stood the mountains arranged themselves along the far side of the valley in a long green line, pocked with granite cliffs and bordered with snow on the higher peaks. The valley twisted off to the west and disappeared around the hem of the western range behind them.

His father stirred and the kid took the horse to a grove of ponderosa pines thirty feet from the precipice. He untied him and helped him down. His father slumped against him and the kid carried him a few yards before he could get his feet under him to stand shakily with one hand on the kid's shoulder. He set him on a log and went back to see to the horse.

He carried the saddle over, spread the blanket on the ground, and eased his father down onto it, propping his head against the saddle facing the edge of the ridge.

"Ah," he said when he saw the valley.

He nodded off with the medicine, and when the kid was sure that his father was deep into sleep he left him to ease stealthily into the trees to hunt. He grabbed a trio of stones that were rounded like small balls and tucked them in his pocket. Then he found a log fallen against a large rock and he lay behind it and peered out through the triangular opening at a stretch of forest littered with bracken, fallen branches, and small pines. He waited. Around him he could hear the sounds of the bush, the snap and crack of it, the swish of ferns where small things scuttled and the rustle of leaves and limb where birds and squirrels made their evening preparations. He closed his eyes and worked at pushing the edges of his hearing out. He could hear things in the distance. A moose bawled in the valley. A bear grunted somewhere down the slant of the ridge and there was a slicing sound where the wind cut through the gap. Then he heard the birds. There was a covey of grouse hunting and pecking around the trees. They moved with their heads down and he looked through the space under the log and whistled once, sharply. The grouse leaped into the branches of the nearest trees and sat there immobile and dull-witted, waiting for the threat to reveal itself. He stood. The first stone felt smooth as a bullet and he hefted it in his palm a few times and leaned toward the biggest grouse perched on a thin limb. He threw and missed by an inch. The bird sat there and blinked. But it fell to the ground when the second stone found its mark. The third stone dropped another bird and he walked around the log to retrieve them. He plucked them clean before walking back toward the camp.

He laid the birds on a rock. Then he gathered stones and made a fire ring and scooped dirt and moss out and made sure there were no roots that might catch. Then he gathered wood, stacking it until he had a good pile. He started a fire with the knife and a rock and some of the moss and small twigs. When it was going well he cleaned the birds and threw the guts in the fire. He skewered them on sticks, drove one end of each into the ground, and tilted them to the heat. As the fire burned down to embers he sat and sipped at the canteen and tended it while the birds cooked.

He stood and stretched, turned the birds on their sticks, and walked to the edge of the ridge. The valley had shifted to a low purple light and the mountains at the far side fell into grey. The river was pink with the light of the setting sun. He stood and watched it ease itself down to slumber. When he turned and walked back to check on his father he found him bathed in sweat, hot to the touch, and clammy. His breath came in ragged gasps. He shivered the length of his body. The kid covered him with blankets. He stirred some and groaned and when he tried to turn on his side the kid could see pain rack him as he clutched at his side and the sweat popped out in globules on his brow. The kid retrieved the canteen and poured some water into his palm and wiped his father's brow. He held it to his lips and his father sipped at it and his eyes flickered. Then he sank back into the hold of the medicine.

The kid watched him sleep, feeling afraid of what was to come and of what it would mean to him when it did. When the fire had died down to a faint orange glow he built it up again slowly and when the flames cast his shadow against the wall of trees he took the first bird off the stick and let it cool before tearing into it ravenously. When he was finished he cut the flesh of the second into strips and then diced them into small bits his father could chew if he was able to eat. He tended to the horse and by then it was full dark. The moon nudged the tips of the trees. He could hear coyotes yap and howl in the valley. The fire threw sparks and he watched them scurry and twist upward and then tumble back down before they flared out inches from the ground. When his father moaned he walked to where he lay and knelt beside him. He was awake.

"Feel like a warmed-over turd," his father said.

"You wanna sit by the fire?"

"Yeah."

The kid helped him to his feet. He could feel the ribs along his back and his hand wrapped easily around his father's forearm. He got him to the fire and set the pack behind him and stoked the fire so it blazed. His father drank from the canteen and he could hear the dry clack of his throat as he swallowed.

"Got me some grouse. Can ya stand to eat?" the kid asked.

"I could try."

He chewed the first dice of grouse with effort. He had to fight the urge to retch but he got it down and the second piece was easier. He couldn't take a third. He sat and stared into the fire and the kid could see the sweat bathe him in a dull orange sheen. He coughed and almost toppled from the effort of it. Then he leaned back on the pack and closed his eyes and the kid tapped him on the knee and held out the medicine. "Ya best take more," he said.

His father took it and sipped at it. He relaxed and for a while he lay in a doze. The kid poked at the fire and got the flame to rise higher. He fished his makings out of his pocket and rolled one and lit it with the glowing end of the stick. When his father spoke again, the words rolled out in a monotone.

"Jimmy used to say we're a Great Mystery. Everything. Said the things they done, those old-time Indians, was all about learnin' to live with that mystery. Not solving it, not comin' to grips with it, not even tryin' to guess it out. Just bein' with it. I guess I wish I'da learned the secret to doing that."

He motioned for the cigarette and the kid handed it to him. He smoked it down to a butt that he had to pinch it with two fingers to hold it and after the last deep haul flipped it into the fire. "I never belonged nowhere, Frank. Never belonged nowhere or to nobody," he said. He gazed into the fire as though it was where his words and the strength to say them were coming from.

"Come a time when I was older when I thought that that was just my draw. Come a time when I believed it was all I deserved on accounta all I done, and I guess all I never done."

A cough racked him and when the kid stood quickly he raised a hand to stop him from approaching. He hacked in small, hard coughs until the spell was over and he took several deep breaths to calm himself. "When the doc told me I was dying I remembered this place. I come here when I was fifteen. We were logger scouts and I come here and found this ridge. Stayed here two days just sitting on the edge of that cliff looking at it all. That's all. Just looking. I don't recall even thinking anything except how good it felt to be there."

The fire burned low and for a while neither of them spoke or moved. The night edged close around them and in the silvered phosphorescence of the moon the top of rocks shone dimly and looking upward into the sky they could see millions of stars and the milky clouds of nebulae and the shimmer of meteors piercing the fabric of it.

"I come to know some peace here, Frank," his father said. "This here's the only place I felt like I belonged, like I fit, where I never fucked up. Couldn't think of no better place to leave from."

He fell silent and the kid raised his eyes and studied the sky again. He leaned his head back as far as it would go and the air was so clear he felt as though he were floating above the earth. The stars almost within reach. He imagined he could hear the crackle of their fire. He kept that pose until his neck ached and he sat straight again and drank in small sips from the canteen.

"I killed a man once," his father said. His voice came out of the dark and shadow.

"On purpose?" the kid asked.

"I don't know."

He reached a hand up and waved for the smoke the kid had just lit. He knelt beside him and handed it to him. He took a long draw. His eyes were closed and he shook when he spoke, and the kid put a hand to his brow and his father turned his head away. The kid sat back on his haunches and when his father turned to look at him again his eyes were hard and set and there was a feverish gleam to them.

"Ain't spoke of it since it happened. But it's what you need to know of me," he said.

His father shifted about to find a comfortable position. When he was settled he set both hands down along his thighs and spread his fingers wide to brace himself. He exhaled and let his head slump forward, held it there a moment, and then inhaled and raised it again and began to speak.

16

WAR. 1951. Neither of them had ever heard of Korea. When the name first rumbled through the talk in the bunkhouses and mess halls they let it disappear. But it persisted. A lot of the younger men were eager to fight. The last World War had been over for six years. Some of them relished the idea of the glory they'd missed out on and others just allowed the notion of conflict percolate within them and the garrulous talk of their fellows to stoke and drive them. They lived for stories in the papers that landed intermittently in their midst. They mouthed the name *Karyong* like a litany when word came of the first fighting and the first casualties. Then the night fight at Hill 677. The 2nd battalion of the Princess Patricia's Light Infantry completely surrounded by North Korean and Chinese troops in two days of blistering combat where ten men died and twenty-three were wounded. It read like a glorious campaign. The fact of the dead fuelled their outrage. The anonymity of the name *Hill 677* gave the image of the battleground the lustre of dreamscape, and he and Jimmy talked of nothing else for days. Soon, there was a steady flow of those leaving to report to the volunteer stations to sign up for the conflict. Men drifted off from the mines, the lumber camps, the oil rigs, road crews, and earthworks. It made work easier to find but harder. There were fewer men for the projects and while the pay remained the same the rigour and the demands on their bodies deepened. Jimmy was the first to raise it.

"We should go," he said. "To that Korea place."

"A guy can get trained for stuff. They even send ya to school if you wanted to learn stuff. Maybe we could be engineers or learn how to drive Cats'n things."

He eyed Jimmy for a long moment. Then he nodded grimly. "Might be a good go. Come back an' earn big. No more bustin' a nut for peanuts no more."

They were eighteen when they went. They were assigned to the Royal Canadian Regiment. They took the train across the country to Camp Petawawa with a group of sixty, the lot of them filled with the keen edge of adventure. They were young and oblivious to danger; instead they were driven by the spark of it, and its presence hung in the air of the coach like sulphur off a struck match, hard in the throat but bracing. The train car was riotous with card playing, wrestling, name calling, and the occasional fist fight, which was broken up quickly and the semblance of order restored until it flared up again. They were mostly dropouts and itinerant workers. The idea of war was beyond them and they only existed for the thrill they felt building in their bodies as the land whipped by and the sheer force of collective bravado became the land itself, the open breech of the sky, what they drank into them, the distance between them and the blood rush of combat shrinking rapidly. At night, as the coaches swayed and the dim coach lights cocooned them in shadow, he could hear the fear in the men around him; the whimpers, the curses, the thump of a fist on a wall, and muttering as they flailed against dreams the colour of ash. They became kids again. He sat and listened and watched Jimmy beside him sleeping. He thought of his father and how he might have felt in similar moments during his war. He thought of his mother. He wondered if she ever thought of him at all in those four years. It was a sad thought and he tried to let it go. He was frightened. The old feeling of confusion rose in him once again, followed by a longing he could feel in his bones. When the black idea of dying coursed through him, he shivered and pulled his blanket tight around him and fought for sleep, the jostle of the train against his spine like small concussions, and he dreamed of explosions and screams and a sky filled with dark birds hungry for dead men's eyes and rotting, smoking flesh strewn everywhere.

They hit Petawawa and were swallowed up in the crush of bodies and the canvas of green the camp was painted in and there was no time for skin. There was only order. There was only detail and the pressure to fit into it and make it part of their consciousness, their way of thinking, their way of being. It was the hardest work he'd ever done. But they fell into the rampage of energy that was basic training. They were muscular and fit and they both loved the running and the exertion. As they had done with the work, they challenged each other for more, and when they ran the obstacle courses and the roadways around the camp, they left the others behind and ran like they had through the bush when they were kids. The years of work had made them tough and the stress of being commanded and driven was as natural as breathing. The feel of the air under barbed wire with the zing of bullets flying over their heads and the concussion of grenades throwing dirt that stung like pellets of shot only made them crawl forward all the faster. They could shoot. They discovered that fast. But while Jimmy was a natural with a weapon, as skilful with his hands as a magician, the arc of a blade in his hands spellbinding in its fluid grace, he felt ashamed that he had to struggle to breakdown a carbine, thrust a knife, or drive a bayonet powerfully through a practice dummy. He could shoot but he did it deliberately, measuredly. Jimmy rattled off rounds and shredded targets. He was the best shot anyone had ever seen. But together they were like ghosts in the trees. They could disappear and not be found, not be tracked, and when they broke training after three months they were assigned to the 3rd battalion of the Royal Canadian Regiment.

"You ever figure we'd be humpin' it in Japan," Jimmy asked.

"Least I hearda it," he said.

They were sent to Nippon Bara for advanced weapons training. They would train on mountainsides under live artillery. Jimmy was jumpy with the feel for fighting whereas he couldn't set his mind to it. He found himself with deep questions. He didn't understand war. Still, he felt loyal to Jimmy and willed himself to concentrate. He focused on what he was being trained in. He became proficient, methodical, dependable, and sure-handed.

Around them the new camp was mayhem. The volunteers had no heads for order, discipline, regimentation, and it became unruly and there were only a handful of them who bent to the idea of soldiery. He and Jimmy became point men. They were sent out early to patrol and return with reconnaissance and the separation from the main body of troops was exhilarating, the feel of being alone in open country heady, and they existed on pin pricks of fear and alertness that spiked their energy, left them breathless in thin cover on naked hillsides. When the boom of artillery echoed through the valleys and the dull thud of shells sent tremors through their bellies they laughed at it and he learned to follow the soles of his friend's boots like blazes on a trail, trusting him completely to lead them home.

"They send us out first on accounta we're Indians, you figure?" he asked.

"Fuck that," Jimmy said. "They send us out first cuz we're soldiers. Damn good ones."

"You believe that?"

"We gotta," Jimmy said. He lit a smoke and studied him, squinting, and he could feel the weight of the question working through him. "It's who we are now," he said.

The soldiers called it "The Twilight War." They set up on a hill outside the city of Pusan, separated from the Chinese forces by a thousand metres. The area between them was ravaged and scarred by artillery, grenades, mortars, and the scrawl of boot prints. They sat in their trenches in the daylight hours and tried to sleep or at least rest and prepare for the patrols that slipped out from both sides into the no man's land that was the valley between them. They could not rise in those hours of light. They learned to duck-waddle or crawl on their bellies to find enough privacy to piss and shit. Sometimes they would have to hunch over and spray or dump into their helmets and toss the effluent over the lip of the trench. Even a helmet raised above that seam would draw a shot from the snipers that were planted everywhere along that ragged line of hills. The artillery bursts were random. It kept them edgy and sleepless. To hone that keen blade of anxiety the Chinese snipers would rake the edges of their trenches, shouting, "Canada kid! Tonight you die." Then follow it with mortar fire and another fusillade of rounds. So that the slant of the sun toward the horizon became the call to arms, the blocking out of anything beyond the moment, the precious seconds of breath and the feel of their bodies baked hard by the same unrelenting sun. Legs and knees, toughened by scrabbles through the rock and brush and bobbed wire, all sinew and tendon and sheaths of muscle clutched around bone. Their feet. The blister and callus and ache of them. They came to order all of this in the slow dip of the sun toward the horizon. Order it into recognition of the other bodies around them, into knowing that the bite of bullet, blade, and bayonet, or the screaming whistle of shrapnel would be there to greet their bodies when the light slipped away into the glimmering, purple greyness their war was named for.

It was the twilight that called them into being. The taunting fire and yelling died with the light, and what remained was a hush they could feel and smell and taste. It galvanized them. They went through the ritual of preparation solemnly, the snick and slip and rustle of canvas, steel and leather bringing them fully formed into the fading light. They gathered in platoons. Hunched together like primates they heard the whispered orders slice through the taut silence and nodded, muttered, or waved their assent. Then they breached the safety of the trenches. They heard the Chinese calling. Their patrols went out at the same time and the no man's land was occupied by scurrying, crawling forces intent on securing the thin band of emptiness. In the gathering twilight they slithered toward each other. Then barrages would start.

Flares sent the skeleton landscape into paroxysms of dizzying red and the high dazzle of white and blooms of yellow that dropped over them like a parachute that sent shadow scuttling into unseen recesses, leaving them pinned there. Men ran in mad bursts for the cover of craters and machine guns rattled off pops of soil behind them like a wake. Bodies sailed. Bodies crashed forward, raking furrows in the dirt. Men were ripped in half or quartered, blood splayed like sudden clouds in the eruptions of light. The encroaching dark was filled with screams and calls and weeping and the hiss of Chinese voices saying, "Canada. You die!"

And as suddenly as it started, the artillery stopped. There were no flares. No light. Only darkness. Full and inescapable dark. So it became a war of inches. Each platoon, wedged between the fallen bodies and the upward thrusts and spills of earth, moved like phantoms closer to the invisible foe, hunkered in the darkness. Men would meet each other suddenly: head on, crashing into each other, wrestling, spinning, whirling in a tangle of limbs and blades and fists. Combat became the push of a blade, the slice, the plunge, the pierce of a bayonet and men lifted on the points of them, spun and shook off and laid to waste while the victor turned from the fatal skirmish, wide-eyed with terror, agape with animal energy. Or it was a silent death. The sudden grasp of a callused hand around the throat. The knife. The muzzle of a pistol or a carbine lodged in the belly or against the temple. Men crept about in desperation, more keenly alive than they could recall being, and when the word came to disengage they crawled backward like crabs until empty yards hung before their eyes and they turned and bellied back toward the shelter of their lines and the drop into the trench that let them reclaim their breath before both sides allowed the other grace enough to gather their dead and dying.

They fought like that for months.

17

"STARLIGHT'S A TEACHER'S NAME." His father's voice came out of the dark. The kid had been lost in the dire images of war. For a moment he didn't respond and when he looked up finally, he could see his father's eyes shining in the light of the fire. "Jimmy told me that. Some nights went by without us sayin' a thing to each other. Nights there weren't nothin' we knew to say. Other times we'd talk. Mostly he'd talk, really."

"Sounds like he knew a lot about Indian stuff," the kid said.

"I reckon. More'n I ever did, least ways. I never even knew where my name came from. Never thought to ask. When I told him that he got right upset." His father rolled onto his side with difficulty. When the kid moved to help him his father shook his head and raised a trembling hand to stop him. "He said that a man oughta know why he's called what he is. You oughta know that too, Frank."

"I always wondered about that name. Surrounded by Smiths and Greens and such," the kid said.

"Some things ya own outright. It's what Jimmy said. His name, Weaseltail, was an honour name. War chiefs got white weasel tails put on the sides of their headdresses. Meant they were honourable men but vicious in fight like a weasel when it's pissed. Sounded like a strong name to me once I heard that."

The kid sat silent. When he looked back at his father he felt drawn into a deep quiet and he could only nod.

"Jimmy said Starlight was the name given to them that got teachin's from Star People. Long ago. Way back. Legend goes that they come outta the stars on a night like this. Clear night. Sat with the people and told 'em stuff. Stories mostly, about the way of things."

"The wisest ones got taught more. Our people. Starlights. We're meant to be teachers and storytellers. They say nights like this bring them teachin's and stories back and that's when they oughta be passed on again."

"I like that story. Makes sense to me how I wanna be out here so much. Under the stars," the kid stood and put another piece of wood on the fire. "But it's another thing woulda been good to know before this."

"I know it," his father said. "Like I said, I never knew where my name come from either."

"Figure that makes us even now or some such?"

"No. Just talkin' is all."

"Well, thanks, I suppose," the kid said.

"I ain't done nothin'."

The kid got one of the jars from the pack and carried it to him then knelt and held it out. His father clasped his hand in both of his and tipped the jar to his lips. When he was finished, he closed his eyes and the kid looked back up at the heavens. He sat waiting. His father began talking and the kid hugged his knees close to his chest.

———

They sat in the trench five yards away from the next huddle of men. Neither of them could sleep. They were desperate for a smoke but the flare of a match drew fire. The soft rumble of men's voices in the darkness. The scrape of a boot in the dirt. Someone coughed into a fist. A muttered curse. Jimmy edged around to face him in the dark. There was enough light that he could see the shadowed outlines of his face and the wet glint of his eyes. Someone went "*Psst*" and tossed a smoke along the floor of the trench. He picked it up and bent his head, cupping it in his hands and taking a draw.

"We're warriors now, right?" Jimmy asked.

"Yeah. Well, soldiers."

"I heard once when the old folks were talkin' that Ojibs usedta bury their warriors sat upright in the ground, facin' east where the sun rose, with all their weapons and shit around them. That way, when they were ready, they could follow the sun across the sky on into the Happy Hunting Grounds where they'd be warriors again. That's how I wanna go out."

"Sounds kinda right, I s'pose."

"If I get killed here, take me home and far out in the bush where there ain't no ugly and bury me just like that."

"You ain't gonna get killed."

"You don't know that. Me neither. But I'd feel a bit more all right with it if I knew ya'd take care of that for me."

The words felt too weighty for his head. He looked up at the stars again. His chest felt hollow with the talk. "I guess," he said quietly.

"Gotta swear," Jimmy said.

"I swear."

"No. I mean ya gotta swear like a warrior." Jimmy took out his knife and slashed a line across his palm. He held it up.

Even in the dark he could see the black of the gash. Then he sat stunned as Jimmy daubed a finger in the blood and reached over to draw a curvy line down one of his cheeks. He repeated it on the other cheek. "Now you do me the same way," Jimmy said.

He took the knife and held it against the skin of his palm. He looked up and could see Jimmy's eyes. He scowled and drew the blade across his skin and felt the bite of it and grimaced. Then he put the knife down, ran a finger through the cut, and traced a line down both sides of Jimmy's face.

"We carry each other into battle now," Jimmy said.

They sat in the dark with their backs against the wall of the trench. He looked up at the sky. It was the same hemisphere but the angles felt different. The stars. He wondered about the light of them. How it falls on people. He wondered if his dead father had been able to make a journey across them, find a second chance somewhere, set his feet down on ground that allowed him to know the story of his name, how it came to be and the teachings that were in it. He hoped so. It made it different hoping that. He held his hand up to his face and licked the wound. Blood. Old-tasting and rich like the sediment of a river. He looked at Jimmy. The blood on their faces meant they were part of the same stream now, bobbing in the current, borne forward effortlessly under the slowly twirling dome of the sky.

The wind cut through the valley. The no man's land between them hung in a desolate silence and there was nervous tension among the men. No one spoke and when the lieutenant duck-waddled through the trench they all turned to stare at him, hands clutching weapons as he made his way past them. He stopped beside him and Jimmy.

"Feel like some action?" he asked.

"Does a bear shit in the woods?" Jimmy asked.

The lieutenant grinned. "Frequently," he said. "I need volunteers for advance recon. I gotta get a fix on the sons of bitches. They're up to something. Every company on every hill's sending out recon. I need to know if you're good for it?"

"We're good," Jimmy said.

"You?" the lieutenant asked him.

"You heard him," he said and nodded at the fixed gaze Jimmy levelled at him.

"All right. You'll be alone out there. I don't need no hero shit. I just need recon."

"Count on it," he said.

"Bring me numbers and bring me location. I'll radio it in and if they break the bastards'll break right into a shit storm."

"Got 'er, Loot," Jimmy said.

"Straight out, straight back. I swear if you don't come back I'll go out there and kill the two of ya myself all over again."

"Love you too, Loot," Jimmy said, and the lieutenant clapped them hard on the shoulder. He stepped off in a crouch to find the radio men.

They checked their weapons. It took them less than a minute. They boot-blacked their faces and tucked in loose edges of clothing and then they bent to retie the soldier's knots in the laces of their boots, squared them so they wouldn't snag. They double-checked everything then they looked at each other and the grim set of their faces made words unnecessary. Jimmy nodded once. They crawled over the lip of the trench.

He could feel the openness. It was dizzying in its threat. The farther they worked their way forward, the more displaced he felt, and in the near dark he followed the dim outline of Jimmy down the slope and onto the hardpan flat. They hit their bellies in a slight gully and caught their breath. Nothing moved. He raised his head and peered over the rim and swept a look back and forth in both directions then signalled with his hand that it was clear. They crawled forward. He could feel the fear in him like ice in his gut. His belly muscles constricted and he felt himself want to scream. Instead, he focused on breathing, inching forward on his elbows, pushing ahead with the toes of his boots. They made steady ground. There was no motion around them at all, no sound but the slice of the wind over empty, and in the full darkness he wished for at least a slip of a moon to slacken the hold of the night.

The first thing they heard was voices. They pressed their faces to the earth. Fear tightened every cord in him and he wanted to run, could feel it building, and he pressed his body into the packed dirt to ease the tremor in his legs. He wanted to cry. He closed his eyes against it and gave a shuddering breath. Jimmy hushed him with a palm on the back. They started to move again, crawling like spiders.

The voices were clearer. They inched over a hump of earth and there were three of them huddled together, jabbering in blunt whispers, and they stopped and neither of them breathed.

The first shell hit in a whoop of earth. It fell behind them, closer to their lines, and another followed it before the sky literally exploded in a chorus of flares and muzzle flash. He raised himself up to break and the Chinese yelled. Jimmy pulled him down, and his carbine slammed against his chest and took his breath away. Rifle fire threw dirt up in splatters in front of them and the Chinese were up and running toward them. Jimmy was suddenly on his feet, but he lay on his side, unable to move. The first Chinese swung a rifle butt at Jimmy's chin but he ducked it and then came up with his knife and plunged it into the man's belly. The dead Chinese dropped and rolled heavily into him and the man's face inches from his own shocked him to his feet. There were explosions behind them and he could hear the hillside clatter with the cascade of dirt and rock and stones. The barrage was deafening. In the flash of light he could make the dim line of hordes approaching from the opposite side of the valley behind the crash of shells and the rattle of machine-gun fire from their troops. It looked like the entire Chinese and North Korean armies were advancing behind their artillery. Jimmy crouched and moved forward and he followed in the same crouch. He saw the silhouette of a man coming at them. There was a snap of rifle fire from the encroaching troops and the man's head exploded when a bullet hit, spraying him with grey gore, blood, and bone, and the dead man crashed into him and they both fell to the ground. He tried to wrestle him off but it was Jimmy who pulled him to his feet and he stood there with his knife in his free hand, looking down at another Chinese soldier beside the others. Jimmy had killed him. His throat was sliced in a hard line, and he thought he could see bone in the flare light.

"Fuck. Come on!" Jimmy yelled.

He gathered himself and they turned and ran back toward their lines, zigzagging crazily while shells ripped out craters all around them and spewed dirt and rock that ricocheted off their helmets. He could hear shrapnel buzz by his head. Rifle fire kicked up earth at their feet. They ran mightily and when Jimmy grunted and slammed into the ground he stopped and turned and found himself standing in a dark pond of blood. He fell down beside Jimmy. Bullets strafed over them. There was artillery fire from their side now. He pulled Jimmy close to him. The blood made purple mud around him. He pulled him closer and dragged him to the cover of small boulders. There was a hole in Jimmy's back and a larger one where the bullet had come out of his gut. He leaned against a boulder and held his friend to his chest.

He heard Chinese voices. They yelled out in broken English.

He tried to move the two of them closer to the shelter of the boulders. Jimmy started to scream and he clapped a hand over his mouth. Jimmy stared at him wild-eyed and crazy. Thrashing. The booming of artillery was everywhere. Jimmy was manic with pain. He held him as tight as he could with one arm, immobilized by the fear thudding in his chest. For now the Chinese had no idea where they were. But if Jimmy screamed he would give their position away. He eased his knife out with his free hand. He rolled Jimmy onto his back and pressed his knee to his chest to pin him. Jimmy tried to grab at him, punch him. He could feel his mouth working under the palm of his hand. His eyes were wide, the whites of them like twin moons. Panicked. He took the knife and held it under his ribcage and Jimmy stopped, his body going perfectly still as he stared at him over the rim of his hand. He closed his eyes. When he opened them again there was peace there and he nodded at him. The knife went in almost on its own and he twisted it like he was trained to do and leaned forward cheek to cheek with Jimmy and heard his last breath ease out of him.

The barrage rammed into the earth and he could feel it shake underneath him and when he rose to run he looked back down at his friend, bullets flying overhead, and he

turned and ran half-crouched under the flare of lights, the
whistle of shells and shrapnel and the screams of men dying
above him on the hills, and he ran screaming and weeping
into the breech of his own private war.

"I didn't wanna die and I sure didn't wanna die by torture
neither. When I got back I told them Jimmy was killed by a
Chinese patrol. I was never so scared in my life," his father
said. "They never found his body. Me, I took to drinking after
that. Drank so bad they drummed me out dishonourable
pretty quick. They said it was because my friend had been
killed and it was. I just never told no one it was me killed him.
I was eighteen years old. I hung on to it all this time."

The fire had burned away and they could see the stars in the
thick purple swaddle of the sky. It was calm. There was an
edge to the air that spoke of frost and in the chill stillness of it
they could hear creatures moving in the bush. A thin scrim of
clouds plowed over the lip of mountain and they watched it
moving by the light of the stars winking out and then emerging
again. When he stirred the coals of the fire, then added kin-
dling and larger sticks, the blaze crackled to life and he saw the
gaunt shape of his father. He was mostly hollow and the fingers that curled around the edge of the blanket were thin and
angled by sharp thrusts of knuckle, the veins on the backs of
his hands black in the firelight so that it seemed to the kid as if
he were held together by rivers of coal.

"Musta been hard," the kid said. "Carrying Jimmy all this
time."

His father shivered in one long, trembling wave that racked
his body. He helped him stretch full out on the ground and

when he got him laid out he stuck a few pieces of birch on the embers and waited while they caught and then added more to them. The fire stoked up well and he could feel the heat of it on his face and he rolled up his mackinaw and placed it under his father's head. He felt his father's brow but he couldn't tell what was fever or the heat of the blaze now. He got the canteen and lifted his father's head and held the canteen to his lips and slowly poured. Some of the water dribbled down from the corners of his father's mouth but he managed to swallow some until he coughed it up, the coughs nearly bending him double. When the coughs settled they tried it again and he took it and held it down.

"They're in us," his father said after a moment. He spoke low now, as if it took all the strength in him to form the words and push them out. "The stars are in us." His father swallowed dryly again and the kid could hear the rasp of his tongue on his palate and the rough clutch of his throat. He pulled the blanket up around his neck and hunched in upon himself more and his father trembled and there was nothing the kid could do but wait it out.

He'd twitch now and then. Eventually he calmed and his breath evened again. Now and then the kid would reach out and heave another chunk of wood on the fire. He gazed upward. The stars arranged themselves into shapes and suggestions and he felt the pull of them like a calling away and he looked deeper into the beaded bowl of the night and saw a multitude of possible worlds hung there, suspended against time itself, and he closed his eyes and tried to feel them inside of himself but all he felt was empty. He reached over and arranged the blanket around his father again, felt the lank bone of his upper arm, his fingers, soon to return to the earth, and he sat and watched him, the clouds of their breaths mingling in the frosted air.

"Jimmy probably would've died anyway," the kid said.

"There's no knowin' that."

"Better off thinkin' that than feeling like a coward all your life."

His father stared down at the ground. When he looked up at the kid again it was bitter and angry and the kid just looked back at him flatly.

"You're hard, Frank. You get that way being out here so much?"

The kid looked out across the valley and then started to roll a smoke. When he licked the gummed edge he eyed his father, who watched him warily. He maintained the look while he lit up and when he exhaled the smoke he let his gaze drift out over the valley again.

"Ain't no trickery out here. No lies. I come to prefer it," he said.

"Christ. You're sixteen."

"Gotta be a special age to brook no bullshit?"

"Not especially. You're still hard though."

"At least I never felt like no coward."

"You never been in a war, Frank."

"Not one of my own leastways."

"What's that supposed to mean?"

"Means I'm still livin' the one you never finished."

"Jesus."

The kid pitched the butt into the fire and got up and stalked off to the rim of the ridge. He stood there watching the sky like a purple stain over the dark humps and crags of the valley and the mountains around it. There was a churning in his gut he didn't like. It made him feel angry and he didn't like anger. He turned and walked back to the fire and sat poking at it with a stick.

His father coughed into his hand. Then he looked at him out of the corner of his eye. "You figure you might be able to forgive me, Frank?"

"I ain't the one that has to."

"I mean about Jimmy."

"I mean about him too."

The kid strode into the bush and returned with an armload of wood. His father lay on his side, clutching his arms about himself and shivering. He used the wood to build a reflector to angle the heat toward his father. The wind dropped, and he could taste far-off snow. He sat close to the fire, warming himself while his father dozed, shivering and feverish. He sat and smoked and watched his father sleep. "War's nearly over," he said.

18

THE BREEZE WAS CHILLY in the dawn and he stoked the embers of the fire and lay in fresh wood. The flames climbed and drove the chill off and soon his father raised his head. Clouds skimmed above them. There was pale sunlight on the shoulders of the mountains.

"You need a hit of that medicine or the hooch?" the kid asked.

"Some of both. Yeah," his father said.

The kid rose and retrieved the bottles. He held them while his father took some of the liquid in his mouth. Both times he fought to swallow. There was a wild shake to his hands. It seemed a struggle for him to hold a cigarette. He held it out to the kid, who pitched it into the fire. They sat there without talking. A hawk soared over the treetops and the horse skittered.

"There's a stream back down a ways," the kid said. "I gotta get some food. I won't be long."

He got no answer so he led the horse back down the trail. The morning was brilliant and the walk energized him. The horse smelled the water and she made him walk quicker to the stream. She drank and when she'd had her fill he tied her to a tree and walked along the rocky shore. He refilled the canteen and studied the water. There were trout in the stream. They were sluggish from the cold of the water and he speared them easily with the knife that he'd lashed to a stout sapling with his bootlaces. He gutted and cleaned them and used a hank of willow threaded through their gills to carry them back up the ridge. His father had sunk into the effect of the medicine. The kid set the fish on sticks leaned over the fire to cook. Then he walked and stooped though the trees to scout mushrooms. He found a big thrust of chicken mushrooms and he skewered them on sticks and went back to set them over the fire alongside the fish. He settled down to watch the fire and turn the sticks. When everything was cooked he polished off the trout and most of the mushrooms. His father would never eat. The shakes were on him hard and sweat poured down his face. Even when his shakes stopped he quivered and his breath was raspy in his throat. The kid could see his eyeballs rolling crazily under their lids. When he reached out to touch him his father convulsed so violently the kid thought he lifted off the ground. His father curled into a tight ball and clutched his arms about himself. The kid got the bottles and knelt beside him and put a hand on his ribs. He could feel the rails of them beneath his palm.

"Ya best have some of this," he said.

"N-n-no h-h-h-hooch," his father said.

"Ya sure?" the kid asked. "Ya ain't good."

"Sh-sh-sh-sure."

The kid managed to roll him onto his back again and straighten his legs. Then he lifted his head and held the bottle of medicine to his father's mouth and watched him wrestle with taking in a few mouthfuls. He let him have as much as he wanted. His father paused and sucked back more. The kid marvelled at the strength of the concoction as he watched his father's face settle and then the racking convulsions ease into shivers until his body quieted and his breathing became regular again. When he was sure that he would be okay the kid laid his father's head back down and tucked the blanket close around him and tried to steady his own breathing. It was a long while before his father moved onto his side and stared at the kid without raising his cheek off the ground.

The kid untied his knife from the sapling and began to whittle away at one of the sticks he'd cooked the mushrooms on. He shaved the bark clean in long strokes and set them in the fire and sharpened one end and poked at the embers with it then reached over and added a fresh piece of wood.

"There's one more thing," his father said.

"My mother," the kid said quietly, looking into the fire.

His father was quiet so long he turned to see if he'd passed out. But he was still looking at him sombrely. He blinked slowly and drew a deep breath. "The old man never told ya nothing?"

"Said he figured that'd be your job. Said it was yer's to do but he'd do it if it come to it."

"Like I said, I owe you. This at the least."

The kid kept whittling away at the stick. "Now yer backed into a corner so ya gotta. How'm I gonna know yer not lyin' just so ya can feel like ya done somethin' proper and good at the last?"

"I wouldn't do that."

The kid laid the knife in his lap. "I got no idea whether ya would or ya wouldn't."

"I couldn't lie about her. I tried to lie to myself a lotta years. Tried to tell myself it was some other way than it was." He raised himself painfully up on one elbow and grimaced. "Guess I figured I might drink it away. Idea never did work worth a damn."

"'Spect not," the kid said.

"Could I sit up a while, Frank?"

"Can you manage it?"

"I figure."

He helped his father over to the log he'd sat on the night before and then stoked the fire higher. He wrapped the blanket over his father's shoulders. Every feature of his face seemed to be cascading downward. His father shivered and clutched the blanket tighter around his neck and set his lips together grimly. His eyes were rimmed with red, spooked and frightened. The kid sat on the ground opposite him and waited. He felt as though there was something he was supposed to say but he didn't know what.

———

Time was a thing he carried. It took him a long time after Korea to realize that. Between bouts of liquor there were stretches of calm that took him by surprise and lulled him. They never lasted. He'd be clear and working, feeling a rough sort of pleasure in a measure of days, weeks, a month or so sometimes. But he could never really shake a foreboding in his gut. It rankled him, the unease, the slow creep of terror, like being hunted, tracked by some prowling beast invisible to the eye, recognized only by the sense of looming danger at his back. Then, always, time's dank shadow would fall over him again and sweep him into its chill. It seemed to seep outward from his bones. He lurched along in its thrall, unresisting, all the way back to the bottle once again. He spiralled downward and the measure of his days was the depth of the shadow itself. He wandered. He sought a place that carried no reminders, believing that a place existed that was barren of memory and recollection. But he bore time like sodden baggage.

In the end, he had to come back to Nechako. He realized somehow that coming and going had become the same direction and he slunk back into the valley with a pocketful of wages and no idea what to do. He only knew that nowhere was a place he occupied. It made one place the same as another. So he settled into Parson's Gap and took whatever jobs he could for as long as he could stand them or until he was fired. There was no word of his mother or Jenks. He'd gone once to the logging camp. It was deserted. There were ghosts of booms on the water, held in the grip of rotting rings they left behind them, buckled some by time and current and placid at their centres so that looking at them from the shore he wondered how much of him or how little was held within their buoyant murk. Jimmy was there. So was his father and the lingering idea of his mother.

Life became the ins and outs of drunkenness and the forced and miserable dryness of work in order to pay for another binge. He made a name for himself. A hard worker. A jack of all trades. Serious. Deliberate. But unpredictable with a pay stub in his hands. He never made more than he could spend in a week. He became a denizen of flophouses and derelict buildings. He was gregarious in his cups, but prone to sudden bouts of solemnity and a simmering anger that kept people away from him. But when he broke he broke all gleeful and raucous. Then he lived in triumphant abandon and he became a storied drinker, ladies' man and raconteur: the highs dizzying in his awareness of the fall to follow.

The crash would find him with other early morning drunks and beggars assembled in the bleary dawn on the river flats at a corner they called The Dollar Holler. He'd hear them coming along the curving road that ran down the hill from town and spilled out onto the flat the mill laid claim to. There'd be coarse laughter, hacking tobacco coughs, curses, and the off-key whistling of an old tune no one recalled the words to and the shuffle of weary feet through gravel, dust, frost. They'd emerge from the fog in ragged lines of three or four, sometimes singly or in pairs, and assemble at the corner. It was next to an open lot where there were cast-off truck seats they gathered around and a small copse of trees at the end that was their latrine. They greeted each other wordlessly. One or two of them would share their makings or hand-rolled smokes and someone would start a jug around wrapped in a brown paper bag. They smoked and drank. They spoke in cryptic, guttural sentences and waited.

"Heard Shultz is hirin'."

"Yeah?"

"Still payin' fuck all still."

"Shit."

"Yeah."

The light would break across the sky and the neighbour-hood of the mill would take on the hues of indigo and ochre until the sun rose beyond the eastern ridge and the world became flares of magenta and pink and orange across the sky. That's when the trucks arrived. They'd spy them coming a half-mile off. On a good day there was a line of them. On most there were two or three. The men would line both sides of the road, wiping at their mouths and raising a toe of a boot to shine along the back of their trousers and slick hair down with spittle on a palm. The trucks would slow and a face would appear to study them as it cruised by. That's when they'd yell.

"Got a dollar fer a fella?"

"Gotta lotta back fer a buck!"

They'd holler. The whole lot of them and the trucks would make a slow turn in the street and head back their way and the men would shuffle their feet and run a hand over their faces and wait until a hand shot out the window and a finger was crooked and the man at the wheel would holler back.

"I need two for half a day. You and you. Get in back."

The lucky pair would run out and hurl themselves into the back of the truck. They'd scramble along the bed and lean against the back of the cab and grin at the rest, strung out along the shoulder of the road, licking at their lips and turning to greet the next truck lumbering their way. Most of them slunk back up the hill into town to the hovels and dim places they called home. It was his only work for a couple of years.

———

He became a regular at Charlie's. It was a ritual for drunks to have one place they never abused. One place they marshalled enough will to protect in their savage way so that there was always a place to go, a stool or a table in a corner to occupy where they could nurse a drink in the smoke and din of beer, cheap wine, and whisky. He liked it. It made him feel a part of something, and he'd eke out a tab from the bartender and waiters and pay it out in full whenever he got paid. He took care to honour that. It made him trusted in a way even though they knew a sot when they saw one. But he was reliable in that fashion and he always had a drink and a warm haven when it was needed.

It was a working man's bar. He could lose himself in the babble of voices, the clack of pool balls, the wafts of music swirling outward from the jukebox, the smell of sweat and dirt, and the electric charge of a fight building until it erupted in a crash of tables and bodies and a spray of blood from fist and mouth and the savage whistle and grunt of men battling until it broke with one on the floor or having been flung through the doors with his coat chucked out after him like punctuation. Then, slowly, peace gathered itself again; the violence was shrugged off and the hubbub returned. He drank it in like a free round. He savoured the manly grunge and preferred Charlie's over other joints and he was known by the denizens as a drunk who minded his own business but one who bore a sudden temper that brooked no foolishness or intrusion. He could set there. Vanish. Be. It was predictable and ordinary in his murky world and he came to rely on it. So that the day when she appeared took him by surprise.

It was a payday. The joint was filled to capacity and he sat in a corner drinking off what was left of three day's pay from The Dollar Holler. His back hurt. He'd dug a trench for a quarter-mile through brush and bramble, stone and dirt and gravel. He'd worked without gloves and his hands burned from broken blisters. His legs ached. The din around him was like the feel of coming to after a punch-out. He leaned forward on the table and drank slowly.

The music was the first thing he noticed. The songs on the jukebox were bouncy and bright with fiddles and pedal steel guitar and drums played primarily on the snare and the kick bass. He heard laughter. Then there was the clapping of hands and stomping of feet just slightly off the rhythm. There was a semicircle of men and their women around the jukebox and he stood and looked over. He had to stand on his chair to see. The tables had been pushed back and in the middle of the clearing, a man and a woman gyrated and spun. The man was ungainly, huge and blocky like a gorilla in a red checkered shirt and blue jeans gone to soot and grease, and he danced in unlaced work boots with the tongues flapping. He lurched after her, his hands held out wide as though he sought to capture her, and he grimaced at the effort it took to fix a modicum of grace to the act of dancing. She was magnificent. She was tall, lean. She had long, straight hair that followed her spins like a wave of dark water and when she bent low to follow the beat, her feet were light and she appeared to float through the dance, sprightly and girl-like but with a wildness and an abandon that was all woman, in the thrust of her hips, the jounce of her breasts in the thin cotton shirt and the sinuous trail of her arms. She danced around her partner with her head flung back, laughing, and the crowd hooted and hollered and urged him on.

"Come on, Dingo! Dance!"

"He don't wanna dance, he wants to rut."

Every time he got within inches of her, she spun and twirled out of reach, one hand tracing his outstretched palm with the tips of her fingers. The crowd ate it up. When the song ended she hugged him, draped herself over him, and from the corner he could see the glazed joy the man took in that, the huge hands on her back, red at the knuckles and raw from the work, and when he tried to kiss her, she laughed and pushed him away with one finger against his massive chest. The crowd broke. People sat back down like hunters easing back behind a blind. When he took his seat there was a man across from him. He was older but with the squinted, bronzed face of someone used to the elements, a face the wind carved.

"Mind?" the older man asked.

He studied him and the man looked back at him with a calm good humour. "Not if you don't, I guess."

"Good. Mind if I buy a round?"

He laughed. "Mister," he said. "I mind it all a sight less now."

When the drinks came they clinked glasses and the older man drained half of his and set it on the table and looked at him. "She's a peach, don't ya think? The girl. The dancer there."

"Yeah. She's a fine one."

"Injun."

"Excuse me?" He raised an eyebrow and the man laughed.

"I mean, she's like you. She's an Indian."

"You figure?"

"Oh yeah. My name's Bunky, by the way." He reached out a hand and they shook.

"Eldon," he said. "Fuck's Bunky mean?"

The older man took off his hat. His hair was frizzled every

which way. "Kid's name," he said. "My pa would say I could go through a whole day an' my hair'd still be bunky, like I just climbed outta the sack. It stuck. I never questioned it."

"Musta got ya punched out a lot, name like that?"

The older man grinned and sipped at his drink and eyed him over the rim of the glass. "There was them that tried," he said. "Never was what ya might call a winnin' bet."

The music kicked up again. It was a slow country waltz and they stood to watch like all the rest. The woman was languid and loose and swayed while she moved. Her new partner was clumsy and hunched over her like a bear, his feet sliding along the floor without lifting. She let her hair trail and closed her eyes with her face toward the ceiling. He could see the jut and cut of the angles on her face from where the pair of them stood in the corner. It was a proud face, jumbled some by drink, but regal and possessed of sureness and knowing and when she opened her eyes and smiled at her partner he could feel his heart clench. When the song finished she retreated slowly to where she sat with six lumberjacks at a table laden with pitchers of beer. She swayed even when she walked.

"Dang fine," Bunky muttered. "Dang fine."

Just then a small man entered the bar. He leaned when he walked, canted at a hard angle to the right as though gravity worked with different properties on him, his feet slapping down like wet fish on a plank. His face was caved from a lack of teeth and the wear of a life lived rough and cantankerous by drink. He glanced around the room with his eyes rolling in his head, wiping at the sheen of sweat on his face and gulping hard.

"Everett Eames," he said quietly to Bunky.

"Know him, do ya?" Bunky asked.

"Some," he said. "He used to be a bush worker."

They watched as Eames straightened and tried to smooth his ragged duffle coat then made his way toward the table where the woman sat with the lumberjacks, all of them with their chairs tucked close to the table as though they couldn't get near enough to her. When he got to the table all the laughter stopped. They could see Eames talking, gesturing with his hands, pointing to certain of the lumberjacks and trying to laugh. The big one in the red checkered shirt stood suddenly and pointed his finger at him, threatening. The room fell quiet.

"Back the fuck outta here, mooch," the big one said. "Work for a drink. *We* gotta."

"Tell him, Dingo," one of the others said.

"Come on, Dingo," Eames said. "I got work next week. All's I need is a fiver. You know me."

Dingo laughed. "Know you as a fall-down drunk prick," he said.

The others laughed. The woman was watching with a worried look. "Don't." He could read the word on her lips from across the room.

Dingo looked at her. "Please," she said. "He just needs a drink."

"You wanna drink, Eames?" Dingo asked.

"Yeah. Yeah, that'd be good," Eames said shakily.

Dingo reached back to the table and grabbed one of the pitchers. He took Eames by the collar of his coat and yanked him forward then took hold of his hair and pulled his head back. "Drink then, ya fuckin' stumblebum!" He started pouring beer into Eames' face and the drunk sputtered at first and then gulped hungrily at the wash of beer, opening and closing his mouth like a drowning man gasping for air. The room exploded in laughter. Eames was soaked. Dingo grabbed another pitcher and started to pour, not noticing Bunky moving through the crowd until he stepped out from between two tables and faced him. "That's enough," he said sternly.

Dingo stared at him in surprise. Then he shrugged and poured more beer on Eames, who sucked at it, swallowing as much as he could. "That's enough," Bunky said again. Harder. Flatter.

Dingo set the pitcher on the table and let go of Eames' coat at the same time and the small man fell to floor and flailed about in the puddle of beer. "Fuck you," Dingo said. "Mind yer business."

"Guess I'm makin' it my business," Bunky said.

The other lumberjacks stood up. The woman watched carefully. Dingo looked back at his friends and then turned to Bunky with a feral grin. "Got you some balls, old man."

"Know what's right is all," Bunky said. "This ain't."

"Could get yerself hurt some here."

"Could."

"Think the weasel's worth it?"

"I figure."

"Got you a lack of friends, I guess."

"Don't need friends. Not in this."

Dingo laughed. He raised himself to his full height and he could see from the corner how small Bunky was in comparison. Dingo cracked his knuckles. Bunky stood his ground. The two men stared at each other and Eames crawled up to a seated position and watched gape-mouthed and wiped at his face. Silence. They could hear the shift-whistle from the mill peal across the flat. Dingo grinned. "Screw it," he said. "You wanna hang with the mooch, hang with the mooch. Just get the fuck outta my face."

"Fair enough," Bunky said. He stepped up to Eames and lent him a hand to get to his feet. Then he led him to the bar and sat him down on an empty stool and waited while the bartender got him a whisky and a beer. The room slowly began to fill with talk and someone plugged the jukebox and Bunky stood by Eames while he gulped down the whisky and washed it down with a swallow of beer. Bunky whispered something to him and clapped him on the back then made his way across the room in front of the lumberjacks, who watched him gravely but did not offer a word. He sat back down at the table and sipped at his drink.

"I was afraid you'd be half killed. That's one big son of a bitch," he said.

Bunky wiped his mouth with the back of his hand. "Half ain't so bad," he said.

"It ain't the beatin' so much as the comin' to and havin' to deal with it."

"Got some history with that, do ya?"

"Taken a few lickin's in my time. I don't favour it."

"Most don't. But ya gotta be willin' to take a few if you're willin' to throw a few."

Neither of them noticed the woman until she stood at the table, looking down at Bunky.

"That was the kindest and bravest thing I ever saw," she said.

"Wasn't nothin'," Bunky said.

"Sure was," she said and pulled an empty chair over and sat down. "Angie Pratt," she said and held a hand out to Bunky.

He took it and held it and shook it firmly. "Bunky," he said. "This here's Eldon."

She shook his hand but her attention was all on Bunky and

he sat there and watched her while she talked to him. She was an inch away from beautiful. He noticed everything about her. Her face was a marvel. It was wide with a bold cut of a mouth and full lips. Behind the scarp of her cheekbones were eyes the rich black of obsidian, so that when her gaze fell on him he felt absorbed. Her hands created a parallel language in the air as she talked, drawing him and Bunky into the centre of her words. He was in love before he knew it as such. He only knew that what he felt shamed him and he looked at the floor. She leaned in when she talked to Bunky and the older man seemed to bask in it. He drank off the last of his beer and stood. When she looked at him there was the hint of a smile at the corner of her mouth. She took his hand. Velvet. He grinned, nodded at Bunky, and left them.

19

HE SAW THEM AGAIN A WEEK LATER. He was at The Dollar Holler, hungover and bleary as the fog and wet he stood in. There were only two trucks. They were in the second. He heard his name and recognized Bunky at the wheel. She sat beside him and leaned forward in the seat and waved. They parked and he shambled across the road. "Got a couple weeks' work, maybe a little longer, if you'll have it," Bunky said. "I'll throw in a roof and a cot, meals and a bag lunch. You let me know what it's worth when you're done with it."

"Doin' what?" he asked.

"Got ten acres needs fencing. Post holes, wire, the works."

"I can do it. But I could really use a drink. Just to settle my guts is all."

Bunky squinted at him. He didn't speak until she put a hand on his shoulder and squeezed. He looked at her and then turned back to him standing in the road. "I'll do 'er this one time. But I need a fence plumb and squared. Got no time fer foolishness."

"Shakin' it kinda rough today is all. I can do the work."

"Get in then. I'll see ya get yer drink."

He started toward the back. He had his hands on the rails of the box when Bunky called to him. "Not there," he said. "Up here with us."

He walked around the front of the truck and climbed in and sat beside her on the bench seat. He could feel the warmth of her leg alongside his and she smiled at him. He stared out through the windshield but he could smell the soapy, smoky haze of her. She offered him a smoke. He fumbled at the pack and she took it back and drew one out and lit it for him and held it. He took it with shaky fingers. Bunky drove hard and deliberate. The road curved and wound through bush cut with wide green spaces where farms sat in sudden bursts of space strewn with the humps of cows, pigs, and horses. After a while they pulled into a long, rutted driveway. Bunky parked the truck beside a barn and there was an open trailer hooked to a rickety old tractor. "She's packed with rolls of wire, posts, the post hole digger, nails, and staples. She's your kit," Bunky said.

They walked into the house. He felt awkward. Angie took a bottle down from the cupboard and poured a generous slug and held it out to him. He took it and drained it in one gulp and she smiled and poured some more into the mug. He sat at the table and nursed it. She doled out some stew that had been burbling on the stove and two hunks of bread and butter. "Get 'er into ya," Bunky said. "That ground tends toward rock an' you'll need all the grit ya can muster."

"Wanna thank ya for the work," he said.

"Was her said we should find you."

"Thank ya," he said to her.

She smiled and sat beside Bunky. He took another slurp of the whisky and then bent to the food. The hooch had settled his gut. He ate hungrily. She refilled the bowl and he sopped up the gravy with the bread. When he was finished he slid the chair back and sat there a moment looking at the two of them. Bunky stood and nodded at him and the two of them walked out the door. They walked, without speaking, to the tractor. Bunky fired it up and he just stood there, watching him. "Ya know how to drive one of these, don'tcha?" Bunky asked.

"I got it," he said. Bunky slid from the seat and stood on the tongue of the trailer a foot behind him. He eased it into gear and thumbed the gas lever up a notch or two and they rumbled across the yard.

"Gates open to yer left," Bunky said, and he steered through the opening and out into a long, wide field. Bunky leaned forward and flapped a hand to indicate straight ahead and he drove easily through the field. His head was clear. He felt better. When they got to the far end of the field there was another gate and he drove through it and Bunky slapped him on the shoulder to halt him. "Dang cows got a nose fer bush an' I can't keep 'em outta there. So I need ya to fence it right up to where the trees start back there. Savvy?"

"Two sides and the back. Figure around a hundred posts."

"She'll definitely keep ya occupied."

"How ya gettin' back?"

"Man can't walk man got no business on the land."

"She's a piece."

"Ah, it's a stretch of the legs is all. Ya need anything just drive back an' look about. I mean to be off soon. Got trees to buck and stack for a friend down the line. I'll see ya near sundown."

"Thanks again."

"Thank me with the job."

"I will."

Bunky stomped off and he busied himself with sorting out the supplies. When he'd got it arranged he took a big roll of twine, tied the end to a post, and walked it out and staked it to the ground when he had it straight and true to the post. Then he stepped out the spacing for the new posts and marked them with a scuff of his boot and a stone. He took off his jacket, picked up the posthole digger, and went to where he'd marked the first set and got to work. The ground was stony beyond the scrim of topsoil. It was gravel, mixed with sand and rocks the size of bread loaves. He bashed away at it and had to get a pick from the trailer and he swung it hard, the clink and the clip of its bite echoing dully off the trees. He'd broken a sweat by the time the hole was cleared enough to get the post-hole digger at it. There was a water jug in the trailer and he leaned against the fender of the tractor and he drank and splashed water over his head and let it trickle down his neck and back and chest. The morning had cleared. The sun had burned the fog away and there were tendrils of it rising like smoke into the hazy near blue of the sky. The grass looked plump with moisture. He set back to work again and lost himself in the feel of his muscles, in the effort of plunging the digger.

He had seven holes dug by the time the sun climbed to noon. He was hungry. He set the digger down beside the last hole and turned to the tractor to find her sitting in the seat. "You work like you mean it," she said. "I brought your lunch."

"Thanks," he said. "I was meanin' to walk in."

"I needed out anyway." She held up a canvas sack and a thermos.

He went to the tractor and drank some more of the water. He rinsed his face and neck and wiped himself with his jacket. She sprang down from the seat and set the sack on the top of the fender. Then she reached into the pocket of her shirt and drew out a flask. He looked at her and she smiled. "He's a good man," she said. "Best I known my whole life. But he doesn't understand a lot of things."

She handed him the flask. He unscrewed the top and took a sip. He closed his eyes and breathed deep and he could feel the burn in his belly. "Thanks," he said.

"I know about the need," she said. "Done my share of hurtin' too." She took a nip from the flask and smiled at him again.

He gazed at her. Then he reached for the canvas sack and opened it. There was a bundle of sandwiches, a container of soup, pieces of carrots and celery, cheese, and an assortment of fruit. He took a sandwich, opened the soup and drank some. He sat on the running board with the sack at his feet. She moved to sit beside him as he drank more of the soup. They both looked down the line of post holes. "Hard job," he said.

"You seem up to it."

"Didn't figure at first."

"You did good."

"You from around here?" He bit into a sandwich and chewed and looked at her.

"I'm Cree," she said. "Well, half. I come from a place called Long Plain, west of Winnipeg."

"Never got out that way."

"You'd like it. Lots of sky."

"Seen me some sky a time or two."

She reached into the bag and took some of the vegetables and ate. He took another slug from the flask and screwed the top on and handed it to her. She squinted at him and he waved his hand. "I'm good," he said.

"What about you? You're from here?"

"Sorta," he said. "Spent a lotta time around here. I'm Ojibway. But I'm half too. I don't have any idea whereabouts I'm from."

"That's sad," she said.

"When you ain't got somethin' it's a waste of time to try'n miss it is what I figure."

"Feels good to miss things."

"Oh yeah. Why would that be especially?"

"Well, it makes you know you're livin'. That you touched something. That something touched you."

He finished the sandwich and took another from the bag. There was coffee in the thermos and he poured some into the lid and blew across it and then drank. He ate a second sandwich and a handful of berries and a chunk of apple. "That's good," he said.

"You have family?"

"You got a smoke?"

She smiled her wide smile again. She fished a pack from her coat and they both lit up and he smoked a while, looking out along the ridge line where it became the backcountry. "No," he said. He ground the butt out on the running board and stood and drank more of the coffee. "Job's callin'," he said.

"You could talk to me, you know." She stood up beside him. She was almost his height and she didn't have to raise her head to look at him. He could feel the strength of her. He wanted to touch her and his hand trembled at his side a little. He trailed the toe of a boot in the grass.

"Not a real good thing," he said.

"Why?"

"Work. That's what I'm here for."

"Everybody needs to talk."

"Everybody needs to work. Seems to me ya can talk yer way outta work real easy. I can't afford it."

"You can't afford a friend?"

He looked at her and she returned it and they stood there and he could hear the sound of the wind in the aspen trees. His heart hammered like a piston. She didn't blink or turn away, just stood there gazing at him, and he could see the tiny images of himself in the shine of her eyes. The idea of being held there pleased him. He walked off a few steps, stopped, then faced her again. "Appreciate the lunch," he said.

She tilted her head and folded her arms across her chest, the wind riffling her hair. He found he couldn't move. "I'll ring the supper bell when it's time," she said. "Unless you come in before."

"I'll work to the bell," he said.

"All right." She turned and walked away across the field and he watched. The sway of her like tall grass. He picked up the digger and slammed it into the earth, the solid thud of it jarring the length of his arm.

———

They ate by candlelight and the glow from a fire in the wood-stove. She'd roasted deer meat and served it with leeks, mush-rooms, and potatoes. There was wine but he noticed they barely touched it so he held back. One glass. Slowly. He saw Bunky watching him. The deer was succulent and he found he had a wild hunger from the work so that once they'd all started he bent his head and dug in and when he raised it again he saw them looking at him.

"What?" he asked.

"Good to see ya chow down is all," Bunky said. "Good day's sweat'll do that fer a guy."

"He's doing a great job," she said.

"You seen?" Bunky asked.

"I walked his lunch out to him."

The older man nodded and set his fork down beside his plate. "That ground hard enough for ya?"

He chewed and looked at them. He took a swallow of the wine and set the glass down gently on the table. "Like tryin' to poke through a mountain face," he said.

"I hear that," Bunky said. "Why you figure I hired it out?" He laughed.

"Coulda got you one of them post-hole diggers that run off the tractor."

"That's not how man's work gets done."

"Easy to say when you ain't the man doin' it."

They laughed. She poured him a little dollop of wine and he looked at her but her face remained neutral, not meeting his eyes and looking at the tabletop. They ate in silence. She ate in small bites, chewing thoughtfully, and it made him slow and set his fork beside his plate between bites. He finished off the wine and she rose and got him a second plate of food.

Bunky eased his chair back from the table and set to preparing a pipe. She looked back and forth at the two of them and he felt awkward so he concentrated on the food and long moments passed without any word said. When he finished he wiped his mouth with his sleeve and pushed his chair back and stood as if to go.

"Appreciate if you'd tell me where I'm to sleep," he said.

"Ain't no mad rush," Bunky said. "I aim to smoke this bowl an' hear a story."

"Story?"

"Angie's a whale of a storyteller. We sit by the fire an' she'll tell 'em after we eat. A pipe goes good with a story."

He stared at the floor. "I ain't really much for it," he said.

"Frig, it'll do ya good to sit a while."

"Stories work to calm you down," she said quietly.

He looked at her but she kept her gaze on the tabletop. She stood and gathered the plates and took them to the sink and set them there to soak. Then she walked over and took Bunky's hand and he stood and they went into the living room, and he followed them and took a seat on the floor with his back to the front of an armchair. Bunky sat on the couch. She took a rocker from the corner and set it to the side of the fire and settled herself. He couldn't stop watching her. She closed her eyes. He glanced at Bunky, and the older man was entranced by her too. His pipe sat in his hand unlit and only when she opened her eyes and looked about did he strike a match and puff it alive. He felt the need of a smoke too and he fumbled out his makings but she reached a package over. "Stories go better with tailor-mades," she said.

He let his fingers trail on hers a second, feeling the electric thrill of it. She smiled. "What's this tale to be then?" she asked.

"I favour a story about the sea," Bunky said. "Never been out to sea. I seen it once though. Kinda always liked the feel of it."

"What are ya talkin' about?" he asked.

Bunky leaned forward on the sofa. "She's a tale spinner," he said. "She spins 'em right outta the air. Tells 'em whole so's you'd think yer readin' a book. You'll see. Flummoxed me the first time she did it."

"You make 'em up?" he asked.

"It feels like they were always in me," she said. "I just reach in and find them and they tend to tell themselves."

She sat back in the rocker and folded her hands under her chin and looked upward and away to the far corner of the room. The two of them watched her and the flicker of the firelight on her face lent it a wavering cast as if she were a shaman or a spell-caster. When she closed her eyes he could feel her go somewhere like stepping through a curtain. He was captivated before she said a word. The unlit cigarette dangled from his fingers and he let it drop to the floor and he crossed his knees and listened.

She told a tale of a being from the sea who lived in the great underwater world. This being yearned to see the colours and hear the sounds of the world above her. But she couldn't figure out how to get there. She tried many ways. Finally she latched on to the tail of a passing whale. When the huge creature breached the waters and then dove lazily back into the depths, the being clung to the tail and let the mystery of the great world above fill her senses. She was dazzled. She let go of the tail and drifted on the crests of waves, looking out across the blue ocean of the sky and feeling the wind on her face and the taste of the breeze. She landed on the beach of a tiny island. She walked there in the thrall of a whole other experience until she longed for her home in the underwater world. But she had to find a way to get back. She swam out and waited for another whale. None came. She became sad and lonely and filled with dread that she might never return to her home. The salt of her tears merged with the salt of the sea and a dolphin came to comfort her. She found she could speak to it and told the dolphin of her journey. The dolphin carried her back down to her home beneath the waves. The being was overjoyed. The dolphin left her with the message that since she had already experienced the air world she could always return there in her mind. The being lived for the rest of her life telling tales about the world above to all who would listen.

The roll of her words rode on the flicker of the fire. Words in firelight taking him back. As the tale wound down to its ending, he didn't know that he was crying until she stopped. He stood shakily and wiped at his face with his palm. They looked at him and Bunky stood and put a hand on his shoulder. Neither of them spoke. He was embarrassed now and he stepped back and scratched his head.

"Told ya it was somethin'," Bunky said.

"Where do I sleep?" he asked.

"There's a bed in the loft of the barn," Bunky said. "I could walk ya."

"I'll find it."

"Sure?"

"Yeah."

He turned to go. When he looked back over his shoulder she sat in the rocker with her hands on her thighs, gazing at him. She watched him without speaking and he stepped through the kitchen and out the door and across the yard toward the barn. He found his way to the loft and lay in the bed and pulled the blanket and comforter around him and stared at the beams and timbers. He thought of her eyes in the firelight. The sheen of them something he recognized. He sought a word for it but was asleep before he found it.

The ground was unrelenting. He pushed himself hard. But the morning only earned him ten more post holes and he was worn and spent by the time she arrived with his lunch. He drank the soup and smoked before he could gather himself enough to eat the sandwiches. There was no flask. He appreciated that. They sat on the running board of the tractor while he ate. The sky was the blue of old denim. There was the smell of clover and muck from the recent rains and he chewed and took secretive glances at her. She had a way of brushing her hair back from her face with one hand, slowly, using the tips of her fingers, closing her eyes briefly, and he was entranced by that. The sheer pleasure she took in it.

"My dad was a working man," she said.

"Kind?"

"Everything. He always said he liked the feel of the earth on his hands. So he did outside work mostly."

"Sounds like a good man."

"He died when I was twelve. Heart attack. Pretty much worked himself to death."

"He was Cree?"

"White. My mom was Cree."

"She's gone too."

She looked at him. He could feel her searching for words. "She left me slowly. Almost like one little bit of her at a time. She kinda gave up when Dad died. I remember that. How she looked. How she slumped when she walked as though there was a weight on her back.

"She had no skills and she had trouble finding work. Dad was the breadwinner. So it was hard for her. She drank and she'd find men and bring them home. I must have had a dozen stepdads. None of them lasted very long. They would always leave her. Just vanish. No words, nothing, and she'd be heartbroken.

"I'd see her standing in the doorway with this look on her face that was all barren and cold like a field of snow. I could feel her struggling to find something to latch on to. It would just end up being another man and another heartbreak. When I was sixteen she just quit. I found her curled up with her arms around a pillow the day after the latest one of them checked out. She just left. Alone and sad."

There was a hawk hovering in the wash of a thermal draft and they watched it. He wanted to offer something and he wrestled with words. It made his gut churn. He found nothing that seemed to fit. "Rough," was all he said in the end.

"I swore I'd never do that," she said. "Never rely totally on a man. So I went to work. I cooked good so I went to camps and crew sites everywhere. Word got out that I ran a good kitchen and I was never out of a job."

"They hassle ya?" he asked. "The guys?"

"They always want something, men. They'll always try to snag a girl. Like it's their right or their duty or something. That's just the way men are. I partied with them but I never let myself get involved with the crew."

"Ever?"

"There were men, yeah. I mean, I'm a woman. But never anyone from the work. When you work around men all the time you find things out."

He looked over at her.

"Like they want to own you until something jars them, something you do that's less than their idea of perfect or that shines less of a light on them. Then it's like you can watch them remove themselves like a wave going back out. Just kinda gone. It's what always happened with my mom. Washed away."

"And Bunky?"

She smiled. "Bunky's a hero, you know? He's soft and gentle but he's got sand and grit in him too. You saw."

"Yeah."

She fished out her smokes and held out the pack to him and he took one. They sat and smoked quietly. "What about you?" she asked. "Family? Women? Anything."

He smoked until the butt was down to his fingers and then he ground it out on the running board. He leaned forward on his knees and folded his hands between them and kicked at a clod and ground it with the toe of his boot. "Nothin' much to say," he said.

He turned to her and she watched him closely. "You draw circles in the sand with a stick," she said.

"Huh?"

"You know. Like a kid. Watching you, you're like a kid with a stick making circles in the sand because you don't know how to shape words yet."

"Meaning?"

"It means I get it."

"Good, because I don't."

"I get that some stories are hard to tell. Like when you heard my story, it took you back to something. To someone, maybe. Back to a story you been carrying a long time."

"Some stories never need tellin'."

She put an arm around his shoulders and put her head against his. He could hear her breathing but all he could do was sit there like stone, his eyes on the ground. They sat like that for minutes and then finally she stretched her legs out in front of her and crossed her ankles. She tapped the sides of her boots together. When he looked at her she had her lips pursed and she looked at him, squinting. "You got it in you to be a hero too," she said.

"I ain't cut from that cloth."

"How do you know?"

"I know."

She rose and brushed off the legs of her pants and when he stood too they were about a foot apart. She looked right into his eyes and he put his head down and shifted his feet in the grass. She raised his chin with one hand. "No one ever knows," she said. "Life asks it all of a sudden when you're not looking."

She stood up on her toes and kissed him. It was cool and damp. It was over in an instant and he stood there with his arms hanging at his sides. She stepped back, then bent to grab up the remainder of the lunch and turned and walked away. He stood watching her make her way across the field. At one point he raised a hand as if to wave then dropped it to his forehead, his mouth open in wonder.

That night as he lay in the loft he could see the edge of the moon through the slats of the barn. It hung in indigo and cast a swath of bluish light across the bed. There was the smell of cattle. The rich, dry odour of oats, straw, and hay curing in the mow. The soft feet of mice in the corners. There was a sound at the ladder. He raised his head off the rough pillow and saw her climb to the top rung and step onto the loft. She wore a white nightdress. She walked silently toward him so that she appeared to hover and he caught his breath. She got to the edge of the cot and he closed his eyes. He could feel her watching him. He flicked his eyes open and she sat on the edge of the thin mattress and found his hand in the dark and held it between the two of hers. Neither of them spoke. She held his hand then opened hers and kept his in her one palm and stroked the back of it with her fingers. He couldn't take a full breath and he felt heavy, unable to move. She took her free hand and put it to her lips then laid it against his cheek. He closed his eyes again and tried to pull the satin of it into him and he could feel her move. When he opened his eyes she was leaned close to him, the wisp of her breathing on his face. He reached a hand up toward her but she brushed it aside and held her position. Her breath was dry: faint cinnamon lingering against a backdrop of wine. He lay with his arms held to his sides, staring straight into the shimmering orb of her eyes. They didn't speak. Instead, she continued to hold a hand to his face. He put his hands to her hips and she let him. He searched for words but there were none in him. The tumble of her hair was like a curtain framing them. The womanly smell of her, all musk and soap and smoke. The sound of cattle rustling in their stalls and somewhere far off the yip of a solitary coyote chasing voles through the field grass. She stood slowly, his hands falling away from her body like a shedding skin, and she stood looking down at him and when he tried to speak she leaned over and put a finger to his lips and hushed him. He grabbed her wrist. They eyed each other and when he pulled her to him she didn't resist, let her body settle against his, and he kissed her and she kissed back, his hands on her shoulders, hers at both sides of his waist. Neither of them moved. When she stood again his palms felt the emptiness of the space between them.

"Don't break the circle," she whispered and walked to the ladder again and stepped down the rungs and left him hanging in the sky of her.

20

BUNKY FINISHED THE WOOD-CUTTING JOB and got busy with regular farm work. It meant he was around the place every day and it was the pair of them now that walked his lunch out to him. They sat in the grass and made small talk while he ate and he fought to keep from looking at her with more than a furtive glance. One day after he finished his lunch Bunky and he walked the new fence line and the older man seemed pleased.

"I could lend a hand if ya needed it, Eldon," he said.

"I took it on, I'd kinda like to finish 'er," he said. "A dozen more posts and then pull the wire. I figure she can't best me now."

"Yer doin' good. Yer a good hand."

"Desperation'll make a man work his tail off, I suppose."

"Well, ya don't look anywhere near so desperate now."

He could only stare at his shoes.

He took to rising early and heading out on the tractor at first light and throwing himself into the digging before the sun came out and hit him with the full heat of the day. But it was more than that. Their kiss in the loft haunted him. He didn't want to risk Bunky seeing it on his face. Guilt wasn't a new thing to him. Dealing with it sober was. He felt as though every move he made in her company threatened to betray him. He was afraid to speak in case he blurted something that would draw attention to his discomfort and the reason for it. So he began to skip breakfast. One morning there was a sack on the seat with bannock, fruit, and a thermos of coffee. He grinned and ate it while he drove. Without drink felt as though he occupied his body for the first time in a long time and each day of work slaked the hard pinch of craving in his gut. He didn't take wine with his supper. He didn't take the beer Bunky offered on the porch when they sat out there late into the evenings. He could feel the older man studying him. He could sense questions in him but they went unspoken. Instead, they talked about the land and how it felt to them to be out on it with their back bent to some kind of labour.

"It comes to fill a man," Bunky said one night.

"I ain't much for poetry," he said. "But I get what you're sayin'."

"Poetry's nothin' but a man feelin' what's there anyhow."

"I guess. Never lent my head to it is all I meant."

"You should. Opens a fella up doin' that."

"Ain't exactly my strong suit."

Bunky puffed on his pipe and nodded solemnly. "That's poetry right there. You sayin' that."

"You're startin' to talk like her."

Bunky laughed and tapped the bowl of the pipe on the

porch rail. "Funny how that'll happen to a man. Never thought it'd happen to me. But I like it."

He took to watching her when Bunky wasn't looking. He found himself pulling tiny details into him; the smallness of her wrist when she stirred a pot, the young girl look on her face when she studied a hand of cards, joy eking when she won a hand and how she could fall so easily into contemplation when something was said that struck her, the depths of her spinning away just beyond his vision like a swirling eddy pulling him to its depths. She caught him now and then. She'd tilt her head. She'd give a small smile and then turn back to whatever she was doing and his gaze would drape her like a cloak.

He drank her stories in. He and Bunky would clomp in from the porch and they would gather in the living room and she would close her eyes and he'd watch her move into another place. She seemed to slip beyond time. When she opened her eyes again she was a totally different creature, and the words when they came were stunning in their flow. If he closed his own eyes he could see the details of the journeys she took him on and he was enthralled. He always felt lonely somehow when the stories ended, lessened abruptly, as if his sole contact with her had been severed, and he'd slump off to the loft in the barn, waiting for her to step out of the moonlight again and touch him. She never did. Instead, she'd look up and watch him leave, the feel of her eyes on him what he carried away.

———

The work took him sixteen days. He was pulling the last strand of wire when she appeared in mid-morning. Bunky had said he had errands in town. There was a breeze from the south and the sun was hot on his back and he'd taken the shirt off and flung it over the last post as a marker. His muscles were taut and hard from the work and he'd lost some of the drunk fat. He felt lean and strong. When she called to him he turned and watched her walk toward him and he wiped the sweat from his brow with a forearm and stepped away from the bundle of wire at his feet. He didn't reach for the shirt. Instead, he stood and tilted the water jug back to drink and then splashed his hair with it and let the water flow over him.

"That's the best part of watching men work," she said. "The pleasure they take in it."

"Yer gonna have to spell that out for me."

She laughed. "Like when you see them half smile when something's hard. When they have to strain with it. Or the look when something's done and it's plumb and square and right and they nod like kids getting coached at a game. Or like now, the splash of water. It's fun to see."

"It's sweat."

"It's manly. I like that."

"That why you chose to work in the camps? So you could be reminded of your father?"

She stared at him. Then she sat down in the grass and folded the flare of her dress close in around her. She traced a finger along the tops of the grass. Then she looked back up at him again. "I told you there was more to you," she said.

"Sorry. Just thinkin' out loud is all."

"Don't be sorry. You saw through something. You spoke it. There's no wrong in that."

"Don't know if it's right."

"It doesn't have to be right. It just needs to be said. People can sort out the right from the wrong together."

"Ain't had much call for that sorta talk."

"Yet," she said.

He sat down on the grass beside her. He crossed his legs and plucked a spear of grass and stuck it between his teeth and gazed up at the sky. "Mosta the big talk in my life got left unsaid. Ya get used to that. Makes it tough to say anything real or hard. After a time you come to prefer it."

"Man talk," she said. "Men think getting to the roots of things is trench digging. It's not. It's plain talk. Like a story."

"I never told no stories."

"You should. When you share stories you change things."

"Says you," he said.

"If you told me one of your stories, you'd get lighter."

"Don't know as I have any worth the tellin'."

She smiled at him and touched his leg. "You could let go of something maybe you carried for a long time. I could know more of you. Get bigger with the knowing of you."

"You're sayin' you want to know me."

"Yes."

"I can't see why ya would."

She took his hand, held it to her face. He watched her breathlessly as she kissed the palm of it. "I don't know why," she said. "I just do."

He reached out and pulled her to him and cradled her face in his hands and looked into her eyes. There was surprise there, wonder. When he bent his face to kiss her she closed her eyes and opened her mouth. She laid a hand on his chest as he eased onto his back in the grass. He rolled over and she lay on the grass with her hair fanned out around her head and he was on his knees looking down at her. She smiled and trailed a finger down his chest. He kissed her again and she wrapped her legs around him and pulled his head to her shoulder and he lay clutched by her with the smell of grass and dirt and stones at his face and knew he would never see the land the same again. When they made love it was gentle and sweet and brought them both to tears. He held her after. He had the scent of their loving in his nose and it mixed with clover and wild raspberries and the breeze. When she rose and arranged herself he could only lie there looking up at her.

"I need to go."

"Bunky," he said, climbing to his feet. "What'll we do there now?"

"I don't know. Yet."

He put his arms around her. The fragrance of her hair. The rim of her ear at his lips. She drew back and looked at him, squinting with the sun on her face. "This was a good thing," she said. "Don't let yourself tell you any different."

"I won't," he said, and she walked off.

"Well, this here's the last meal we'll share. Here anyways," Bunky said. "Dig in, Eldon. You earned it. That was some fencin' you done. Proud of ya."

"Thank you," he said. She'd roasted moose Bunky had killed the previous autumn. There were turnips, corn, and mashed potatoes and he ate slowly, enjoying it, making it last. She hovered around the table, adding portions to their plates. He eyed her. The memory of her body under his. He looked at Bunky, who ate with his head down. After a while

Bunky looked up across the table and set his utensils down. "You ain't looked in the pay envelope," he said, easing his chair back. "All these days in the sun'n the dirt, that's the pure sum of it. Yer ticket."

"Not real sure what I need most right now," he said. He reached out and pulled the envelope to the side of his plate.

"Well, she's a good haul, I figure. Get ya anything."

"Don't want much," he said. He thumbed open the flap and looked at the wad of bills crammed there.

"No matter. A man's got cash in the hand, his mind'll sort what to do with her."

He scratched at the back of his head and looked across at the older man. "I thank ya for this," he said. "I ain't felt better in a long time."

"Ya done good for yourself. All's I did was give ya work."

"That's lots," he said. "Most don't."

"Man's past ain't his measure."

"Most don't think that neither."

"Well, I'm a different sort. Kinda always have been. Me, I figure ya prove who ya are in the day yer in."

"Thanks for that too then."

"Ain't nothin'."

"It's lots."

They bent to their plates again and he stuffed the envelope in his chest pocket. She came and joined them at the table. She had a small bowl and she picked at it.

"You ain't hungry?" Bunky asked.

"I nibbled all the while I cooked," she said.

"Get you a cook's belly," he said with a laugh.

"Hopefully not," she said and reached a hand out to touch his. They shared a look across the table.

"What say we have us a smoke, Eldon," Bunky said.

"No," he said. "You two go on ahead. I wanna clean up."

"You ain't paid to do that."

"Don't need payin'. Something I just wanna do is all."

She stared at him and he picked up his plate and took it to the sink. "Well, I'm never the one to argue with a man wants to do extra," Bunky said. "Let's us smoke then, girl."

He could hear them stand and walk out to the porch and when they were gone he gathered the other plates and scraped them into the bin and stowed the food stuff in the fridge. There was a feeling in him like waiting for a punishment. It felt better to keep moving and he ran the water and held his hands under and let the heat calm him. He took his time washing the dishes and he could hear them talking in low tones. He wondered if she was telling him what happened between them and then he heard him laugh and tap the toes of his boots on the boards of the porch. He dried the dishes. Then he used the soapy water to clean off the counter, the cutting board, the stove and fridge, and finally the sink itself. He towelled the tap and faucets to a sheen and set the towel on the rack to dry. He craved a drink for the first time in days. His gut was agitated. His head was full of thoughts that sped past each other. Trapped. He was shifty-footed and it scared him and he walked out to the porch and leaned on the rail and faced them.

"Think I'm gonna walk," he said.

"She's near to sundown," Bunky said.

He couldn't lift his gaze from his shoes. "No matter. Feel like a walk is all."

"Do you want company?" she asked.

"No," he said. "Thanks, but no."

"Well, come in when yer done. We'll play some cards and maybe have one last story," Bunky said.

"I think maybe not. I think I'll just book in. Kinda tired."

"You should be. That was some work. You okay?"

He puffed out his cheeks and looked around at the barn and the fields and took his time speaking. "Feels good out here," he said. "I kinda feel like walkin' it some."

"Kinda suck at goodbyes myself," Bunky said. "This was nice. Havin' you here. Yer a good man."

"Am I?" he asked and risked a look at the older man.

"I got no call to argue the fact," Bunky said. "Hire ya any time. Tell others to give ya a go as well."

"That's good of ya."

"You done it fer yourself."

"All right then."

"All right. Ya feel like it, come in anyhow once yer done."

He turned and walked across the yard. There was a feeling in him like a bruise, a purple ache that set between his ribs. He tasted a cry building at the back of this throat. It was too familiar and made him fearful. So he strode past the barn and out into the field and aimed for the line of the ridge. Ground squirrels nattered and whistled at his passing. The grass was wet with dew and his pant legs were soaked but he strode fast and purposefully, the feeling in his belly churning and rank like something turned to spoil. He wanted to scream, to run into the trees and let branches cut him, sting him like lashes. But he stopped at the line of them and turned and looked back at the farm. It sat in the hushed fall of evening, the lights from the house like pale yellow eyes. He thought he heard her laughing. He thought of her touching Bunky in that gentle way she had and the idea of that made him half crazy. She'd stay with

Bunky. She'd choose what was predictable and safe and he didn't blame her for that. But he'd miss these days. He'd miss her. He'd miss the lightning bolt thrill of her in his arms. He felt the impending separation like a shearing away of something pliant and soft inside himself and he wanted to drink.

He dreamed of a valley. It shone in the glow of a setting sun. There was a river wending its way through with the backdrop of mountains and the smell of gum and sap and the feel of the breeze on his brow. He could hear the yap of wolves at play. He sat on a rock that faced the east and he watched the line of shadow creeping westward in time with sun's fade behind the lip of another ridge to the west, the cool air like a curtain descending. The blink of the light of emerging stars in the purpling mantle of the sky. The susurration of the rising wind in the treetops. He closed his eyes and drew it into him and felt peace and he raised his face to the heavens and sat open-mouthed and breathing, seeing nothing but hearing the motions of life around him everywhere. He heard footsteps approaching from behind him and he listened, unafraid and trying to discern shape and substance from the fall of them, slipping through the rough tangle of root and stone, dropped branches and the dry husk of moss. He opened his eyes and he could see her standing on the top rung of the ladder. She clambered up and walked toward him stealthily, soundless and assured. She touched him and he turned and she kissed him and he fell into it again. Her hair draped around their heads, shutting out the world so that all he could see was her face, her smile, the line of her lips, and the glimmer of her eyes. He kissed her, uncertain if he dwelt in dream and not wanting to move for fear of waking. Her hands on his chest, his ribs, his belly. Her tongue trailed down his neck. His hardness. Her hands on it and she took control and eased the night shift she wore over head and the spill of her breasts taking his breath away and then the soft wet of her all round him, within him.

They drifted with it. He lost all touch with earth and existed in a primal sphere and she bit his shoulder and thrust at him with her hips and he kissed her neck and her nipples and they rolled into the straw beside the bed. She laughed in his ear. She turned over and knelt on all fours in front of him and he felt wild with the churn of desire and he put his hands on her hips and sank into her and let his body loom over her and she leaned forward and put her head on her forearms. He put his head back, closed his eyes, and thrust slowly and he could hear her moan. There was no space that they did not fill. He knew he would never relinquish this feeling until the light of a lamp edged the shadow away and they heard the older man gasp and say, "What the hell?" and the spell was broken.

21

THEY SAT IN THE HARD LIGHT OF THE KITCHEN. None of them could speak. Bunky sat with his unlit pipe in his mouth, glowering. His eyes were shining. He kept thumping the table with the side of his fist and the two of them could only look at it, both of them snared in the beat of it. He slammed it down a final time and stood, leaning on the table and shaking. She moved toward him and he glared and she stopped, one hand extended toward him, and she withdrew it slowly and let it fall to her side. Bunky stepped around the table and stood over him in his chair. His fist was clenched hard, red and splotched with white from the grip. It shook in the air and Eldon looked at it and lowered his head, waiting for the crush of it against his skull. But the older man cursed once and stepped away into the corner. The two of them looked at each other, faces fallen and empty of words.

"This is how you repay me?" Bunky asked. "The both of you?"

He turned from the wall. His face was etched deep with pain and anger and the wildness of despair.

"I'm sorry," he said quietly. Pointlessly. "I'm sorry."

Bunky shook his head. "Ya can't be sorry for this. Not this. Neither of ya."

"It wasn't his fault," she said.

He stared at her. He tried to laugh but it came out as a dry huff and he stalked to the door and turned and looked at them again. His leg quivered. "I loved you," he said. "I give ya the whole deal. Trusted ya. Love ya best I could."

"I know," she said.

"Do ya? Do ya? If ya did how come this then? How come!"

"I don't know."

"You?" Bunky said, pointing a finger at him.

"It just happened," he said. "Weren't no plan."

"No plan. Well, maybe ya got a plan now then. What're ya gonna do now?"

"I don't know," he said. "We never talked on it."

"Fuck and run? Is that it?" Bunky said. "That why you

took the walk tonight? Figure out how ya were gonna get outta here?"

"No," he said. "Try'n figure out where to go my own self."

"Why, if this was what ya were gonna do anyhow?"

"Thought she loved you. Didn't wanna get in the waya that."

Bunky laughed then, hard and bitter. "Sure didn't look ya had me much in mind up in the barn there."

"I did. Well, not there. Not then."

"No. I wouldn't suspect ya did. Ya love her?"

He looked at the floor under the table. "Yes," he said. He raised his face and looked at her where she stood leaning against the counter with her arms folded across her chest. She was staring at the floor too but lifted her head at the sudden quiet and met his eyes. "Yes," he said again.

"And you?" Bunky asked.

Her face was soft and limned with the light. "Yes," she said.

It broke him. Bunky fell against the jamb. He put a hand to his face and when he opened his eyes they were sorrowful. He heaved a breath into him and walked back to the table and sat and put his head in his arms as he began to weep openly now. They could only watch. When it subsided he raised his head and wiped at his face with a sleeve. "Ya come like hope to me," he said. "All of a sudden and strong and I come to believe in it. Believe in you."

"I know," she said.

"Thought this place might turn out to be a home. Wanted that with all my might. I love ya too. Even if you don't hold it for me."

"I know." She said it to herself.

"Know a lot, don't ya?" There was bitterness in his voice.

"Sometimes, things come along of their own accord," she said. "There's nothing we can do to prepare for it. Nothing we can do when it drops into our world unannounced. None of us meant to hurt you. None of us knew this was coming," she said.

"I'm s'posed to draw comfort from that?"

"No. I'm just saying how it was."

"What do you want to do then? He ain't what ya might call a real goin' concern."

"I know that too," she said. "But I also know I gotta live this through."

He looked across the table. "Whatta *you* say?" he asked.

"I want her," he said. "Don't got it figgered how I'm gonna work it but I know I want her."

The older man shook his head sadly. "Can't be no booze-hound. Not now. Not with her. Can ya keep sober?"

"I can try."

"Better do more'n that. You hurt her with drinkin' I'll come find ya."

"We'll take care of each other," she said. "We can both work."

He shook his head again. "Like that's all of it."

"I know what the state of it is," she said. She stood taller now and there was a resolute set to her. Her shoulders squared and she looked directly at him. "I love him. I feel like there's a big part of him I recognize and know even if he doesn't. That's enough for me."

"It better be," Bunky said. "I don't see a whole lot more comin'."

"You said I was a good man."

The older man stared hard at him. "Gonna take some convincing now. Where'll ya go?"

"Follow the work," he said. "I know how to do that."

"I don't want her walkin' or takin' no bus."

"What're ya sayin'?"

"I'm sayin' if yer hell bent on goin' I can't say nothin' or do nothin' to stop neither of ya. That's just the set of things. But I don't want her walkin' nowhere. I'da never done that. So I'm givin' her the stake truck." He reached into his pocket and laid the keys on the table. "Got me the old pickup anyhow. She's reliable. Loyal even, ya might say."

He looked at her when he said this and she broke a little too. "Thank you," she said quietly.

"All's I ask is that ya leave now. Don't dilly-dally. It plum hurts me terrible to have to look at ya both. Can't be wakin' up to see ya leave. Go now." He slid the keys across the table and stood. "Now it's my turn to walk. Don't be here when I'm done."

Bunky turned toward the door and took a step, but she moved to block his way and they stood and looked at each other. His face quivered. His shoulders began to shake and when she reached out to him he broke wide open and bawled into her shoulder. She cried too and hugged him hard. They stood like that for long moments then he peeled himself out of her embrace and strode to the door, wiping at his face. He turned at the doorway. "You take care of her," he said, pointing a finger. "I ever learn she's been disrespected, I'm coming to find you."

"I hear that."

"Ya stole my love," he said. "Ya broke my damn heart. But I can learn to live with that. Got to, least ways. But you be a man about this. Or else."

Then he turned and strode out the door and they stood in the silence he left behind, staring at the black space of the doorway until she moved finally and went to gather her things. He walked to the barn and gathered his own few belongings.

When he got back to the house she was standing beside the truck, looking out into the dark of the fields. There was a thick roll of bills in her hand. "He left this on the seat," she said.

"Don't know that I can take it," he said.

"It's a lot of money."

"Don't figure it covers any of what we done."

"It's a good stake. We can get set up with this."

"Blood money," he said.

She nodded. "It's his way of still wanting to take care of me. He can't let me go without knowing I'm okay."

"Are ya okay?"

She stared out into the darkness of the field. Then she turned and put a hand on his arm and looked at him. "I want to be able to explain this to him one day. Right now I can't even explain it to myself. But that's all right."

He had nothing to say to that. He laid his bag of belongings behind the seat of the truck. When he looked at her there were tears on her face. He wiped one away with the curl of a knuckle, and she smiled and got behind the wheel while he strode to the other side and got in beside her. They drove away into the black canyon of the night.

"WHERE DID YOU GO?" the kid asked.

"Followed the work like I said." His voice was hollow, empty. He could barely hear him.

"Did ya drink?"

"Not for the longest time. I made a promise."

"You could hold to that?"

"Had to," he said. There was a long silence and the kid could hear the snap of the wood as it died down to embers. "She was a wonder, Frank. You gotta know that."

He coughed then, a long, racking cough that made his shoulders shake, and the kid looked at him but all he could feel was a wave of rage in him. He stood up and strode over to a pine tree and broke off a couple of the lower branches. He whacked at the ground with them and snapped one with his boot and tossed it deeper into the trees. He walked back to the fire and hunkered down and poked at it with the end of the one remaining branch. Then he broke it over his knee and tossed the lengths into the fire without speaking or looking across at his father. They both watched while the wood took and flamed upward. "I *shoulda* known all that way before now. I shoulda been able to have an idea about her instead of a head full of nothin'," the kid said. "I had a fuckin' right."

"I know it," his father said. "Been times I tried to speak of her but the words would never come. I never had the sand to open up to it. I was scared that if I did I'd fall right back into the hurt of it and keep right on fallin' way beyond any bottom I ever landed in and not know how to find my way back up again."

"I hope that ain't supposed to be a comfort," the kid said.

"I don't know what it is."

"You *should* know," the kid said and stood up suddenly. The motion made his father startle and he groaned at the pain it caused and gripped at his belly and gritted his teeth. The kid just looked at him balefully. "You don't get to say things like that and just die. You don't get to get off that easy."

It took his father some time to regain composure. He wiped at his face that was glazed with sweat and his hand shook. "I know what's owed," he said. "I know that there's no way in hell I'm gonna be able to make up to ya what I took by not bein' around. But I can't give ya years, Frank."

"I don't want years. I wanna be able to quit lookin' at women I see and wonderin' if that's how she looked." The kid punched both fists against his thighs and turned around and back again. "But you can't give me that neither. Can ya?"

He waited. His father's breathing was shallower now and he laid there with his eyes closed so that the kid stepped around the fire to lean close enough to see if he was still there. He poked him and his father opened one eye and stared. "Can ya move me to the rock, Frank?"

"You're damn poorly."

"I wanna sit and watch the light break over the valley when it comes."

"That'll be a while," the kid said.

"Even so."

The kid rose and retrieved the last bottle of Becka's concoction and he held it to his father's lips. He could only manage a small sip. The kid set a few more pieces of wood on the fire and then helped his father struggle to his feet. They shuffled across the open space to where the rock sat near the rim of the ridge. The valley below them was an open yaw of dark. Nothing was distinguishable. The sky was a dazzle of stars. The kid helped his father to a seat on the rock and he felt him shiver. It was more of a spasm and his father shuddered with the force of it. The kid wound the blanket tight around him. "She'da been proud to know ya as her son."

The words hung in the air and the kid slumped to the

ground beside him. They both gazed out across the open valley. His belly felt raw and he rubbed at it and had nothing to say in reply so he sat there mutely and looked up at his father, who rocked slowly back and forth with his hands clutched at his own gut. "I want years," his father said. "I want all of 'em. Every single wasted, drunken one. But I can't get 'em back. I know it ain't no, whattaya call it, legacy or nothin', but all's I got left is the story of her now." He looked up into the sky and began talking again.

"She got on as a camp cook and me, I landed work at a sawmill. She didn't wanna stay at the camp so we found us a cabin by a lake with a thin, unmarked road leading down to it. It was a trapper's cabin. Hadn't been used in a long time. She come to love it right off. But me, all I could see was a mess.

"But she got me goin' on fixin' it. We got to it every day after work. That girl could use some tools and it surprised me. She taught me to chink walls with mud and newspaper and moss and strips of cedar bark. She showed me how to mix mortar for the chimney stones and how to split cedar shakes for the roof. We even lifted the floorboards and insulated the space down there. Then we done the same with the walls and she helped me tote gyp board from the truck. Took three months to get it ready to take a winter.

"We dug us a couple flowerbeds and a garden plot for the next spring. She even had me dig out a root cellar for the turnips and potatoes and onions she was gonna grow. She taught me to make chairs outta willow wands and we set them on the porch we built so we could look out over the lake come evening.

"Funny thing is that in all that time I never thoughta drink. I had pocketfuls of cash from the job but it all went to her and she spent it on makin' that rat hole of a cabin into a home. Never seemed like work neither. Seemed natural. Like breathing. Even the shitty jobs never got me down like they usedta. Never had me no trade but I worked hard an' my reputation got good and after a time I was seldom out of work for more'n a day or two. The jobs were never no hell but it was cash money an' meant we could be okay."

He stopped talking and the kid could see how harrowing it was for him to be back there. He was shaking but it wasn't just the sickness. His eyes were wide and he stared without blinking at a spot just beyond the rim of the ridge, barely breathing, his jaw slack and quivering. The kid wanted to do something to break the awful silence but he fidgeted and couldn't think of anything. In the end he just sat and waited for his father to continue.

"I recall standin' on the porch early one morning with a mug of coffee, looking out across the lake, an' I felt like for the first time I could stand this life. I could settle. Every time I'd drop her at the camp I'd find myself not hardly able to wait for when I'd pick her up again. Strange. Me always wantin' to come back. I spent my whole life runnin' away not runnin' to. She brung that alive in me, Frank.

"It got me to wonderin'. Got me wonderin' if time could make goin' back to other things possible too. Goin' back to other people, other places. My mother and such. Never ever thought them kinda thoughts before. Found myself wonderin' if returnin' was somethin' a man could do, if ya could walk back over your trail and maybe reclaim things. They were odd thoughts but she hadda way of getting them into my head."

"Did ya tell her?" the kid asked.

"Nah. I never figured anyone'd care about what was goin' on in my head. Not even her. Guess the strangeness of those thoughts made me kinda ashamed."

"She mighta liked to know. Mighta been good for her to know how she was gettin' to you."

"Yeah," his father said slowly. "Still an' all, I never could cotton on to the idea of just spillin' things out."

"Your loss," the kid said.

His father just stared poker-faced at the fire and for a moment the kid thought he'd been too hard. But his father began to speak again.

"She found out she was pregnant in the fall of that first year. I just sat in the willow rocker on the porch not able to say anythin'. I stretched out a hand and cupped her belly and if I never felt no baby then, I sure felt her roundness and the idea of magic goin' on right beneath my hand. I ain't never been humbled like that ever again.

"I recall that night so clear. Layin' beside her, holdin' her, listenin' to her breathin' with my hand still on her belly. Felt like I was parta her too, just like the life she got inside her. Like you an' me was the same right then, Frank, on accounta we both needed her fer life. An' that thought scared me more'n I ever been scared and I woke up to fear."

His father paused and the kid regarded him wordlessly. When he lifted his head and turned to look at him the kid could see the desperation in him and he moved in front of him in case he lunged for the edge of the cliff.

"You were scared ya couldn't be what ya had to be," the kid said.

"More'n that," his father said. "Scared I couldn't be

what I never was. I never told her about Jimmy, about my mother, even though she told me I could tell her anythin'. I was ashameda myself, Frank. Bone deep shamed. I was scared if I started in on tellin' about myself I'd break down an' I wanted to be strong for her. I really did. But layin' there knowin' how weak I really was brung on the dark in me. The dark that always sucked me back into drinkin'. I woke up to the belief that I'd always lose or destroy them things or people that meant the most to me cuz I always done that. Now there was her. Now there was you. An' there was still me.

"Her sleepin' beside me with you in her belly scared the livin' beJesus outta me. Felt like I was on a runaway train headin' into the darkness and was no way I was gonna be able to stop it."

The kid turned his back and looked out across the empty space above the valley. He could feel his gut churn. He didn't want to hear what was coming but he couldn't shake the need to. The confusion swirled in him and he put his hands on his hips and lifted his head and looked up into the sky. The stars offered no comfort, and the chill of the wind seemed to seep in and fill him. Finally, he turned and knelt in front of his father, who was slumped on the rock, the blanket clutched about him like a shroud.

⏤

At first it was a beer or two at lunch. Then it became more. It just did. It just seemed to happen and it wasn't long before he was in the lure of it; the ongoing thought of it, the amber glow of a glass, the low burn of booze hitting his belly, the cottony feeling at the sides of his head that chased all thoughts away.

"Are you okay?" she asked.

"I'm fine."

"You worry me."

"Just tryin' to relax is all."

"I need you with me, El. Don't let that stuff take you away."

"I won't."

By the time she was due he was drinking in secret; furtive gulping and then the aftertaste of guilt and shame that only made more possible. He couldn't tell her about that either. He couldn't sleep. The certainty of failure, the landscape of his secrets, became the terror that kept him awake.

He was in town at a tavern one night that was slick with rain. It had grown late and he found himself broke without anyone he knew to borrow from. So he stumbled to the truck and aimed it along the highway to the unmarked road. He drove clutching the wheel hard with both hands and fighting against the reeling sensation in his head. Their gravel road was loose with mud from the downpour and steering along the ruts was a heaving, tossing affair that made him sick to his stomach. When he got to the cabin he wobbled out of the truck and lost his footing in the grass and pitched face first onto the ground. It made him laugh. He raised his head and wiped the muck away and saw that the door to the cabin was thrown open and there were no lights.

He scrambled to his feet and lurched to the porch calling her name and clawing toward the door frame. He almost fell over her. She lay a few feet from the doorway with her hands clutched to her belly. When he tried to move her she screamed. It took everything he had to get her to the truck.

The continuing rain had turned the muck of the road into a thin grog and he slid about and got stuck. He grabbed a handful of pebbles and small stones to stick under the wheels and somehow gained sufficient purchase to keep moving. She was groaning beside him as he drove. He got stuck again and it took a desperate back and forth to get moving again and each hurl forward drew another harsh gasp and scream from her. He put a hand to her head. It was blazing. When he made the highway she'd curled into a ball on the floor and he drove as fast as possible. The rain splattering down like paint and the booze making every motion slow and lugubrious and he lurched into the parking lot of the small hospital barely able to see.

The baby was in full kneeling breech. She fought gamely to deliver him. It took everything she had and when they finally turned to an emergency Caesarean she ebbed away. He was pacing in the hall when the doctor told him, sobered some by coffee but still lurid with whisky. He couldn't concentrate. He half grinned at the doctor, who took him by the elbow and led him to an alcove and spoke to him plainly, sternly, until the weight of the words hit him square in the chest.

"She had a chance if she had made it here in time," the doctor said.

"I was at work," he muttered.

"You're drunk. Did you get that way on the job?"

"I ain't all that bad."

"You need to get yourself together."

He stood and dropped one shoulder so he could angle out through the doors without falling. The pain was roaring in him and he only knew one way to quiet it.

23

"NEVER GOT TO SAY GOODBYE," his father said.

The kid slumped to the ground and sat with his head to his knees and his arms wrapped around his shins. There were no words. There was only that ache in his belly like hunger only deeper, set more in the bones than in the flesh. He rubbed at it but it only felt cramped and dull and empty. He raised his head and looked at his father. His face was desolate. The kid could hear the rattle of his breath. One bony finger tapped anxiously on his thigh and the kid watched him and waited for more words but there were none coming. That angered him. He waited and he felt the pressure of rage build up in his chest and he rose quickly and strode off.

He wandered along the line of the ridge and into the trees. The deep shadow calmed him. He leaned his back on a stout birch and kicked at the moss and grit with his boot heels. Family. The story of him etched in blood and tears and departures sudden as the snapping of a bone. When the tears came they were sudden as that. He let himself cry and the feeling of it scared him. The release uncontained, erupting over him. When it ended he was spent and he slumped down and sat on the moss. It was quiet. The forest was still and cool and he rubbed his hands together to warm them. His father would die, and he would never know his mother. He would never know her touch, the feel and smell of her or know the sound of her voice. He would never know the way she looked. She would remain as shadowed as the trees and rocks and bracken that surrounded him. There was a hole in his history and there was nothing that would ever fill it. He stood quickly and kicked at the tree, a shower of twigs and dead leaves fluttering down around him. He picked up a handful of stones and threw them at trees and across the open space as hard as he could. He picked up more and hurled them until his arm succumbed to the effort and he leaned over with his hands on his knees and drew deep, quaking breaths until he calmed again and felt strong enough to return to the man who was his father.

His father sat exactly like he'd left him, with the blanket snug around his shoulders. The kid didn't trust himself to speak. There was an odour coming off him. It was mouldy like compost but higher like rot, as though his flesh would die long before his heart. "Christ, I'm thirsty, Frank," he said.

The kid walked back to the fire, stoked it, and retrieved the canteen and the bottle of medicine. He turned toward the rim of the ridge again and saw the outline of his father perched against the great gulf of the sky and the swooning depth of the valley in front of him. All that emptiness. He walked slowly and when he got to his father he nudged him lightly on the shoulder and he startled and looked at him sideways all gape-mouthed and wild. "Here," the kid said softly. He held out the canteen and his father slumped in relief.

"Thought you was somethin' else," he said.

"Like what?" the kid asked. He stepped in front of him and held the canteen to his father's lips. He could only sip at it. When he was finished he tried to splash some of the water on his face but his hands shook too violently. The kid put the canteen on the ground and heard quiet retching and when he turned he saw his father bent forward vomiting on the blanket that was covering his legs. Some of the spume landed on the kid and he wiped a hand at it. It was gritty-looking, like coffee grains, and smelled like blood and the odour he'd detected earlier.

His father groaned. The kid helped him sit back up. He calmed after a few moments and the kid took the ruined blanket and replaced it with his own coat. He gathered the edges around his father and pulled it as snug as possible. "I got the medicine," he said.

"I don't think I could keep 'er down," his father said. He was shivering again and the words came out in blurts.

"It's here anyhow," the kid said.

"All right."

"I could get you back to the fire. She'd be warmer for ya there."

His father shook his head. And held the edges of the coat and huddled tighter on the rock. "No. Thanks. I'd rather be here." The light had eased upward and the kid could see a thin scrim of indigo to the east.

The kid leaned on one knee in front of his father. "Did you ever tell that Bunky what happened?" he asked. "Mighta been someone to turn to."

"Never thought to. The man woulda had no time for me certain."

"You're sayin' that ya never once thought about him. Scared shit like you was, ya never once gave him a thought. I think you're lying."

His father tried to glare, but it didn't have much force.

"You might as well just go on and tell me who the old man is then." The kid stood up and faced his father square. His fists were clenched at his sides.

His father lifted his head and looked at him sadly. He swallowed and the kid could see the effort it took. He closed his eyes. "He's Bunky. He's the man I stole your mother from," he said without opening his eyes.

The kid blinked and just stood looking at his father, whose eyes were still closed. He walked a few steps to the edge of the ridge and stared out across the valley, then turned and faced him again. "That's kinda how I had it figured. But how'd I come to be there, you talkin' like he hated you an' all?"

"I took ya there when ya were a week or so old."

"Why? On accounta you were scared that you'd hurt me?"

His father's chin jutted out and for a moment the kid thought he would press himself to his feet. "No," he said firmly. "It was more'n that. I didn't want to hate you."

The kid startled. "What?"

"Every time I looked at you all's I could see was her. Hell, I was drunk, Frank. Drunk and sick and tired and hurtin' like a bastard. Like all my skin been scraped off. I couldn't move without hurtin'."

"You thought *I* killed her. Comin' out breeched like that?"

"No," he said slowly. "I thought I did."

"I don't get it then."

"I thought me lovin' her killed her. Looking at you reminded me of that."

"And he just took me in? This man who had no time for you?"

"It took some doin', but he done it for her. He loved her. Maybe bigger'n me. Maybe his was the right one all the time and I buggered that. So I brung you to him. Only thing in my life that I can say I'm proud of."

The kid could see the exhaustion in his father's face, flat like panes of dark glass. When his father started to speak it was in a voice cracked and worn and he had to strain to hear him.

"I was scared the day I drove back to Bunky's place. I had ya with me in a bassinette the hospital let me have. I jury-rigged it with twine and leather strapping so's you'd be held in place while I drove.

"I couldn't just drive right in there so I left ya in the shade by the trees at the head of the driveway and walked in. It was early morning. Didn't think at first there was no one around an' I stood at the edge of the yard tryin' to decide what to do. I walked over to the barn an' looked in an' he weren't in there so I headed fer the house. He musta heard me close the barn door or somethin' cuz when I was about ten yards from the porch he stepped out the back door an' raised a hand.

"'Ya kin just stop right there, Eldon,' is what he said to me. 'I got nothin' to say to ya no more.' He told me I hadda lotta nerve even showin' up there.

"'I know I ain't welcome,' I said. 'I wouldn'ta come if there were any choice in the matter. Believe me.'

"I recall him puttin' a hand on the backa one of them rockers an' when he looked up at me I could see how turned against me he was. He said he wasn't partial no more to no sad stories so a drunk could get himself a drink. I told him I weren't after no drink, that I'd come to talk about Angie and that he hadda hear me out.

"I watched his face just at the mention of her name. He asked me if she was sick or hurt, if she needed anything. I could tell he woulda dropped everything to go to her.

"It weren't easy comin' outta me. I stood there in the yard feelin' like I wanted to just turn tail an' run an' him starin' hard at me like he'd pound the words outta me if I didn't soon spill 'em on my own. I didn't know how to start in an' all I could get out was that she was gone. He figured I meant she run off more like. That she finally had the brains to leave me.

"I told him then that she was dead. That there was a baby but that she didn't make it, that I weren't there when the baby started to come. He took it hard, Frank, and when he started to blame me I didn't offer no other account. I watched him stagger like gettin' hit with a bullet. He grabbed at the porch post for balance then he slumped down into one of them rockers with a hand to his mouth an' breathin' so ragged through his fingers I could hear him from where I stood. Then he closed his eyes. He was shakin'.

"'You were drunk.' He stood up slowly. 'When she needed you most you were drunk. I could kill you,' he said to me.

"'Wish ya would,' I told him and meant it. 'It'd make everything easier,' I said.

"He looked at me for a moment. 'You don't get to have anything easier,' he said. 'You don't deserve easier.'

"And we stood for the longest time saying nothing further. I started to walk away then and when I turned he'd already headed back toward the house.

"'I got the boy,' I said. 'He's in the truck down the drive.' I told him that I didn't have it in me to take care of a baby, that all I could think of to do was drink.

"Bunky stopped where he was without moving.

"'I got no time for no newborn either. If that's where yer headin'.'

"'Would ya just see him even?' I asked him.

"I remember hearin' a rooster crow and the clatter of cowbells in the field an' that silence between us a lot louder'n any of that. I didn't think he was gonna move or say anythin' more so I kinda half turned to leave. 'He's her son,' he said. 'Least I can do is see him since ya brung him out here. Might do to get him outta that damn truck too, ya dumb son of a bitch.'

"We walked down the drive without speakin'. He was all straight, like he had a poker down his back, all business, and I could feel the anger comin' off him. When we got to the truck he just stood there leanin' against the door frame an' lookin' at you through the open window. I didn't know what to do. He stood there an awful long time an' when he turned to me there was grief in his eyes an' he took out a hanky from his back pocket.

"'Fetch him up to the house,' he said. 'I got good fresh cow's milk. We'll feed him and then you can be on your way. You got a bottle, don't ya?'

"He didn't give me time to answer. He just marched back up the driveway without looking back. So I got your bassinette untied and followed him up to the house. We sat in the rockers on the porch. Bunky held ya and fed ya. I was no hell at any of it. Bunky'd even changed yer diaper and I sat and watched as he give ya that bottle, runnin' his finger down the side of yer face. He looked plumb happy doin' it and I recollect feelin' lost on accounta all I could feel was sore and ragged and rough inside.

"After a while he said, 'I'll do it. Not for you. For him and for her. He'll be my responsibility,' he told me. 'Not yours. Not ever.' So I told him he wouldn't get no trouble from me and he just looked at me hard and said he'd better not.

"Then he said he'd raise ya cuz he owed her. I didn't get it an' I asked him and all he done was keep on lookin' down at you for the longest time. When he looked up at me again he clutched ya to his chest and put his chin on the top of yer head and just watched me. Then he said that she brung him to life. Said he was movin' through his life by recollection until she come along and showed him how to look at things again.

"'I got bigger on accounta her.' That's what he said. 'I got made better.'

"I knew what he meant, Frank. I got made better too. But not better enough on accounta when she needed me most I wasn't there an' she died cuz of that. I looked at the two of you on that rocker an' all's I could do was walk away. All's I could do was walk away because I guess I come to know right there that some holes get filled when people die. Dirt fills 'em. But other holes, well, ya walk around with them holes in ya forever and there weren't nothin' in the world to say about that. Nothin'.'"

The light had begun to climb higher in the sky and they could see shadow relenting and giving way to dawn. Birds twittered and there was a soft soughing of breeze in the top branches of the trees. The kid sat and watched morning break slowly and hunted for words but the trail was empty and he found nothing. He looked at his father's ravaged face. Trembling harder and gaunt as empty saddlebags, he fought the spasms in his gut and the kid thought he might tumble off the rock.

"He said he'd try'n teach you Indian things even though he wasn't no Indian himself. Said he'd show you your mother's way as best he could. Said he'd love you like his own. Far's I know he done all that."

"He did," the kid said.

"He told me I could come whenever I wanted long as I wasn't drunk or drinkin'. I come a few times but after a while I couldn't hold to that promise. When you were older he let you come see me where I was. Didn't want to but he let you anyhow.

"He's the one called you Frank. Franklin. Said there was a man one time stood out in a thunderstorm with a key tied to a kite. Said that man was trying to catch the lightning. Said he knew the world would change if he caught it. Took courage, he said, to want something for others like that. So he named you for that man."

"Ben Franklin."

"Yeah."

"How come he never told me?"

"Guess he figured that was up to me."

"You never give up nothing until now."

His father closed his eyes again. The kid tried to see himself in him. All he could see was a shivering, dying man. All he could see was woe. His father shuddered and the force of it racked his whole body and the kid went to him and helped him stand and then walked him slowly back to the fire. It had died down. When he had him settled he went into the trees and came back with an armload of wood and kindled the fire and watched it catch. The morning had broken fair. The sun cast a spindle of light across the top of the ridge on the far side of the valley. His father groaned. He got the bottle of medicine and tilted his father's head back and waited while he sipped. He made him take as much as he could. Then he laid him with his head leaned against the pack. When he was out he went into the trees again and came back with four saplings. He stripped them of bark with the knife then built a lean-to over his father to shelter him from the sun. He covered the frame with spruce branches. His father slept in the shade of it, his breath raspy and thin, shuddering now and then and moaning.

He thought about everything he'd been told. It was grim but more than he'd had before. It felt alien, like listening on someone else's story. The skeletal man who slept in front of him seemed to resemble nothing of the man who'd walked through the tale he told. He wondered how time worked on a person. He wondered how he would look years on and what effect this history would have on him. He'd expected that it might have filled him but all he felt was emptiness and a fear that there would be nothing that could fill that void. His thoughts turned toward Eldon Starlight and there was only pity there for a life with benchmarks that only ever set out the boundaries of pain and loss, woe and regret, nothing to bring him comfort in his last days. He thought of his lost mother, and wondered how it might have felt to touch her, to put a hand or the other on her shoulder and claim some of her energy as his own, or if, as an infant, enough of her spirit had clung to him despite all the lean years of absence to carry him forward without loneliness. He hoped so. His life was built of the stories of vague ghosts. He wanted desperately to see them fleshed out and vital. History, he supposed, lacked that power. He rubbed his palms together slowly then held them out to the fire.

His father slept on. The kid sat by the fire and whittled saplings with his knife. Hours passed and when he looked up his father was staring at him from the lean-to, his eyes glimmering so that he looked mad with the sheen of sweat on his brow. The kid stared back at him. Neither of them spoke.

Finally, the kid got up and walked to him and let him drink from the canteen. He only managed a small swallow or two then pointed to the fire and the kid hooked his hands under his arms and lifted and walked him to the fire and sat him on the ground beside it. His father hunched there, nodding as though hearing the words of a silent conversation.

"You shoulda told me the whole story a long time ago," the kid said.

"I don't know that I coulda." His father stared into the fire. He coughed and his hand came away sprayed with the grainy clots of blood and he stared at it until the kid gathered some moss and wiped it away. His father put his hand against his chest and the kid could see that it pained him to breathe. "She was the breath of me, Frank. I don't know as I took another full one all this time."

The kid nodded. "I ain't never had no hurt like that. But I think I get it now."

"I'm surprised you don't hate me outright." His father coughed into his hand again and wiped his palm on his pants. "Could ya walk me back to the edge, Frank," he said.

The kid got up and stretched out a hand and his father took it. He could feel the finger bones and the dry rasp of his skin against his palm. He pulled him to his feet and then hooked an arm around his back and up under his armpit and began to walk. They picked their way across the thirty feet of space and came to the edge.

In the valley below the river was a mercury ribbon. It fluttered through the valley and here and there they could see the crosshatch of trees and shrubs and bushes and the dim whiteness of stones along the banks. The mountains behind it were a black wall. The kid took his father as close to the lip of the plummet as he dared and they stood there latched to each other, staring away across the great vast space.

His father stepped to the very edge, still clinging to him. Then he nudged him aside and the kid watched as he closed his eyes and stood there wobbling on the edge of that drop. He wondered if he needed to reach out and grab him but his father slowly raised his arms to shoulder height and held them there with eyes closed and his head tilted back, moaning something soft and low that the kid leaned closer to hear.

"I'm sorry," he whispered. "I'm sorry."

24

HE WORSENED AGAIN once they got back to the fire. He vomited more and eventually there was nothing left to heave but a thin trickle. When he spewed, his stomach caused him horrific pain and he clutched at it and rolled on the ground. By the time night fell completely, not even the heat of the fire was enough to warm him. The kid covered him as best he could and stoked the fire high. Then he lay down beside him on the ground and pulled him close. Eventually he settled and the kid could hear his steady shallow breathing. He held on to him. When the kid dropped off to sleep himself he didn't know. He dreamed there was a man and a woman seated on a blanket. They were talking and their heads were bent close together, but he couldn't see their faces or hear what they were saying. Then he was on the porch of a house he didn't recognize. The sun was going down. The sky was alive with colour and he could see it bending and receding above the fields. A woman was there. She stood in the middle of the field, looking at him. She waved with both arms and he waved back at her but it was his father she was waving at. He was striding across the field and then broke into a run and the kid closed his eyes.

The kid heard him leave in the darkness. There was a huff of breath, a short jolt, and then quiet. He lay there awake and looked out at the night and felt the stillness. It was heavy as a thick blanket, and in the depth of that quiet he was afraid to move, afraid to break it, of sacrilege, of piercing something that settled over him seamlessly, attached him to his dead father, who lay in silhouette against the glint of the moon. After a while, he rose and fumbled about for a stick of wood and pitched it sideways into the fire. It sent embers arcing high into the night and he watched them climb and peak and fall. Then he pitched another and the flames licked at the bark and slowly erupted into flame all blue and yellow and on into orange as it caught and held and ate away at the chill and dark around him. In the wavering light his father appeared to breathe and the kid caught his own breath. But there was only stillness.

After a time he reached out a hand and traced his father's face with his fingertips, like memorizing it with his skin. He followed the scarp of bone over the eyes and onto the broad plain of his forehead and stopped at the bramble of hair. Then he took two fingers of the other hand and traced his own face at the same time. With his eyes closed he could feel the plummet from the brow to the nose and the long slide to the dip down to the mouth, full and plump and broad. Then the hollow at the top of the chin. He followed the squared nub of chin to the cascade of skin of the throat, to the poke of Adam's apple and into the basin of the clavicle. "Shh. Hush," he said for no reason he could think of and gently closed his father's eyes.

He put a hand against his father's chest and held it there a long time and only when he felt the air change and the shadow ease in the first pale aquamarine of morning did he raise it and let it settle against his own chest. Then he stood looking down at his father. Quiet. He took two fingers and knelt and laid them against his father's lips again.

"Shh," he said again. "Hush." Like a benediction.

25

IT TOOK HIM ALL MORNING to dig the grave. The ground near the precipice was stony and hard. He poked around with the edge of the pick and found a spot with give and started to hollow it out. There was a layer of dry, crumbly soil about ten inches deep and once he got to the bottom of that he hit the sand and rocks. He had to root about and find the edges of the stones in order to dig around them, to get a grip so he could lift them out, and some were as big as loaves of bread. He thought of his father fencing ten acres in his days at the farm when he came to know his mother. This was less digging than it was leveraging out a hole. He got to about five feet and struck a bed of rock. For a while he tried to find the end of it with the folding shovel but it was huge and he gave up and sat at the edge of his dig and looked out over the valley. The grave was dug within six feet of the edge and the view to the east was astounding in the clear autumn light. He drank from the canteen and sloshed a handful of water over his face. He didn't want the varmints or wolves or bears to get at his father's remains. He spent hours trundling rocks and stones from among the trees to the gravesite. There was a moss-covered rock shaped like a football that lay in the shadow a few hundred yards away and he took the rope and the horse and managed to haul it over. It would sit perfectly atop the stones if he could get it up there.

When he had enough stones assembled he ran water over his hands to clean them and then walked over to where his father lay under the lean-to. He bent down and looked closely at him.

"I don't know what the fuck I'm doing," he shouted. He cried then, feeling the raw edges of a new hurt deep within him.

He took the coat that covered his father and laid it beside the lean-to. Then he squatted and pushed his hands under and pulled him toward himself and lifted him, cradling him as he stood with the insignificant weight of him in his arms. He walked slowly across the clearing to the grave and when he got there he set his father down and stood looking at the hole.

It seemed a poor end and he took the hatchet and stalked off into the trees for an armload of boughs and moss and he lined the bottom of the hole with them. Then he pulled the makings from his back pocket and opened the bag and sprinkled a pinch of tobacco on the bed of boughs. He wasn't much for prayer and it was the only ritual that he knew. It was an act of honouring. He looked up at the sky and followed the line of

horizon along the saw edge of mountain and thought about
what he might say. All he found was a quiet place inside him
like the silence his father lay in and he let himself have that.
Then he lifted him and lowered him into the hole feet first
and clambered in with him. The space was small but he
managed to fold the body and seat it and arrange the arms
and hands across the chest. He set his father's head against
his kneecaps. When he was satisfied he climbed out of the
hole and stood looking down at the shape of his father in
the grave. There was a small breeze now blowing off the
land and across the chasm and the kid gazed out and away
across the valley.

He worked fast and when the last few shovels of dirt
obscured his father from view he felt empty. He piled as much
as he could on top of him and then began to arrange the
stones into a mound. There was anguish in him now that he
had never felt before, an aching down the middle of his throat,
and he let himself weep. He cursed at the world, at his own
sorry history, and at himself for caring. Then he took hold of
the large rock he'd hauled over and he squatted around it and
pushed upward with his legs, screaming as he lifted it. He
held it momentarily in his arms, grimacing, letting himself
feel the hard burden of the rock and the pull of the muscles
in his face and the long tendons in his neck and arms. Then
he set it down on top of the mound of stones.

When he stood up he felt weightless. The sear of sorrow
gone now and replaced with the clear wash of air in his lungs.
He stepped to the lip of the ridge and stood there in front of
that incredible space.

"War's over, Eldon," he said finally. "I hope when you get
to where you're goin' that she's standing there waitin' for you."

It was all the prayer he had in him. And though there were more words to say he couldn't reach them now and so he stood in the stillness, looking out over the valley a last time. Then he marched to the campsite to clear it and gather what was left into the pack for the journey back.

26

IT TOOK HIM TWO FULL DAYS to get back to the farm. When he got there it was mid-morning and he eased the horse out of the line of trees at the edge of the field and sat there looking at the old buildings and the sweep of the acres, gone brown and mouldering in the late fall chill. The cows were in the outside pens. There was a thin curl of smoke from the chimney of the house and he dismounted and walked the mare across the field and into the pen at the back of the barn. He could hear hammering coming from inside. He removed the tack from the horse and hung it on the top rail of the fence and brushed her out. He patted the mare on the rump and she walked off toward the water trough and he slipped quietly through the open back door of the barn.

The other horses were gone, likely sent out into the back pasture. The stalls were empty and he could see the old man working with a pile of new lumber, replacing boards on the partitions and stalls. He stood in the shadows and watched the old man work. His face was rough from not shaving and his clothes were rumpled as if he hadn't changed them in days. He was intent on the work and did not notice the kid enter.

The old man hammered a single nail loosely into both ends of the plank. Then he lightly pounded one end to a post and walked to the opposite end, lifted it into place, and hammered the nail in before going back and securing the first end. His movements were familiar, a smooth and effortless rhythm afforded to the task at hand. He was bow-legged and bent some with age but he knew how to work. His face was intent and the kid remembered that look from all the years of farm labour they'd done together. Work was serious business. That's what he'd taught him. "Ya just get'er done," was his favourite saying and the kid had accepted it as a motto by the time he was ten. He had the old man to thank for the feeling of bending his back to a chore or a task and the sense of rightness that came from it. Watching him now, the kid saw how much of the steadfast old man was a part of him and he slipped into the tack room and retrieved his tool belt and put it on. When the old man's back was turned he walked over and hefted the next board in his hands and stood there, holding it at the ready. When the old man turned there was only a momentary hesitation, a surprised flick of the eyes and the hint of a grin at the corners of his mouth. Then he took one end of the board and they walked it into place together and nailed it.

They worked in silence, going through the pile of boards quickly. They hauled the old boards out to stack in the back of the truck and the old man pointed to a five-gallon pail of paint and the kid trundled it into the barn while the old man retrieved brushes from the shed beside the house. The kid stirred the paint until the old man stood beside him again.

"He's gone," the kid said without looking up.

"I figured," the old man said. "I hope it wasn't too hard for ya."

"Yeah," he said.

The kid hauled the pail to the far end of the corridor. They went to work again. They painted opposite sides of the boards and every now and then their eyes would meet and the old man would nod. They painted hard and fast and when they reached the end of the job the kid resealed the pail and carried it to the shed where the old man was washing out the rollers and brushes with a hose.

"You must be near to starved," the old man said.

"Near enough," the kid said. "Whattaya got?"

"Got some deer left over that'd make a dang fine sandwich and I done up a soup the other day that needs to be ate." He handed the hose and a basin to the kid and waited while he washed up and handed him a tattered towel to dry with before going through the ritual himself.

"I got to get the mare squared away," the kid said.

"I'll get the food set out then," the old man said.

The kid stood in the tack room after he'd stabled the horse. Their riding dusters hung side by side. The old man had always preferred a rope hackamore to a bridle and it rested on the same hook and draped atop his duster. The kid went over and took it in his hands. It was coarse and dry. The kid had used a hackamore for years. The old man had taught him to ride bareback first. Said it let him learn the rhythm of a horse better. It had. A hackamore made a rider work more closely with a horse, know it, understand its moods and temperament, and learn to cooperate with it and vice versa. So that when he went to a bit and bridle at twelve the old man had just cocked an eyebrow at him. "Ya want a horse on a bit in the backcountry," the kid had said. "Something happens out there like comin' upon a bear or a cougar a guy wants to know he's got control. 'Sides, it's better for the horse to know there's a boss out there."

"Makes me wonder who'd be the boss of the bear or the cougar," the old man had said. The kid wondered at the nature of things that stuck in the mind.

When he got to the house he slipped out of his boots. The old man was rattling pots around in the kitchen and the kid set the cutlery on the table, the heft in his hand reassuring and solid. The old routine felt easy and natural. The old man ladled soup into bowls and carried them to the table while the kid fetched the sandwiches. The plates and bowls were heavy clay pottered by a neighbour long dead, the old man had once told him. While he sipped spoonfuls of the soup, the kid watched the old man eat. He moaned lightly while he chewed. When he bent his head to the bowl he scooped soup quickly, the clink of the spoon against the bowl in counterpoint to his satisfied grunts. The kid set his spoon down. "He told me, ya know."

The old man gazed at him and pushed his bowl aside. "I always hoped he'd be the one to," he said.

"You ever see her in me?"

"Near every day."

"Did it hurt like it hurt him?"

"I could see you move, see ya change, and it was like watchin' part of her claim its place in the world."

The kid nodded. "I heard how you got your name," was all he could think to say.

The old man rubbed at the bald top of his head down to the rim of hair above his ear. "Kinda lost its use same time as the hair left," he said.

"Did he ever tell ya the whole story? His life. What happened to him. What he done."

"That's what he always kept locked away. He had a weight to him like he was luggin' sacks of grain uphill but he never spoke of it. Not to me leastways."

"I don't think he ever told no one."

They finished their meal in silence and then stood and walked out onto the porch. They sat in the rockers and the kid looked around at the farm. He lit a smoke and he began to tell the old man the story of his journey with his father. The old man listened and did not interrupt and when he was finished the old man asked if he wanted to walk a while.

They walked the perimeter of the yard, past the chicken roost, the tool shed, the tractor shed, and along the line of rail fence to the barn. The kid regarded everything solemnly. "I don't know as he ever got what he wanted in the end," the kid said.

"Whattaya think that was?" the old man asked.

They stopped and they both put a foot on the bottom rail of the fence and gazed out across the acres. The kid shook his head. "Don't know. It's all jumbled up in there. Maybe I was s'posed to forgive him."

"Do ya?" the old man asked.

"Don't know that either. Kinda like a thousand-pound word to me right now."

"It's okay if ya figger I oughta been the one to tell ya. It's okay if ya think that. I wrestled with it for a lotta years, waitin' on him to break and let ya know the lot of it."

"You don't need forgivin'," the kid said. "You were my father all these years."

The old man's eyes shone. "It's what I hoped to be," he said.

"There's a stone in the pack," the kid said. "It's from the grave. I brung it for ya."

"For me? Why'd ya wanna do something like that?"

"I figured you mighta lost something too."

The old man clamped his jaws together. He nodded. The cattle were moving from the back pasture and they could hear them bawling through the trees. "We'll keep it on the hearth," he said. "That way we can share it, talk of it if we need to. Thank you, Frank."

The kid looked down at his feet. Then he raised his head and looked at the old man and they held the gaze silently.

"I ain't sure how to feel," the kid said.

"Sometimes when things get taken away from you it feels like there's a hole at your centre where you can feel the wind blow through, that's sure," the old man said.

"Whattaya do about that?"

"Me, I always went to where the wind blows." The old man put a hand on the kid's shoulder and turned him to face him square on. "Don't know as I ever got an answer but it always felt better bein' out there."

The kid nodded. They looked at each other. The horse neighed softly in the barn and the old man pulled the kid to him and clasped his arms around him and rocked side to side. The kid could smell the oil and grease and tobacco on him and it was every smell he recalled growing up with and he closed his eyes and pulled it all into him.

—

He walked out into the pasture and got the old man's grey mare, brushed her out and saddled her, and led her out to the paddock. He pulled a hat down low over his eyes and mounted, urging the mare to the gate, and he leaned down and opened it and rode through into the field. The light across the horizon was a wide flush of pink and magenta beneath the banked tier of cloud and the lowering sun threw shards of light upward so that the sky seemed curtained. He rode across the field to the line of trees. When he got there he turned the horse and regarded the farm. He let his eyes trail across the fields to the back ten acres his father had fenced and thought of that time when he had been almost happy. Then he wheeled the horse and kicked her up the trail.

He sat the mare easy. The roll of her gait was comforting and they climbed steadily. When they breached the rim of trees at the top of the ridge, the last of the clouds parted and sun reclaimed the western sky. The clouds were dappled now in a burnished gold and he thought that this was all the cathedral he'd ever need.

The ridge formed one side of a deep narrow valley. It was a half-mile across at its widest point and there was a stream that ran its length through thickets of alder and red willow with a swath of meadow, level and true as a table, leading to the scree and talus that marked the bottom of the far ridge. It was the old man's favourite ride when he'd gotten too old for riding into the depths of the backcountry. He nudged the horse forward and kept his eye on the vista.

The light weakened. He could feel the thrust of evening working its way through the cut of the valley and he watched the shapes of things alter. The sun sat blood red near the lip of the world and in that rose and canted light he sat there filled with wonder and a welling sorrow. He wiped his face with the palm of his hand and he stared down across the valley.

Soon the light had nudged down deeper into shadow and it was like he existed in a dream world, hung there above that peaceful space where the wind ruled, and he could feel it push against him. He closed his eyes for a moment and when he looked down into the valley again he thought he could see the ghostly shapes of people riding horses through the trees. They angled east into the valley with dogs strewn out in ragged lines ahead and behind them and children running after them waving sticks, the shouts of them riding the wind to the rim of the ridge. Close on that the clack of the horses' unshod hoofs on the loose and scrabbled stone and the drag and bump of travois poles and the shouts of young men on rearing ponies. There were women walking stately beside the horses, stooping to gather herbs and berries in hide pouches slung against their hips, the dip and sway of their travelling song finding the push of thermals and rising to him. He watched them ride into the swale and ease the horses to the water while the dogs and children ran in the rough grass. The men and women on horse-back dismounted and their shouts came to him laden with hope and good humour. He raised a hand to the idea of his father and mother and a line of people he had never known, then mounted the horse and rode back through the glimmer to the farm where the old man waited, a deck of cards on the scarred and battered table.

ACKNOWLEDGEMENTS

In the Ojibway world you go inward in order to express outward. That journey can be harrowing sometimes but it can also be the source of much joy, freedom, and light. There are many who have been there to share on my inward journey and without their light I may not have found the wherewithal and courage to brave the darkness and shadows. Suffice to say, the re-emergence has been amazing and this story was born out of long nights of soul searching and reflection. I am grateful as always to my steadfast, indefatigable agent and friend, John Pearce, who's been there every inch of that inward journey and always when I re-emerged to take up the writer's craft again. You made me strong enough to write this book. As well, to those great friends who have also been part of that journey and always been there for me though sometimes I didn't know it: Nick Pitt, Rodger W. Ross, Dawn Maracle, Shelagh Rogers, Charlie Cheffens, Joseph Boyden, Thomas King, and Fiona Kirkpatrick Parsons. I owe my current state of openness and light to the presence of Rick Turner, Arjun Singh, Waubgeshig Rice, Kim Wheeler, Daniela Ginta, Blanca Schorcht and Vaughan Begg, Mackenzie Green, Michelle Merry, Deb Green, Jane Davidson, Herman Michell, Peter Mutrie, and, especially, Yvette Lehmann.

Thanks to all the folks at Westwood Creative Artists, the Thompson-Nicola Public Library in Kamloops, and all my students and workshop participants for the ongoing motivation to be more.

Heartfelt gratitude and deep indebtedness to my uber editor, Ellen Seligman, for finding me and this book. I owe you many dinners. To all the folks at McClelland and Stewart and Random House of Canada, the Canada Council, the B.C. Arts Council, thanks for the support.

Lastly, this book would not have been possible if it weren't for the presence of Debra Powell in my life during its writing. Long may you shine.

RICHARD WAGAMESE is one of Canada's foremost writers. He's been a newspaper columnist and reporter, radio and television broadcaster and producer, documentary producer, and is the author of eight previous novels, including *Keeper'n Me* and *Indian Horse*, which was a recent Canada Reads finalist. He is also the author of acclaimed memoirs, including *For Joshua*; the bestselling *One Native Life*; and *One Story, One Song*, which won the George Ryga Award for Social Awareness in Literature. He has won numerous awards and recognition for his writing, including the National Aboriginal Achievement Award for Media and Communications and, most recently, the prestigious Molson Prize and the Canada Reads People's Choice Award. He lives in Kamloops, B.C.